ABAN'S
ACCENSION

Also by Shireen Jeejeebhoy

In Print and Ebook

Lifeliner

She

Concussion Is Brain Injury

Time and Space

In Ebook

The Job Sessions: Why Do The Innocent Suffer?

A Nibble of Chocolate

Eleven Shorts +1

ABAN'S ACCENSION

SHIREEN JEEJEEBHOY

ISBN-13: 978-0-9877110-5-2

http://jeejeebhoy.ca

Dedication

For the teachers who taught me more than the curriculum

Ms. Buchanan

Mr. Rumsey

Mr. Payne

Mr. Richardson

Mr. Cooper

Mr. Carter

Mrs. Semenovs

Prof. Kerpneck

Prof. Duffy

ACKNOWLEDGEMENTS

Aban's Accension is the second novel I wrote but not the second to be published. I took my time in getting it out because I wanted to do justice to my characters of Aban and El and to pour over them the attention they needed from me and from my graciously giving beta readers.

I want to thank Duke Vipperman, whose conversations with me about many matters have always stimulated my 'little grey cells' and whose insights helped me form the character of El; and Greg Ioannou who taught me how to structure a novel and helped me put together this story. I want to thank my beta readers Ann Benoit, Andrew Fogg, Olive Jeejeebhoy, and Ben Babcock. Your attention to the characters and details and constructive feedback were invaluable to me. I also want to thank the Wattpad community whose votes and comments buoyed me up and encouraged me to bring this book out in paperback.

National Novel Writing Month 2010 created a deadline for me to finish my outline, settings, and character backgrounds in order to begin writing on November 1. Without this global event, where we all write together yet alone, where we encourage each other and receive tips and guidance from the NaNoWriMo folks, I would not have gotten any of my novels written. Thank you! And last, but not least, I want to thank my editor Pam Elise Harris, who I found through BiblioCrunch. As she did with *Time and Space*, she did a bang-up job here too.

Note: The title is not a typo! Accension is an old word, meaning to kindle or set on fire.

1

THE DREAM

A black sink. That's her first thought. A black sink. She squints down. The blackness is moving softly, its edges . . . there are no edges. A ping of fear rises in her, then settles softly back into simple observation. The empty deep swirls beneath her. She is hanging over and in it, its inky fluidic space sucking out the light from around her, vacuuming away all hope. Motion catches her eye to the left and behind her. She moves her eyeballs left and sees two creamy, ribbed things undulating toward her, slowly. Their blurred triangular shapes swim in a straight line. A second couple hoves into view: two by two they come. Maggots. She flickers her feet, trying to rise, to get out of their way, but she's stuck, gripped by an unknown force and the niggling thought of, does she really want to move? Aren't they fascinating, these effervescent couples with their soft bodies and hypnotic movement. She stops struggling.

The line is long now stretching into the unseen distance, growing like a scarf flying out of a magician's pocket. She's not sure if the line of pairs is above her or in front of her. Her eyes watch them while her mind disengages. It is so easy to disengage, to see them as having nothing to do with her.

They're just maggots swimming by. The void beneath her feet does not exist.

They turn.

The front of the line has now gone way past her on her right, and so when they turn, they are on her front and right flanks. She doesn't like that. Her mind re-engages. She can no longer pretend that they have nothing to do with her. She wriggles; she flaps her feet; she stretches her neck, arches her head back. But it's hard to resist this formless place. Fear rises in her throat.

She wakes up.

And finds herself struggling with her sweat-dampened sheets, the bottom one all wrinkled, the top one holding her down, pinning her arms to her sides. Panic grips her until she wakes up enough to relax and release herself from the tight top sheet.

Her chest rises and drops heavily, up and down, up and down. Gradually, her hearing returns, her sight broadens. She hears: the cicadas singing outside in the sultry air. She feels: the air inside her bedroom sitting on her like a wet fleece with no breeze blowing in through the open window to bring relief.

She jumps out of bed to fill her mind with the busyness of brushing teeth and putting on her multi-pocketed, baggy army pants and favourite T-shirt proclaiming "The Secret is My Birthright."

2

THE LETTER

ABAN hesitates on the last step of the staircase, her right hand on the square newel post, its wood worn comfortingly smooth by many years of hands resting on it. It's the mail on the scuffed wooden floor that's stopped her. This morning's letters are lying there, higgledy piggledy, in front of the radiator with its slab of wood on top—their hall table. And she wonders: why does Dad always drop half the letters on the floor when he brings in the mail? Why does he toss them, the ads too, toward their hall table? It's like he doesn't care that half fall on the floor. He goes around them as if they're not there, just goes back to the kitchen like it doesn't matter. Aban will pick them up.

"Yeah," she mutters to herself, "I'll pick em up."

In all the years she's come down the stairs and has automatically picked the mail up off the floor, this thought has not occurred to her. Now it's followed by others: Is he, like, clumsy? Does he drop them deliberately cause she'll pick them up anyway? It's not like anyone else does it. It's like it's her job to pick them up and take them to Mom at the kitchen table. They're never for Aban; she never looks through them first.

Mom would be mad if she did. Aban shakes her head clean and moves again.

She bends down and, one by one, pokes her fingers underneath the letters' edges until they're all in her hand. She throws the ad mail into the scuffed recycling box at the side of the radiator. She flips through the letters surreptitiously, quickly, and suddenly pauses. A bright white envelope with blue lettering stares up at her. It's addressed to her, in her full name. It looks, it looks . . . legal. She looks at the return address. "Myerstein and Associates at Law" it reads. From a Toronto address too, some place called "First Canadian Place." Sounds posh and arrogant. What can it mean?

"Aban," her mother cries down the hallway from her perch at the kitchen table. "Are you going to stare at those all day or bring me my mail?"

"Coming, Mom." She shakes her head and sorts the letters into an alphabetical pile for her mother, taps them even, picks them up in her right hand and carries her one letter in her left hand, slightly behind her back. She walks down the hall and places the pile squarely in front of her mother, who sets aside the section of the paper she was reading and takes them as is her due. Aban sits down in her chair and stares at the letter, forgetting to hide it underneath the table. She doesn't understand how she can have a letter addressed to her.

"Why are you staring at my mail?"

"It's not for you."

"Your father's then."

"It's not for him neither."

"It's for you?"

"Yes."

"Must I ask you twenty questions? Who from?"

"Some lawyer, some big law firm in Toronto."

"Let me see."

"No. It's for me."

"Aban, it's best if I look at it first. You never know what lawyers will send you, and I don't want you being upset. Law firms in Toronto only mean trouble."

Aban obeys Mom always but not today. She rips the letter open with her fingers, uncaring of the ragged edges. Astonishment doesn't impair Mom's reflexes. She lunges across the table for it but fails, as Dad flaps the paper he's reading into a higher position. He reaches around the paper for his milk-drowned muesli with his spoon, scoops up a full spoonful, and brings it back around the paper without spilling a drop. A loud slurp emits from behind the Sports section. Aban glances over at him, and Mom almost gets the letter this time. Aban leans back fast, dangerously so, in her chair. She unfolds the letter and begins to read it silently, her lips moving.

Finished, Aban lowers the stark white sheet of paper to stare at Mom, who has both a furtive and angry look on her face. "Grandma was alive? You said she was dead."

"No, you said it."

"You never said different."

"It's not my fault you assumed."

"But, but . . . I was a kid."

"You're still a child."

"I'm twenty."

"You see, you talk like a child."

"Why did you say she was dead?"

"I didn't say it, Aban, you did." Mom settles back down into her seat and resumes spooning up her muesli in that careful way she has while lifting the top of the paper up from the table to ostensibly read it.

"Dad? Did you know she was alive?"

He doesn't reply, just remains behind his paper.

She returns to the letter. "It says here that she died, like, this year, and, like, she left her, her entire estate to me."

"What?" her parents chorus, dropping their papers and complacent expressions.

"She left all her stuff to me, including some house on some street in Toronto."

"Well, you're not going," Mom declares firmly. Dad glances over at Mom expressionless then lifts his paper back up to his face.

"We had nothing to do with that woman for a good reason, Aban. And you won't have anything to do with her now."

Aban peers at the letter again. She feels something, some feeling she hasn't felt before. It stirs in her, and she's uncomfortable. She drops the letter down next to her plate. She gets up and moves to the kitchen counter. She takes the loaf of bread out of the bread drawer and hacks off a thick slice. She never can slice neatly; the edges are always messy. She senses Mom's disapproval seeping through her back although Mom's back is to her. No matter how much Aban tries, how many times Mom has shown her, Aban can't slice bread. It's the first and only thing Mom taught her to do in the kitchen. Aban bundles the loaf back into the bread drawer and places the slice into the shiny toaster oven. She shuts the lid and turns it on, turning her head away from the sight of her fingerprints on the silver-coloured metal. She waits. It dings, and she opens the oven to remove her slightly toasted slice of bread. She pulls a jar of cherry jam toward her, unscrews the lid, and knifes out some jam to spread on the toast. Uncharacteristically, she leaves the lid on the counter, the jammy knife next to it, and carries her toast back to her place at the kitchen table. Mom comments that it's going to be another hot day and exclaims that it's all the fault of climate change that they've had no rain this summer. She snaps the paper to punctuate her point. Aban drops the toast on her plate and lets it lay there as she stares at the open letter. Mom hadn't removed it. Mom knows she won't go.

But she wants to.

She shifts in her seat and takes a sip of the chicory Mom had poured out for her when her parents had sat down for breakfast earlier. As always, it's lukewarm. But she barely notices. That letter is scorching her side vision. She picks up her toast and bites into it, jam spilling onto her hand. She keeps biting and chewing, biting and chewing until the toast is gone. She licks the jam off her hand.

"Aban!"

Aban grabs a wrinkled cloth napkin from the holder in the centre of the table and finishes wiping her hand. She drinks her chicory in one long pull. She bangs the mug down on the pine table with its scratches and dents and looks guiltily at Mom's disapproving glare over her paper.

Aban wipes her hands back and forth on her worn khakis and peeps at the letter again, its two short edges sticking innocently up into the air, its middle flat on its back on the table. She wipes her hands again. She frowns and unwillingly picks it up.

The lawyer in highfalutin English explains that he is the executor of her grandmother's estate, the estate of her father's mother. Her grandmother has left a substantial amount in funds, most of it residing in a savings account at some bank Aban's not heard of. But then what does she know of banks; her parents do her banking for her. Well, Mom does. When Aban had first begun working at her parents' shop in town, Mom had said to her that she'd hold onto her earnings to pay for rent and food for her own good. Aban had acquiesced, for Mom was right all the time, and anyway Mom would never do something to harm her. Mom looked out for her, not like other kids' moms.

Then why didn't Aban know her grandmother was alive, that she could've seen her anytime when she got old enough to travel on her own?

But when has she travelled on her own anyway? Everyone knows she's not old enough yet; she has to be in charge at the shop first and to save up. Besides, as Mom has told her many times, and Dad agrees, Toronto isn't safe. Toronto is a bad place where people get mugged, and cars run you over.

"I'm going," Aban declares to the ceiling.

"What?"

"I'm going to Toronto, to see this lawyer about her, about my grandmother."

"We've had this conversation already. Rip that letter up. You're not going," Mom flaps the paper back into a reading position to emphasize her point.

Aban looks over at Dad. He hasn't moved, if anything his paper looks iced over.

"Dad? Should I go?"

"Do as Mom says, Aban," he mumbles at her through his paper. "She knows best in this. We had good reasons to keep you away from her, as Mom explained to you. Don't stir things up now." He resumes reading, or so she assumes.

"Look, Aban, we've gone over this before," Mom says.

"Not with me."

"We didn't have to. We—your father and I—discussed her back when you were little, after a particularly distressing visit from her. You were upset. And I won't have you upset. She had been trying to push her views on to us, telling us all about her bourgeois ideas, and then she'd started talking to you about it. I told her expressly that she was not to talk to you about certain subjects, and she ignored me. I will not have anyone ignore my wishes. You are my daughter; I am the only one who decides what you will and will not learn about. I know what upsets you and what doesn't. I didn't want you learning about these things and being upset by things too old for you."

"What things?" Aban doesn't remember anything about her grandmother, yet she has the feeling she'd last seen her when she was nine years old. A memory floats up: she's performing a ritual for her dead grandmother. She's throwing flowers into a stream that runs in the woods behind their home. Mom's sharp voice jerks her from that memory.

"None of your business." Mom's right hand, the one with the large opal ring on it, slaps down on the table. Aban jumps. "We made our position clear with her. She knew what our views were. I had moved your father away from that place, away from her. I didn't want her influencing him or you at any time of day or night. Being further away from her, making it harder for her to see us was good. I could limit her visits that way. I told her that she could come visit us if she wanted to see you, but we did not have the time to visit her. We were busy opening up our new shop, setting up our lives here. But when she came, she had to obey our rules, and being out of her element, she had no choice. Or so I thought. If she wanted to see you, she had to obey me. I told her what subjects were off limits. I didn't want her interfering and upsetting you. But she wouldn't listen to me."

Mom inhales sharply and leans forward. Her voice quavers with indignation. "She had the temerity to speak of Atasgah, against my express wishes, and she upset you, making you ask us all these questions, wanting to travel to Toronto to learn more, and . . . and . . . indulging those thoughts. I wasn't having any of that. We had just opened up our shop and had ordered a full inventory with the money from your father's inheritance from his father. It was stressful starting in a new place, alone. But we found peace in our little shop with its crystals and rune stones. We still have that lilac crystal, our first one, as a talisman to our new life. But whenever she came," Mom pauses, anger sticking the words in her throat. She swallows. "Whenever she came, she shattered the peace we were so carefully building up. After she got through with you, all we heard from you were these arguments and questions. You were so upset. You were only nine, but she could get you riled up and asking questions, questions, questions. All these questions that I didn't want to deal with! I shouldn't have to deal with.

9

Worse, she had the temerity to talk directly to you instead of through us. She was disturbing the peace of our home and our shop, so I warned her she could not come again if she continued. Your father was in agreement. He agreed with me that his mother couldn't come over anymore, that our family was complete with him, me, and you. We were good enough for us, and she had to show us respect and to do things my way if she was to come into our family, to be part of our family—else she would suffer being alone. Well, she didn't get the message. She wouldn't stop. She wouldn't show *me* respect." Mom pauses again, her chest heaving in indignation and rage. "So she suffered." Mom settles back in her chair.

Aban sits, silent.

"Your father agreed with me. He told her not to come anymore. We weren't going to have anything to do with her anymore. It was not our fault you assumed she'd died. It was easier that way anyway. It was better for you. Now rip up that letter."

"Okay," Aban says. The large, livid opal on Mom's right ring finger mesmerizes her. It seems to be shooting tongues out at her. Mom had never known her own mother; this opal is her only link. She shivers.

Mom is watching her. Aban drops her eyes, licks her finger, and uses it to lift crumbs off her plate while she watches Mom watching her watching Mom covertly back until Mom, with a satisfied half-smile, disappears behind her section of the paper. Dad hasn't moved; he hasn't flipped a page of the paper he's so avidly reading. Quickly, she slips the letter off the table and into one of her pants' pockets and rips up the envelope loudly.

3

TORONTO

ABAN half-closes her eyes against the early morning sun entering the Greyhound bus window on her right. She leans her head against the warm glass and turns it away from the rising sun and pale blue sky. The seats are filled with regular commuters all reading their newspapers or holding flat glassy things. The commuter beside her has one. Aban arches forward surreptitiously and sees the print change on it as the commuter swipes her finger. Weird. The commuter looks up at her, and she quickly shrinks back. When she feels it's safe again, Aban looks past her seatmate into the other seats. Another commuter has wires disappearing into his ears. The wires remind her of headphones but without the fat, round parts on either side of his head. Aban furrows her brow: the commuter's head bobs rhythmically like her former classmates used to bob their heads when she'd catch a glimpse of them from a distance. A sudden spurt of words takes her eyes off him toward his seatmate, who seems to be talking to a ghost. She hears a flip, and the woman behind those two, barely visible from her angle, is raising a small phone to her ear. Mom has one of those things for work but had told Aban that they're an expensive toy and not for her.

She rubs her hand on her seat. The fabric is soft. The big cushy seats with their multi-coloured fabric block out much of the noise but not the low whine of the engines as they roar down the highway. She looks out the window. The sun has grown stronger, and she can barely see against the light. Why is she here? She rubs her hand over her face and wipes the thought away. She had left the house early before her parents had gotten up. She doesn't know why she needs to go to Toronto.

There are so many cars going the same way.

As the sun rises higher out of her eyes, she sees that the green trees and wild brown grass have given way to houses. Cookie-cutter buildings rise up into view on either side of the elevated 401. The traffic slows, and the bus becomes boxed in by cars and trucks. So many trucks. Her bus curves off the highway right, then curves left underneath a bridge and up onto another, smaller highway. It feels claustrophobic, with cars and trees and narrow-feeling lanes hemming them in. But it soon presents her with a view of a tree-filled valley with a thin ribbon of a river meandering through its brown bottom. She'd thought Toronto was all buildings, all cars, all bad people. This glimpse of nature puzzles her.

The bus enters the chaos of the city and slows down more. Too soon, it is pulling into a station, parking underneath an overhang, and the commuters are getting up and getting off. Fast. Aban shuffles behind them down the aisle, down the steps, and onto the concrete pedestrian area. She looks around perplexed.

"Do you need some help?"

Folks in Toronto are friendly? "Um, yeah."

"Where do you want to go? Do you have a map?"

"Map?" No, she'd totally forgotten to buy a map in her rush to get out and to the bus before her parents awoke. She shows the man the lawyer's return address that she'd ripped off the envelope and stuffed in her pocket in her dramatic rip-up at breakfast two days earlier, before Canada Day. The country's national birthday is receding quickly from her memory, even though it was only yesterday.

"First Canadian Place. That's easy. You go out the station here, through those doors, turn right, walk up to the traffic lights, and you'll see a red and white bus stop sign. Wait there and get on the Bay bus. Don't bother asking the driver to announce the stop. He'll probably forget. Just listen to the automatic announcements. When you hear King get off; the big white building is First Canadian Place. Good luck." And the man is striding off. Aban hitches her army pants up, stuffs her hands in her pockets, clutching her wallet that is deep in her pocket, and follows him out of the station before he hurries out of her view. She looks around, her eyebrows puckered, spots a line of people down the street, and follows his directions, nerves fluttering her stomach; but this urge that took hold of her earlier keeps her in line, moving her feet to follow the self-assured people getting on the bus.

At King, she hears the bus's automated voice call the stop and gets off the bus, relieved that she's made it safely to the lawyer's street. She stops. The buildings are so tall. They loom over her. They—the cars, the people, the different sounds coming together in one cacophonous noise—confuse and overwhelm her. She hunches into herself and looks around until she sees imposing white across the street. She peers up cautiously and follows a wall of white stone and glinting windows up and up and up until her neck hurts, it's craned so far back. She takes a deep breath, lowers her head, and heads to the intersection. She crosses the street with the men in suits and women in dresses, almost tripping over tracks running down the middle of the road, and hurries through the nearest door.

She's in a bustling place with people standing in front of marble-white slab counters, people standing behind the same endless counters, people hurrying past the counters over gleaming white floors, no one looking at each other.

Now what?

"Can I help you?" A woman in a blue suit is standing in front of her. Wordlessly, she shows her the return address. "Ah, I know that lawyer. Come with me. I'll take you to the elevator to his office. When you get to the fortieth floor, his office will be right in front of you."

Aban follows the woman, trying to keep up. Torontonians all walk so fast. Suddenly, she's in front of the elevator, and the woman is gone. The doors in front of her slide open, a flood of people flow around her from behind and get on. The doors close. She hasn't moved. She waits long minutes for that same elevator to come back—she dares not try to get on another one in case it takes her someplace else—and when it arrives, she joins the flood this time. Almost every button is lit up in the gleaming, stuffed cage, and she tries to squeeze into herself away from the mass of people until they arrive at the fortieth floor. She exhales as she rushes out before the doors close on her.

A closed glass door with large letters spelling out the name of the lawyer's firm faces her. Its partner stands open. As the woman had said, the office is right in front of her. She walks through the open glass door to a high, long wooden desk, behind which sits a coiffed woman with a headset on, answering a constantly ringing hushed phone.

"Please hold. May I help you?" The woman looks up at her with a question on her face.

"I want to see, um, Mr. Myerstein."

"I'll transfer you. Do you have an appointment?"

The woman talking to her and the phone at the same time confuses Aban, and she doesn't answer.

"Do you have an appointment?"

"Uh, no. He sent me a letter."

"What's your name? I'll see if he's free."

"Aban."

The receptionist raises her eyebrows, clearly waiting. Exasperated, she says, "Your last name?"

"Mukherjee."

The receptionist presses a button. "Hello, Mr. Myerstein, there's a young woman here called Aban . . . Yes, I'll tell her to wait."

"He'll be right out. Hello, Myerstein and Associates, how may I help you?"

Aban looks around her, pulling her rapidly chilling T-shirt off her sweaty skin. This one proclaims "Save the Pandas," not one of her favourites, but it had been dark when she'd pulled it on.

The air in here is so cold, so chemically-smelling compared to the stifling air outside. She'd thought home was hot. Toronto is hotter. A memory of herself as a child begging for air conditioning rises up. Mom and Dad hadn't believed in it back then and still don't. Every summer, they say it destroys the planet. Now she knows it smells weird too. She wanders over to a black leather couch.

"Aban?"

She halts and turns to see a balding, paunchy man in a well-made blue-black suit coming toward her, hand outstretched. She puts her own limp hand in his.

"It's nice to meet you. Your grandmother regaled us all with tales of you when you were young."

Aban says nothing.

"Let's go to my office where we can talk comfortably." He strides swiftly down a maze of corridors to a tall, reddish wood door standing open, showing a view of a large lake in the distance, its surface a flat sheen. Aban hurries desperately after him as he waits for her at the door. Just as she catches up, he flies toward his chair behind an expansive desk. She follows him in and sits down in the chair indicated. Piles of paper stand on the floor, precariously on bookshelves, on his desk. He shifts a pile to see her better, leans back in his chair and then abruptly shifts forward, clasping his hands on the desk.

"Your grandmother was adamant about leaving all her assets to you. As her executor, I handle the dispersal of her assets and the paying off of her debts. She didn't have any debts as a matter of fact, but there are certain expenses incurred when a person dies and leaves a substantial estate. She decided against setting up a trust fund, which I told her had certain tax advantages. But your grandmother was stubborn, liked to do things her way. She wanted to leave you everything as is, and she had a video made to introduce herself to you. She worried about how much you'd remember. Although she herself had an excellent memory her whole life, stretching all the way back to age two, she worried that being so abruptly cut off from her, in the way that you were, that you may not remember anything so as to protect yourself, psychologically speaking you understand."

"I thought she was dead."

He nods, "She wondered that. Come, let me take you to our video room." He stands up, his chair shooting backward to thud against the bookcase behind him, comes around his desk, and gestures her out the door. He soon passes Aban and leads her through the maze again. She puffs to keep up.

They enter a darkened room, with sun shades drawn down and a large conference table taking up the centre surrounded by the most extravagant chairs she's ever seen. The table is reddish-brown like the tall slab doors and glows softly in the low light. He gestures toward the chairs to sit. She sits down in the one closest to the door, one that half-faces away from the table, and it moves unexpectedly backward. She almost falls off. Aban freezes her motion and glances at the lawyer. He doesn't seem to have noticed. She grabs the edge of the table and pulls herself back up, shifting her bum properly onto the chair then pulling herself forward. Meanwhile, he's typing behind a black open lid of something at the other end of the table, and suddenly this woman's face appears in a large flat screen up on the wall. Her still image seems to look right at Aban. She shrinks into her chair.

"Come closer," he instructs her. She obeys. "Are you familiar with computers?" She shakes her head. "Okay. Well, don't worry about it. Here's the remote." She takes the small, plastic contraption gingerly that he holds out to her. He frowns at her and half-jokes, "You have seen a remote before? For a TV?"

"We don't have no TV."

He schools his brows. "I see. Well, here, press this button," he points to one with two vertical bars on it side by side, "when you want to pause it. Press this one," he points to one with a solid right-facing arrowhead, "when you want to play it again." He instructs her too on the double-arrowed buttons that face in opposite directions of each other. The whole thing frightens her, and she puts it down determined not to have to use it. He notices and tells her that it will stop automatically. He picks up the remote, presses it, and the video begins to play. She stares at the screen while he quietly leaves the room and closes the door behind him with a soft click.

"Hello, Aban," says the image. "I'm your grandmother. Grandma, you used to call me. I don't know if you remember me. At night, as I lie in bed, wondering what you are doing, how your day went, I like to give myself the thought that you do remember me and that you miss me maybe a little, as I miss you every day. It doesn't matter why I was cut off from you. We all have to be true to ourselves; we cannot change who we are fundamentally and what matters to us in order to accommodate other peoples' prejudices, for therein lies the slippery slope to becoming someone we are not and don't know how to be. But it does have consequences. And I was sorry that it probably lay more heavily on you than on me. Adults can adjust to these kinds of fallings out; children don t understand and get confused or worried or unhappy without knowing why. I prayed every night that you'd be surrounded by peace and love that would wipe away any tears, ease any worries, smooth away your confusion, and bring joy to your life. I hope that my prayers were answered." She pauses. Aban shifts in her chair and looks away from the screen, down the table, down the long bare table. "Grandma." She mouths the word. It sounds kind of strange yet comforts her. She starts tracing her forefinger on the gleaming top.

Grandma's voice halts her finger, but she doesn't look up.

"On your eighteenth birthday, I had a small celebration with a group of friends where we remembered you. I pulled out the photos I had taken of you, and I talked their ears off about your funny habits and cute way of doing things. I told them about how you loved to read and how you'd get real annoyed if we pulled you away from your book in the middle of a chapter. I think you were reading *Anne of Green Gables* when I last saw you. I gave it to you because I had read it and enjoyed it so much as a child myself."

Aban frowns. She hardly ever reads fiction, just the pamphlets and books about climate change Mom gives her to read and books by her own mentors like Deepak Chopra. Aban doesn't go to movies, but Mom took her and Dad to see Al Gore's *An Inconvenient Truth*. "Truth is always so inconvenient, but necessary," Mom had said. "Fiction is for trivial minds."

"We had chocolate fudge cake, with lots of chocolate butter icing, your favourite, and El blew out the candles." She pauses. Aban looks up from underneath her lashes to see her grandmother dabbing her eyes with a handkerchief. The image on the screen wipes her nose and then smiles, a small, sweet smile with sadness in her light eyes, a colour not far off from the image's grey hair, which is pulled back with strands sitting up here and there.

Aban's stomach growls. She's never had chocolate. What's this woman talking about? And yet . . . and yet the way she talks about it, it sounds familiar. Bile rises in her chest. She lowers her eyes and scrubs at the table where she'd been tracing patterns.

"I had thought that after your sixteenth or maybe eighteenth birthday, you'd come to Toronto and seek me out. But you always were intuitive about what your mother liked. Oh sure, like any child, you tested her. But fundamentally, you wanted to make her happy. I liked that in you. And so I wondered if that was why you didn't come. And then I realized you probably thought I was dead. I could not come to you; I could only pray that you would come to me. One night I had a dream that I would not see you in this life. When I awoke, I decided that I may not see you again, but I would have you see me, or at least I'd give you the opportunity to see me. I would not let evil triumph."

Aban s breath halts. Is Grandma calling Mom and Dad evil? Shouldn't she apologize or something? How can she say that? What does she mean anyway? She shifts in her seat, and her pent-up breath whooshes out. She checks out the blinds in the room. Cracks of light show through but not enough to mask the picture on the screen.

The voice continues, "And so I told Myerstein that I wanted to leave my entire estate to you. I thought at first of simply leaving Atasgah to you, but we live in the real world, and in the real world things cost money. I didn't know how much you had or if you have a job or are in school. And who else would I leave my money to anyway? You are the dearest person to me. Yes, I am surrounded by my loving sisters and brothers; El means the most to me. But you are the one I think about every night as the city falls still."

Aban looks back up at the screen, frowning. She's never heard those kinds of words before, aimed at her, in that way.

"I hope that you will accept my gift, the only one I can give you, and use it to learn about me. I know it means moving to Toronto, a big, noisy, oftentimes harsh city. But my tenant El will be there to guide you. You see, my only stipulation in my will to you is that you let him continue to rent out the bottom floor for up to one year. He may choose to leave earlier than that, but I ask that you give him at least a year."

Grandma remains smiling as the video stops. She really hasn't stopped smiling, Aban realizes with a jolt. When Aban's looked at her, that is, her grandmother's face has been smiling, her lips curving upward, her eyes bright, even her hair with its springy strands looks happy. Aban's never met a person who non-stop smiles. Even when her grandmother's eyes had grown sad, her face continues to reflect, to reflect . . . Aban searches for the right word. Joy. Wetness stains her eyes. She wipes her hand down her face absently, erasing the wetness and the frown, as she continues to stare at the screen with the smiling face on it. As she stares, some of Grandma's words return to her consciousness. Tears ooze out her eyes.

She doesn't like them.

She doesn't like the feelings.

She doesn't like what Grandma said about her childhood. She makes it sound like Mom was lying. Aban stands up abruptly and stumbles to the door. She turns the knob and lets the hall light blind her and laser out the unfamiliar emotions.

A young woman pops up into her view. "Hello, Mr. Myerstein asked me to take you back to his office when you were done." Head down, Aban follows the young woman back through the maze, this time walking at a saner pace.

4

THE WILL

MR. Myerstein regards Aban for a moment from behind his paper-stacked desk, his fingers tented before him. Suddenly, he leans forward, threading his fingers through each other to clasp his hands on top of the desk but doesn't say a word. She doesn't blink. Her eyes take in that his hands have a fine cloak of black hair and that the sun is burning up the back of his head and throwing a shadow onto the desk. But she keeps herself disengaged from him, from this situation. She slouches down in her seat.

He seems to come to a decision and sits up, while reaching for a single sheet of paper. "The will is simple," he explains in his rapid-fire speech as he looks at the paper in his hand. "Your grandmother leaves all her assets to you. She had changed them all into cash to make it easy for transfer to you and so that you decide what you want to do with the money. She thought you might like to go backpacking across Europe or do a Master's." He darts a look at her from under his eyebrows. "Are you in university?"

Aban shakes her head no.

"You graduated high school?"

21

"Yeah." Backpacking, what would that be like? A Master's? Her? Mom always said she was an average student, not university material like her and Dad. Dad always nodded to agree with Mom, and then he'd say he liked his little girl the way she was; he didn't need no intellectual for a daughter. She swallows the memory into the churning of her stomach.

There are so many papers on this lawyer's desk. I guess smart people like paper, she thinks.

"Well, you can go to university if you like now." He clears his throat. "You also inherit her house. And as I explained before, there is enough here to pay for the upkeep of her—your—house. The house has no mortgage or lien on it. So, you can live in the house, sell it, rent it, go to university, travel the world, whatever you like. She hoped you'd use it to expand your horizons, to see life differently from what your parents would've shown you."

"My parents showed me life fine."

"I'm sure they did. I'm sure they did." He quickly waves away his previous remarks. "Here," he passes over the piece of paper. "This is the will in its entirety."

She reads it slowly. There are lots of words in it she doesn't understand, but she isn't about to let him know that. Her eyes fall on a row of numbers. Numbers she gets. She gasps when she gets to the last line and reads the sum total of her inheritance.

"All this?" He leans over to look at the line she's pointing to.

"Yes. That is the total accruing to you after all expenses are paid."

"And the house too?"

"Yes."

She stares at him, then back at the will, then back up at him.

"Have you finished reading it all?" he asks.

She shakes her head mutely and reads it all again, frowning in her effort to understand. She gives up. She raises her head and lowers the will to her lap. He hands her a set of keys. "These are for the house. One is the front door key; one is the back." He stands up. "Come, I'll take you down to the bank. The manager is expecting us."

She freezes in her chair. He stops at her elbow and regards her profile a moment. He awkwardly places a hand on her shoulder. "I know this is much to take in. But you can call me anytime if you need help, and the bank manager is a good gal. She'll make sure you know what's what, financially speaking. I took the liberty of mentioning you to her as she was your grandmother's manager and just in case you decided to come down." He pats her shoulder then takes the two steps to the door, opens it, and waits.

Aban wobbles up slowly and shuffles out the door. Suddenly he's in front of her, and she once again has to hustle her legs to keep up. He isn't that tall, but he does beetle along. She arrives panting at the elevator as the doors are sliding open. He extends an arm in to keep the doors open. Aban stumbles into the golden box, Mr. Myerstein on her tail.

They ride down the elevator silently and swiftly, the descent popping her ears. She bangs her ears with her left hand, the will in her hand slapping the side of her head. She lets her left arm drop as she shakes her head like a confused puppy. Sighing under her breath, Aban stills herself and stares at the elevator floor. She grips the keys in her right hand compulsively and crumples the will in her left hand. The elevator stops a few times on the way down, with a gentle sudden brake as if on springs that bounce mushily. People get in and out, couriers in their uniforms and packages under their arms, women in short-sleeved dresses wafting gagging perfume, men competing with their cologne. She watches in her detached way the lower parts of their bodies enter and exit, move and shift in the confined space.

The doors slide open at the lobby floor, and whoosh the crowd pulls them out. Aban loses Mr. Myerstein for a moment then catches sight of his bouncing suit jacket bottom. She half-jogs to catch up or to at least keep him in sight. They enter the bank that she had entered what had seemed so long ago that morning. He leads her to a desk and asks for a name she doesn't catch.

A blue-suited woman comes out from somewhere, shakes hands with him, shakes hands with her, and escorts them to her office.

"Well, I'll leave you two to work the financials out." Mr. Myerstein addresses the women. He turns to Aban, "She knows all the details, and she'll arrange to have the funds transferred to your bank account."

"I don't have a bank account."

They both look at her baffled. He recovers first, "Well, Mrs. Rogers can set you up with one. This is too much money to put under your mattress bank." He smiles to lessen the sting.

"I don't have a mattress bank," she replies woodenly.

"You do have a little money, right?"

"Yeah, I got money. Mom and Dad hold on to it for rent and food and stuff. They're saving up the rest for me. They give me fifty dollars every month to spend how I like."

Mrs. Rogers and Mr. Myerstein look at each other, eyes wide, his knowing.

"Hey!" Aban shouts at them. "There's nothing wrong with that, you know."

"Of course," Mr. Myerstein smiles at her.

"They look out for me, you know. Mom is good with money. I'm not."

"You can be. You will be, Aban." Mrs. Rogers replies gently, reaching out to touch her arm. "I'll teach you everything you need to know, and anytime you need help, you just call me, okay?"

"But Mom will do this."

"I'm sure she will. But wouldn't you rather learn?"

Learn? Her? She stares at this woman who's contradicting Mom. Aban shoves her hands into her pockets, unheeding of the will almost ripping as it crinkles and crackles in her rough movement, and looks down at the grey-carpeted floor.

"It's not that hard. Look, why don't I open up a bank account for you. We'll put, let's say, a small portion of your grandmother's estate into it, something that you feel comfortable with, and I'll show you the basics today. Then later, when you're feeling more comfortable with your inheritance, you can come in with your bills—"

Aban raises her head sharply, "Bills?!" Her hands come racing out of her pockets, will and keys still clutched in them, the will a little worse for its rude treatment.

"Not to worry, Aban. Just regular bills, you know, things like property tax, water, hydro, heating, regular stuff, all stuff we pay for when we live in a house."

"Oh." Her heart beats fast and loudly in her chest. She can feel it. She doesn't like it.

"Mr. Myerstein, I've got everything under control here."

"Good. Here is my card, Aban," he hands her a textured stiff white business card with blue print on it. "Call me anytime. Anytime."

Aban stuffs her keys in her right-hand pocket where her wallet is, shifts the will into her right hand, and takes the card in her left. She stares at it a moment before abruptly stuffing it into her left-hand pocket. She resumes crumpling the poor will.

Suddenly, Mr. Myerstein is gone, and Mrs. Rogers is doing things on a keyboard in front of a flat screen like the one Mom uses in the shop. Mom doesn't let her touch it, saying the one time she tried it, she'd caused her endless hours of work cleaning it up. Dad had joked Aban's not a computer person, just like him. Let Mom take care of it, he'd said to Aban before disappearing off to help a customer. She still doesn't understand how a computer can get a cold, but since then she doesn't dare touch one.

A young woman comes in to the office and hands Mrs. Rogers a bunch of stuff. "Thank you, Dorrie. All right, Aban. I have here your account information. I need you to sign here and here," she says as she points to lines on the sheets of paper she hands over to her. "You can use the pen beside you." Aban hadn't seen the pen in its neat little holder at her right hand. She takes it and signs, bending her head right down almost to the paper, not sure if she's doing the right thing, not sure why she's signing, why she isn't taking it all to Mom to handle? The best thing is to take it to Mom. Why'd she ever come?

Mrs. Rogers retrieves the signed papers and taps some more on the keyboard. "Okay, we're all done." She hands over a small box of cheques. Aban takes them gingerly. "These are your first set of cheques. I recommend using Quicken. It's an easy computer program to track all your spending." She perceives Aban's panicked look. "Or you can write them down here in this handy ledger, see here." She riffles through the cheques to the back and shows her the blue-and-white cheque-sized lined pages. "You write the cheque number here," she instructs as she points to each part with her black plastic pen. "Then the date here. What it's for, here. If it's a cheque from this book here, then write the amount under 'Subtractions.' If you're depositing something, write the amount under 'Additions.' Then calculate the balance and write it in there."

Aban blurts, "I'm not good with money."

"That's all right. It's just like adding and subtracting numbers in grade school. And that's what calculators are for, for us adults." Mrs. Rogers smiles reassuringly at her. "Don't worry. You'll be fine. As I said, take some time to get used to having an account, spend some money, and then when you get your first bills, bring them here, and I'll help you with them."

Aban nods, staring fixedly at the cheque book, then at the unfamiliar plastic card that Mrs. Rogers hands her. She has no idea what to do with it. She flips it over and over.

Mrs. Rogers says, "Here, why don't I show you how to use your new Interac card, all right?"

Aban nods.

"First, you'll need to choose a PIN number." Mrs. Rogers hesitates at the confusion returning to Aban's face. "PIN, that's your personal identification number. It's easy, don't worry. Think of a four-digit number, not your birthday mind. Have you thought of one? Okay. Got it? All right. Now put your card in this small machine. Here, I'll do it for you. Type in the four-digit number you thought of, and now you can use your card. There, that wasn't so hard, right?" Mrs. Rogers smiles at Aban. Aban s expression turns wooden. The emotions and thoughts are back where they belong: stuffed away. She feels better.

She follows Mrs. Rogers out of her office, through the bank with its efficient-looking people who know where they are and where they re going, to a row of large machines lined up against a wall, each with a number pad below a screen. Mrs. Rogers takes the card from her limp hand and puts it into a slot, "You put it in here, like this. See, it shows you which way the numbers should be facing. Here, give it a try. That's it. Don't be afraid to give it a slight push if it doesn't go in." Aban obeys and watches fascinated as the machine swallows the card. "Now, you press your PIN number on this pad here. Make sure no one can see what you're typing in, okay? The machine is set up to hide what your hand is doing, but if you don't lean forward and shade it with your other hand, people can still see, especially at some ATMs."

Aban creases her forehead slightly. She doesn't understand these letters Mrs. Rogers keeps spitting out.

Mrs. Rogers notices. "ATMs? That's what these machines are called, ATMs. Now see here on the screen," Mrs. Rogers points to the screen at each option in turn. "You can withdraw, deposit, check your balance. Let's check your balance first, shall we?"

Aban obediently presses the button next to check balance.

Mrs. Rogers clears her throat and continues. "Now here we can see the balance on the screen or print it out. I recommend that if you print it out, you keep the printout, don't throw it away. It's important to properly dispose of all secure and private papers. So now we see the balance here on the screen."

Mrs. Rogers pauses but seeing no response from Aban rushes on. "Now, let's take out a little spending money for you." She presses buttons swiftly. "Now here you see you have a choice of amounts. The machine only dispenses twenty-dollar bills, so the amounts are all in twenty-dollar increments. How about one hundred dollars, how does that sound to you?" She doesn't wait for an answer before she presses the button next to $100.

The machine, the ATM, Aban reminds herself, spits out the card, which Mrs. Rogers indicates for her to take, then the cash, and then the receipt. Aban holds the card in one hand and five twenties in another. Mrs. Rogers pulls out the receipt and tells Aban to put the card and cash away in her wallet. Aban doesn't know what to do with either the card or dollars. "Um . . ."

"Here, let me hold your card for you," Mrs. Rogers says suiting action to words. With relief, Aban reaches into the capacious front pocket of her army pants, pulls out her wallet, slides the cash into the bill fold area, then takes the card Mrs. Rogers hands her along with her business card and forces them into one of the empty card slots. She takes the receipt too from Mrs. Rogers, hesitates over where to put it, decides on an inside pocket, pulls out a couple of twenties to stuff into her left-hand pocket, and slides the wallet back into its accustomed place.

When the chore is accomplished, Mrs. Rogers reiterates that she must remember her PIN number, never give it to anyone else, never write it down, especially on the card. Then she's gone with a friendly wave.

Aban slowly walks away from the machines. No, ATMs, she reminds herself. She heads toward a revolving door. She leans into it, and it revolves her slowly out of the bank and onto the sidewalk at the corner of King and Bay.

The heat wallops her.

She almost revolves back into the bank. But she doesn't. It scares her more than the instant sweat springing up under her arms.

Aban stops a metre beyond the door, and someone bumps into her with a muttered "excuse me." She stays put, gazing at the cars rumbling over the tracks in the road, lifting her head to look to the top of the black tower across the way reaching to the sky, lowering her eyes to the sidewalks where masses and masses of people hurry by in the still hot air, and then staring at a red and white long metal car clattering past on tracks, its stiff-angled pole ripping along the wire overhead. Her heart pounds against her ribs.

This is where she was born.

But she doesn't remember Toronto, and she knows nothing about her birthplace. Her parents never talked about it other than to dismiss it as the big city where people get mugged and mown down. She feels utterly lost in this alien world where people take for granted that everyone uses computers and has bank accounts. She feels small and useless.

"Excuse me, get out of the way," a man yells at her as he jostles her and hustles past. Her body absorbs his push, and she remains in place, not liking where she is or all these unfamiliar churning feelings that have risen back up. Her world had been predictable, her emotions and Mom s thoughts comfortable until that letter came, that letter that had revealed her assumption about Grandma's death had been a lie, that Mom and Dad had let her believe that lie, that the protection Mom and Dad had given her had been not protection of her but of them, of their feelings, of their fears.

She doesn't even know how to operate an ATM.

She doesn't remember Grandma.

Grandma.

The name feels familiar in her mouth; it gives a warm, yet confrontational feeling. For a moment, she feels safe. But a small man head-butts her back, mutters "sorry," and swishes past her, his briefcase hustling her leg forward. This time she notices she's in the way, and she's back to feeling foolish. How could Mom and Dad have let her believe Grandma was dead? How could they keep her from knowing her? Suddenly, she needs to see. She needs to see where all this began.

She lurches away from the ever-revolving door and the unhappy people coming through it. She looks around for a cab. She knows cabs.

5

THE HOUSE ON GREENWOOD

ABAN stands at the side of the busy street, wondering how to catch a cab. Back home, she simply calls up Eddie. Suddenly, she realizes a green-and-orange car with a lit sign on top and a painted name on its side has sidled up to her. She opens the back door and slides onto the worn grey vinyl seat, her knees almost knocking up against the back of the seat in front of her, the air pungent and stuffy. A throw made of big beige and brown beads covers the driver's seat, overlapping the sides and top underneath the head rest, and some sort of doll swings from the mirror. He addresses the windshield, "Where to?"

"Uh," she digs first one hand then the other into first one pocket and then the other until she finds the will. She unfolds it and squints at the wrinkled paper as she searches for the house address. "Uh," she stalls again.

The driver twists around and barks, "Where to, miss?"

"Two eighty-five Greenwood Avenue."

The driver shifts the car into gear with a crunch and lurches forward, squeals a U-turn, pushing Aban into the door, and stops abruptly at the light she'd been standing near. It's red. She decides a seatbelt would be a good idea. She pulls and tugs at the belt until, with a massive jerk that sends her almost sprawling across the seat, she gets it to stretch the right length. She rights herself and digs into the grimy seat where it meets the back, looking for the clip, and just then the cabbie leaps the car forward and brakes hard, lurching her forward and half off the seat, her grip on the belt keeping her on. She shoves herself back onto the seat properly and hastily digs down again and yanks free the clip. The cabbie accelerates again, his car's tires jouncing over tracks, but she retains her seat and her grip. With a huffing click, she puts buckle in clip and sits back with relief.

At that point, she sees the counter.

Her mouth opens silently. She's never seen such a high charge for a cab at the beginning of a ride. That's what Eddie charges her for a whole trip to the grocery store and back when Aban has to do the big shopping for the family, when Mom is so busy at the shop that she has to entrust Aban to buy food for them all. With a jerk, the cab brakes and accelerates forward once more, flinging her head back against the seat. She pushes her hand deep down into her left front pocket, searching for the money she put there. She fingers the slippery texture of the bills. Reassured, she leaves her hand there and watches buildings fly by: a cathedral set back from the road with a large garden flowing from its side with trees and flowers so lush they look like they have a secret source of water; a stone building with straight, flat columns book-ending tall windows; brick-fronted little shops. It's too much. She brings her eyes back into the cab, and that s when she notices the tiny TV above the front seat in front of her, like a miniature Buddha version of what she has seen in shop windows. In a cab. She cannot comprehend the idea of a TV in a cab with commands to touch here. She lowers her eyes and finds rest in the sign in front of her, the one draped over the back of the seat telling her who her cabbie is and all the rules. There are so many rules and rights for her as a passenger; it's boring to read them all. She looks out the window again, and the cab seems to shift as if something is making it move from side to side. This goes on for a while. Suddenly, the cab veers to the right, throwing her to the left, and for a moment she's looking out the front window. Rails snake into the distance in front of them; the cab is riding next to them, then with a lurch he's on them and speeding faster. She's about to move back into her seat properly when she sees they're going up an incline toward another main street and a bridge with a curving, verdigris sign, declaring something or other. She flops back as they zoom up and underneath it.

She slouches down in the seat as much as the belt will allow, shoving her right hand into her pants' pocket. She wonders why she is going to see the house. It's not as if she's going to move to Toronto. Mom is right; Toronto is big and noisy and smelly. And stifling. And she's going to die in this cab. The buildings are shorter on the street here, not like those tall things back where she started, but they look so rundown with faded windows, barred windows, and scruffy people leaning against the walls in front of shop after shop. She knows the homeless are victims—she's heard so much about how Toronto is full of them, poor people too, about how you're supposed to pity them—but she feels apprehensive, shut away from them in this cab. Mom will say, "I told you so," when she gets home. And she'll be right. What is Aban thinking?

She's thinking; that's the problem.

The driver makes a sharp left turn. The belt grabs her right shoulder hard, the pain blanking out her thoughts, her confusion, her questioning.

They're flying uphill now as the sky darkens with clouds, the rundown shops having turned into scruffy houses. She stares at those clouds. This summer has been long, dry, and hot. Mom had said it would rain soon, and those clouds seem to say she's right. Aban hadn't brought her rain slicker. She'll arrive home wet too. Mom will say, "I told you so." She jams her hands deeper into her pockets.

The cab veers into the curb and stops. Hard. She rocks to the left and forward, the belt grabbing her shoulder, trapping her hands in her pockets. The driver says nothing.

"How much?" Aban asks him.

He gestures impatiently to the trip counter. She looks to where he's pointing. Thirty dollars! She peers out her window, seeking the house numbers in the dark. "Where is two eighty-five?" He points to his left. She turns her head to follow his finger and examines the quiet street. She doesn't see any cabs.

"Um, can you wait?"

"Wait?"

"Yeah, wait," she says with a spurt of assertiveness.

"Pay me first."

"I'm not going to be long. I just want to look at the house before I get my bus." She goes to open the door and can't. She panics, "Open the door!"

"Pay me first."

Uncharacteristically and from somewhere deep inside, she-does-not-know-where, she warns, "I'll scream."

"Go ahead, scream. You're not getting out till you pay me."

She opens her mouth, inhales strongly, and the door lock pops up. She shoves at the door and stumbles out into the swirling, hot air. Tufts of garbage spiral along the dirty sidewalk. She walks forward to the front of the cab and stares across the street until she finds her number.

At first, the red-painted brick house seems huge, like some worn dollhouse grown giant. Then she realizes it's two houses stuck together. Three stories high it rises; a gable window graces the brown-tiled roof; and two chimneys, one behind the other, sit on the side. Two windows cut out rectangles on the second floor, and the first-floor window is partially hidden by the front porch. Black metal, like some sort of metal table leg from the local pizza parlour Mom let them go to five years ago, holds up the two far-apart corners of the sagging porch roof. The whole is mirror-imaged on the right. Thin slats painted white and fastened together separate the porches of the two houses, yet the divider doesn't seem to provide any support to the roof at all. In Aban's town, people talk to each other, well, not her too much, but here it seems that even when you share a house, people don't want to know the others exist.

Aban leans to her left slightly to peer down the narrow alley that runs along the length of Grandma's—no her—house, separating it from a squat two-storey house beside it. The brick on the house's left edge is dirty brown. The house is old but not nice-old like Mom and Dad's. Aban shoves her hands back into her pockets.

She can't see the grass in front. Or whatever is growing there, for a white unsteady picket fence runs along the entire front edge, sequestering the lawn from the sidewalk. It's so small, that patch between the fence and porch, and the gate looks saggy. Dad would never let anything get so rundown. What kind of person was Grandma?

But something pulls her toward this old house. She takes a step onto the road.

What is she doing?

She yanks her foot back onto the sidewalk. She has to go home; that yucky cab driver will run her down if she crosses the road. She takes her hands out of her pants and steps backward until she bruises her right heel on something short and hard. She doesn't turn to look at the littered garden right behind her; instead she stumbles to the cab, yanks open the door, slides in, and barks, "Bus station," before she slouches down and shoves her hands into her pockets. The driver clicks the gear lever down and shoots the car forward and downward under the railway bridge then upward, making her slide further down the seat. She makes no move for the seatbelt this time.

6

THE MOVE

THERE'S only one customer in her parents store, and Aban is restless, itchy. She moves off her stool behind the cash register. The customer is picking up the small, dark-grey rune stones with their foreign inscriptions, looking at them, turning them over, then frowning. Aban looks around for her parents. They usually take care of the customers, and Aban usually ignores them. Yet today, she sees this one is in need of attention. Dad is minutely adjusting the placement of the skull-sized quartz crystals, his back studiously to the customer. Mom comes rattling through the beaded curtain at the back with a fist-sized purple quartz, its cavity filled with reflecting teeth, and takes it over to Dad. She doesn't notice the customer. That is . . . different. Mom always notices; even in the back of the back end of the store, she notices. It's like she has a scent for money coming her way.

Aban shrugs and wanders around. She knows not to approach the customer. Still, she surreptitiously watches her.

The customer picks up a rune stone and walks over to Dad. She asks a question that Aban doesn't catch. Dad hesitates in his adjustments but leaves his hand hovering over his giant crystal. He clears his throat. Impatience clouds the customer's face.

"It's a rune," he says loudly enough for Aban to hear.

The customer opens her mouth as Dad's hand descends on the sharp, sparkling pink quartz he was playing with. The customer closes her mouth, and she lets her hand holding the rune drop. She watches him uncertainly; she shifts her weight backward. Suddenly, Aban knows that the customer is about to leave the store, and any time Dad loses a customer because he has become so absorbed in his crystals that the human next to him asking questions becomes a mere mosquito, Mom belts into him until well after dinner. Aban's aversion to arguments triumphs over her fear of Mom's tongue for daring to speak up when it's Dad's or Mom's place, and she approaches the customer as she wanders away from Dad.

"Um, can I help you?"

"Aban, let your father speak," Mom hisses into her ear.

Aban jumps.

The customer halts.

Dad clears his throat and removes his hand from his sparkling rock.

Mom smiles up at Dad.

The customer remains rooted, one foot heading out the door, one foot aimed toward Dad.

Dad clears his throat again and says, "Yes, well, runes are, runes are stones with these Viking inscriptions. They will give you insight and answers to your questions."

Aban hears no more as, feeling foolish, she now wanders away, unconsciously performing her usual stuffing-down of another unwanted emotion. She pushes her backside onto the stool in front of the cash register and picks up her magazine from the shelf underneath it. But as she flips the pages desultorily, she glances at the computer screen beside the register. Graphics slide across its black, shiny surface, changing shape, changing colour. The word "Windows" appears and vanishes as the graphics move. Unbidden, a thought escapes out of her subconscious: "what are the graphics hiding?" Without realizing it, she lets go of the magazine with one hand to let it creep toward the keyboard underneath the screen.

"Aban, what are you doing?"

Aban jumps. "Um, reading."

"I hope you were not considering touching the computer. You remember what happened last time?" Mom snaps.

Aban thinks but doesn't voice, "That happened a year ago. I'm older now."

"You broke the computer. I couldn't even figure out what you did, it was so bad. I tried to quiz you on what you did. But you shrugged, protested you didn't do anything. Like always, you didn't remember. It took me hours to fix your mistake. Why do you think you can have anything to do with the computer when I cannot even trust you to work the cash register properly? How long did it take me to teach you how to work it? Do you remember how long it took for you to learn it?"

"Not long," Aban mumbles within the space of the breath Mom inhales.

"You can't work the register properly, so how can I trust you with my computer, an important business machine crucial to the success of my store? It's not a toy, Aban. It's a business machine. You can't just play with it. Last time, it almost cost us the store. I can't let you do that again."

Aban stares at the cash register.

"Do you hear me, Aban? By touching the computer, you are taking on the responsibility of the store. And we both know that you cannot handle that responsibility. It's too much for you, never mind that you are not capable of working a computer. You don't have even the most basic skills to work it, especially when you need me to take you places, remind you to do your homework—"

"I'm not in high school."

"Aban, that is not the point. You don't remember what you read. You didn't even remember what you did with those kids in your classes when I asked—"

A spurt of injustice opens her mouth, "I told you about the party!"

"What party?" Mom asks sharply.

"Nothing," Aban mutters, her outrage petering out, her heart beginning to thud.

"Nothing?"

"It was in high school."

"When?"

"I don't know."

"You don't know?"

"It was, like, um, back in grade ten. I didn't do nothing," she says to the cash register. "I never went again. I promise."

"You promise?" Mom's voice is implacable.

"Yes," Aban replies.

Mom eyes her for a minute while Aban inspects the cash register drawer and keeps herself still. Finally Mom says, "This is what I mean. You don't pay attention half the time to what your father and I tell you. I still have to look out for you, remind you to do things—"

"No." Her voice drops to a whisper, ". . . not the big stuff anyway."

"This is my store, my computer, my decision. Don't touch the computer."

Aban takes firmer hold of the magazine with the hand that had strayed toward the computer keyboard and raises the glossy publication to her face, automatically making herself forget where she is, who is near her. Mom watches her for a moment before turning around and heading to the back. The door chime sounds, but Aban does not so much as glance up as she rereads the article on pandas in zoos for the third time. Her heart slows down.

You will never be happy here.

The thought barges into her mind the next morning. It brings thinking with it. Aban stops chewing her toast and focuses her eyes on what they are aimed at: Mom. Complacent, neat, rigid, always needing to be in control, like with the newspaper section she's reading. She reads the Business pages first; then Dad can. She reads the Main page second; then Dad can. She doesn't read Living or Entertainment, so he gets to read those first. And the Sports pages. They don't think about Aban, about how she might want to read the paper too. As soon as they finish their morning muesli and morning newspaper read, they throw the whole paper in the large recycling box that dominates the mud room. Aban has her magazines—*World Wildlife Fund, Greenpeace*—and her books—*The Secret, An Inconvenient Truth*. Deepak Chopra's books have their own shelf in her room. Mom gives her a reading allowance to buy whatever she wants, as long as it's not some silly fiction, and as long as she doesn't spend too much time reading. "There's a time for everything," Mom always says.

Mom had home-schooled her until grade nine, then let her go to the local high school. "You're ready," she had said. "I can trust you," Mom had said. But Mom had still taken care of her. She had made Aban her lunch, even having Dad bring her to the store to eat it, after that girl had tried to get her to go to her house, so that she wasn't "influenced," Mom's word, into doing bad stuff. Even today, Mom makes Aban her lunch and eats with her. Mom made sure they were teaching her correctly too at that school. At the end of grade twelve, Mom gave Aban a full-time job in their crystal and stone shop as her high school graduation present. Out of her salary, Mom pays for and drives her to her saving-the-environment and green workshops. She doesn't have her driver's license yet cause Mom doesn't think she's responsible enough to get it. And anyway she doesn't need it. Mom drives her, or Dad if Mom is busy. They even let her set up a section in the store for her fundraising efforts for the World Wildlife Fund and Greenpeace. She doesn't have to worry about cooking or her laundry. She has it good here.

Are you sure?

She wrinkles her brow. Yeah, she's sure. Mom always looks out for her, protects her, guards her to ensure the world doesn't get her. She's grateful. Well, not grateful exactly, just accepting. Aban shakes her head of these intrusive thoughts. She resumes chewing her toast. But that voice, its urge, some sense halts her chewing again.

Go get the suitcase, go pack, move.

She scrapes her chair back.

"Aban, what are you doing?" Mom asks, her chunky metal green and bronze bracelets banging each other and the table as she lowers the Business section, while Dad lifts his head and peers over the Entertainment section. Breakfast is over only when Mom gets up.

"I'm going to pack," she says.

"What?"

"I'm going to pack, and I'm going to move to Toronto, Mom."

"You are not."

"Yeah. I am. And you can't stop me."

"As long as you live under this roof and you want to be considered part of this family, I can, and I will." She slams the tabletop with her free hand, her necklace of large green and brown stone beads swinging forward for emphasis.

"I'm going."

"We've talked about this already. You had your little rebellion, and you were almost kidnapped by that cabbie. You've seen how dangerous Toronto is, how dangerous people are there, with their attitudes and ideas, and now you want more? You're not going." She snaps the paper back up.

"I am too."

Aban stands up, her legs trembling, and edges to the basement where she remembers seeing suitcases years ago. As she stumbles down the dark steps, Mom suddenly gets up and thunders after her, every bead and bracelet jangling. Dad brings up the rear slowly.

Aban flips on the switch at the bottom of the steps, and a couple of bare light bulbs blink on, illuminating the air around them and not much else. She peers around, sort of aware that Mom is talking but shutting out the details of her words as she often does. She'll tune in when it's important. She sees a pile of rectangles in the far corner.

"Aban! You are not to touch those!"

Aban jumps. She half-turns.

Why are you stopping?

She swivels back on the ball of her foot. Mom's authoritative words mean she's heading in the right direction. Aban covers the remaining distance to the rectangles in a few long, strong steps. She squints down at the jumble of hard-sided suitcases with metal handles and clasps, coloured blue and blood red. They're covered in dust and dirt and sticky cobwebs. She brushes off the top one with her hands. But after a few strokes, she feels the dirt accumulating on her palms; she turns them up and looks at them. Ugh. Black. The sides of the suitcases where she'd brushed them are no longer peppered with dust, but smeared black. She lifts the top one, a blue one. Dust sprays into the air. They all sneeze, first Aban, then Mom, then Dad.

Aban carries it awkwardly past Mom, who grabs at it. They tussle, beads and bracelets clanging a chorus to their grunts. Aban sneezes again, and she almost releases the suitcase handle as her eyes water.

"You are not going, Aban." Mom grates at her. "This nonsense has to stop now. I've made my wishes known. I'm only saying this for your own good. That woman harmed you in life, and if she forces you to move to Toronto, she will do so in death too."

Aban lowers her head and grips the case tighter, bringing her left hand to join her right. She yanks the case out of Mom's hands as Mom's swift, savage words sail over her head and don't land in her ears.

Aban moves past Dad, who merely says, "Aban, I don't know what we did to make you want to leave us, but please don't go."

Aban stops and stares at him, about to say something when she hears Mom lurching at her. She scuttles forward and up the steps, suitcase bumping against her right leg, not pausing when she reaches the hall, and continues through into the kitchen and then into the mud room. She keeps hold of the case as she grabs a rag, wets it in the utility sink, and scrubs down the suitcase. Mom and Dad join her. Dad looks mournful, his hands jammed in his pockets, his head limp. Mom hasn't stopped berating Aban with warnings and threats of what will happen if she leaves.

Aban grabs another clean rag, not letting go of the case, keeping herself between the case and Mom's futile grasping hands. Aban pops open the clasps, which surprisingly are not rusted. She wipes down the inside, snaps it shut, hefts it in both hands, and brushes past Mom and Dad as she walks to her bedroom, this time on steady legs. The noise of Mom's anger and the silence of Dad's sad steps follow her.

Aban plops the case on her bed, pushes the little metal prongs to the sides, and the clasps pop open. She starts piling in her briefs, white tube socks, T-shirts, and army pants. All her winter clothes are packed away, and she doesn't want to fight Mom to go get them. And anyway, she's coming back. She's just going to visit. She glances around her room to see if she's missed anything, and in that moment, as her eyes sweep past Mom standing angrily in her doorway, Mom's words filter through.

"You will regret this, Aban. We love you, but we cannot help what will happen to you if you obey the siren call of that woman, that woman who would not respect me or my role in the family. She broke up the family because she wouldn't respect me. Do you hear me? Do you hear me, Aban? You're not going to do the same thing to me. You're not! Do you understand? I am your mother, and I know what's best for you. I am your mother, I raised you, I know better than you, I grew up in Toronto, I know what that city is really like, and most of all I know what your grandmother was capable of, the things she'd say to upset you and turn you against me. She's still trying to do that with this will. Why are you doing this to me? You're letting her turn you against me. I'm warning you, she'll upset you again if you go live in her house; she's trying to control you by telling you you have to live with a tenant, one you did not choose yourself, and one I don't know. I can't guard you against someone I don't know. He could be a rapist or a robber. You don't know what he is. A man. That woman—your father's mother, not mine—always had poor choice in friends, inviting those people to her house and letting them have the run of her place. Her tenants will be worse. You'll see. I know better than you in this, Aban. You don't know what you're getting yourself into. I do. I was right about your trip to Toronto, and I'm right about this. You'll see. How can you worry me, upset me, have me wondering what is happening to you, and I can't do anything about it? You will listen to me." Mom leans sharply into Aban's bedroom, her necklace swinging toward Aban.

Aban jams her hands in her pockets all the way up to her wrists, her fingers curling into fists hidden deep inside. She stares at her suitcase expressionlessly, head down, her side to Mom.

Mom straightens up, her body relaxing, her necklace coming to rest against her heaving breast. Her voice drops down to normal levels. "This life we have, this life we have as a family is the best one for you. And it's the best one you'll ever have because we love you, and I will do anything to protect you. Anything. But how can I if you're in Toronto, away from me? Ask Dad, he will tell you how bad Toronto is."

Dad clears his throat from where he stands behind Mom and speaks to the air above Aban's head, his wire-framed spectacles dropping down his nose, "Your mother knows best," he croaks. "We moved away for your sake. It was safer here for you." He clears his throat again. "But even here, your grandmother was making life unpleasant, so many arguments with your mother," he sighs and stares wordlessly for one or two minutes. He clears his throat and resumes, "I had to tell her to go and not come back. It was hard, but life became safer, quieter after she left. You're better off here with us, just the three of us. You're better off without her."

"Dad's right, Aban. You listen to him. You leave, you'll have the kind of life your grandmother had. Is that what you want? To live without us and be consigned to that kind of life? You want to be away from your family? Without us, what kind of life will you have? Alone, that's what you'll be. No one will care for you like we do; no one will love you like we do. Your life will be lonely. Lonely. You hear me? Without us, you'll be in a constant struggle. With us, you won't have to."

Mom stops for one or two minutes to let her words sink in. She's found it an effective tactic in the past. Silence is lethal.

"It doesn't have to be that way, Aban. Stay here with us; tell that lawyer he can have that estate; you want no part of it. Don't let a whiff of her money taint you. We have plenty of our own; we don't need it." Mom's voice deepens, slows. "But go, and you will not be part of this family. Any. More."

Aban stands rigidly. With an effort of will, she flattens her fists, pulls out her hands, and reaches for the suitcase lid with her right hand. Her hand hovers over it. Her left hand joins it. She slams the lid shut.

She must go.

She doesn't know why, but that thought, those unbidden words, "You will never be happy here," keep repeating in her head, like a neon sign blinking red. She snaps the clasps closed. Mom snaps her mouth open and yells, "Aban!" Dad drops his head and pushes up his glasses. He steps away and disappears downstairs. Mom steps into Aban's bedroom and blocks Aban's path. Mom glares at her daughter while her daughter grips the case with both her hands and examines the blackened wood floor, examines the cracks between the boards, gazes at the streaks of the old honey colour.

"You're not going. I'm not going to let you."

Aban doesn't move. Neither does Mom. Mom frowns at this unexpected behaviour. She has done everything to stop her, yet it's not working. She doesn't understand why not. It always has in the past. Panic grips Mom's chest, fear surges adrenaline through her, and she yells, she screams obscenities and threats, she throws her arms around, her bracelets slamming up and down her arms, her necklace swinging from side to side, her hands almost hitting Aban's head, slapping her shoulders, chopping the air. Aban stands still, unyielding.

Mom stops. She breathes heavily. She opens her mouth for one last volley. She says deliberately, "You bitch. You go then. You are not part of this family anymore."

Mom swivels on the ball of her foot and stalks out, slams down the stairs, and out the front door. Opening time for her parents' shop is soon, Aban thinks. Mom can't be late.

Aban doesn't move for several long minutes as the reverberations of Mom's exit die down. And then she lifts her head and blinks, as if the sunlight shining through the window had suddenly strengthened in intensity. Hesitatingly, she walks forward across the room and through her bedroom door. She shuts it behind her, noiselessly, not looking back. She walks down the stairs and into the kitchen, holding on to the suitcase with both hands all the while, letting the now-heavier case bump against her leg. She puts it down between her feet in the kitchen in front of the solid black phone on its own little table. She lifts the receiver and dials a number.

"Hi Eddie. It's Aban. . . . Yeah. . . . To the bus station. I'll wait outside my house."

7

ATASGAH

THE sign is what distracts Aban. Nailed above the peeling painted door, in cerulean blue it reads, "Atasgah." Aban stumbles on a board and lands on the front door with an unintended knock, not feeling the key fall from her hand. She straightens up and looks behind her. No one has seen her. She turns back to see a pair of arms coming at her, enfolding her. And a joyous voice booms into her ear, "Welcome, Aban!"

For a moment, bright light as if from the sun, flashes into her eyes and fills her, and then she is being released. Aban wants to run. But she's frozen to the old boards.

The strange man smiles into her face, his smooth, supple skin masking his age. He holds her out, the better to see her, "Welcome, Aban!" Sweeping his arm back into the house, he adds, "Welcome to Atasgah."

Aban blinks at his bright white shirt, speechless.

"Come, let me get your suitcase." He bends down first to retrieve something shiny, and she feels her flaccid hand being taken and turned, her key being dropped into it, her fingers being closed around the key. He grabs her suitcase, takes her other hand, and leads her in. She stops where he drops her hand to close the door. He strides by her, carrying her suitcase, heading toward the staircase in front of them, against the right-hand wall.

"Your grandmother told me many stories about you," he says as he climbs the stairs, in expectation that she will follow. And she does; her feet moving without her will.

"She was fond of you and treasured her memories of you and her together. When she felt her time was near, she gave away much of her furniture. She wanted to leave you her house, but she did not want to impose her taste upon you. Here is your kitchen," he sweeps a hand in front of him as they reach the top of the stairs, but he continues on, turning left and walking down a narrow hallway with the staircase balustrade to his left and doors on his right and ahead. "And here is the bathroom, and next to it a guest room. And in front of you is the living room. You will love the light in there. It brought much joy to your grandmother. She would sit in the sunshine for hours, reading."

He doesn't halt as he talks. He enters a doorway at the end of the balustrade and says, "Come, we go up these stairs."

Aban gropes her way after him up an enclosed narrow stairway.

"Your grandmother liked to sleep on the top floor. She said it gave her a feeling of being closer to heaven, of being part of the beauty of the cosmos. She also said it was poetic somehow to walk through the cramped dark to get up to the light. Ah, here we are."

They have reached the top of the stairs. He passes the open doorway ahead of them and again turns left and walks down a narrower hallway toward a door on the right. He swings it open and gestures Aban in. She enters to see a softly lit room, for though the sun is high in the sky, this room faces west protected by the trees standing outside. Before her is a bed with no headboard, no footboard, no skirt. Yet it's welcoming with its cover of red and blue and green and yellow patchwork quilt. Next to it on the east wall is a pine nightstand with a cosy lamp nestled on top. To her right on the other side of the door, on the north wall, is a small dresser glowing with the warm honey tones of pine. Past it on the west wall is the window dressed with long, gauzy drapes and a cream-coloured blind rolled to the top. Beside it at the end of the bed is a chair with a floor lamp bending over it. She hears a soft fall behind her and turns to see him straightening up from placing the suitcase next to the bed.

Aban stares at him. He seems to read her confusion.

"I'm El. Your grandmother's tenant. I've been waiting for you your whole life and hoped you would come today."

How creepy, she thinks. Her face remains still.

Yet El smiles and replies, "One can anticipate with rejoicing as a parent waits for a child, not for possession but to meet them again. And today there is a wedding. It is truly a time to rejoice. The bride and groom have sent many invitations out, but few have replied. And many of those that have replied have said they would not come. They have baseball games, open houses to see, hockey camp, and work that cannot wait. The bride and groom told me that these people are not worthy to be invited; none will taste their hospitality again. They are angry too that they asked them in the first place. But if you do not invite, then you will not know who will come and who will reject. They have asked me to invite my friends, the poor, the homeless, the lonely. For they want to celebrate their good news with all of their human family."

Aban blinks rapidly. What's he talking about? Family is Mom and Dad, not people off the streets. Then she remembers: Mom had told her she was no longer part of the family if she left. Did she mean it? She fingers the quilt's ragged edges and the narrow ribbons outlining some of the squares. The ribbon is a pretty blue. It reminds her of . . . of something. She frowns.

"Come to the wedding." His voice jerks her head up.

She's never been to a wedding before. As her mind veers away from the thought of weddings, for the first time, Aban focuses on him, takes in his black suit pants that hang just-so over his brogues and his pure white shirt with its long sleeves that ends in stiff cuffs held together by simple steel studs. His collar is held closed by another steel stud. Suddenly she feels shy and grubby.

"Come as you are. You will be welcomed. They want you, not your wardrobe. But you must be tired and sticky from your journey. It is hot out. Wash first, put on fresh clothes, and join me downstairs. I will be waiting." He disappears through the door; his footsteps ring as he walks on the scuffed wooden floor of the hallway and jogs down the stairs. Quiet descends.

Automatically shutting her mind off from thought, Aban snaps the clasps open on her suitcase. She rifles through her clothes until she finds a plain white T and a plain pair of khakis with not too many pockets on it. Grabbing clean underwear and socks, she carries the lot down to the bathroom, where towels await her, she notices with a start, realizing that she had forgotten to pack any. She has the requested shower. Though her short damp hair quickly creates humidity around her face, she does feel better afterwards. Aban dresses herself. She takes her wallet and key out of the pants on the floor and shoves them into her right-hand front pocket. Sitting on the damp bathroom floor, she pulls on her white tube socks and then puts on her shoes and laces them up. She scrambles up, and taking a deep breath, she opens the bathroom door and lets the steam out.

She thumps down the stairs to the bottom where El is waiting for her. Aban stops on the bottom step and rests her right hand on the smooth, yellow-painted round knob that tops the newel post. He beams at her.

"Come," he says. "Follow me. We will go on the TTC to this wedding."

El is holding a decorated tall, narrow bag, weighed down with something. Her eyes fasten on it.

"Do not worry about a gift. Your presence will be gift enough. This is a bottle of red wine for the dinner after the wedding."

Wine means nothing to her. Her parents drink beer: Molson Canadian. The kids at high school drank beer at that party. She'd been the odd one out at that long, boring party she'd snuck out to. Her one friend had told her how to sneak out, had said how all the kids did it, it was normal. But she hadn't dared drink once she was there. Mom would find out, and then she'd find out about the party too. And she did find out about the party. Mom always finds out things. Aban drank Coke instead; Mom wouldn't ever know. Coke didn't smell on the breath. And she'd wanted to know what it tasted like. It was good. Her classmates were lucky; they could drink it anytime. That was the only time she'd drunk Coke. Mom always said it was a symbol of corporate exploitation and evil sugary drinks was worse than any drug. She'd stared at Aban in that way of hers when she'd told her again after that party, like she knew. Mom always finds out stuff.

Aban breathes raggedly.

"Come."

Aban looks up and sees El standing at the open front door, his arm stretched out to her, his palm up. Aban's breathing calms. She follows him out, and he locks up. Across the porch, down the steps, and through the listing white-picket-fence gate they walk, one in front of the other. He turns right and heads to the bus stop at the corner, two doors down.

They wait.

The humidity slowly sticks their shirts to their bodies.

They continue to wait.

The bus roars into hearing and grumbles to a stop. They climb on. She has a moment of panic; she hadn't thought about how to pay. But El pays for both of them, asks the driver for two transfers, and hands her one before leading her to a double seat halfway down the dark charcoal-painted bus. It lurches from the stop, and she falls into her seat, hitting him.

"Sorry," she mumbles.

El grins at her and playfully nudges her shoulder with his own. She hunches into herself. He doesn't mind, and they sit there for a while in silence, he holding the tall, narrow bag, she shoving her hands deep into her pockets and sliding down into the seat.

He begins to talk.

"The bride and groom met through me. To your grandmother's house, to Atasgah, one day they came at her invitation. She held many dinner parties, and she invited people who didn't seem to go together. These two, people would have said, do not belong together, yet your grandmother saw them as going together when I had met them separately one day and told her about them. He is a man of action, as they say. He likes to do things and rarely stops to think. She is a thinker. She likes to sit and read and think about what she has read. He is younger than she. She is fatter than he. Since they have been together, he has grown up, learned to listen, learned to slow down and think before he speaks and acts. She has grown thinner and has learnt to use her hands, to put her mind toward action not just toward her own thoughts. They have rarely been apart in the last nine months, and today we rejoice to see them wed."

He sure likes that word, "rejoice," Aban grumbles to herself. What a stupid word, she huffs to herself, not admitting that she doesn't know what it means.

"Come on, Aban, we are at our stop."

He stands up eagerly, forcing her to stand too. He leads her to the back door, which he opens effortlessly, and she follows him out and across the street, not looking at her surroundings but only at his back. They wait at another stop but not as long this time. A large metal vehicle rumbles up to the stop on rails.

It's that long red-and-white car she saw the first time she was in Toronto, when she came to meet that lawyer, Mr. Myerstein. The doors whoosh open, folding and bending to the sides. Narrow steps ascend high to the driver, who is staring straight ahead.

As they cross the strip of road to climb the steep front steps, he says, "This is a streetcar. Torontonians call it the Red Rocket. It's a symbol of Toronto. It holds many more than a bus does. It sits up higher and flies along the road, to the peril of those who do not look out. But it can only go where the rails take it."

They sit in another double seat; this time she is next to the window, and Aban looks out on the rundown shops going by as the Red Rocket clatters across intersections and along the street. Again, silence reigns between them though El's presence seems to be touching her. She hears a baby cry and turns her head to see a young woman struggling with a stroller past the driver. She feels El's leg tense up as if he is about to move, but a woman with grey-flecked hair nearer the stroller leaps up and offers her seat to the young woman with the child. Aban's eyes follow the old woman as she walks to the back of the streetcar, and she encounters El's profile as the woman walks past them. Aban drops her eyes.

Aban doesn't like parties. Her mouth turns down at the thought. They're all about people getting drunk, and they talk about stupid things, things that don't matter, things Mom hates and doesn't think she needs to know about. Mom doesn't like her going to parties. She feels her heart thudding against her ribs. She raises her hand to her chest, but the thought keeps unfolding. A wedding is just a big party, a big frivolous party. Weddings are stupid. Mom had always said marriage is an outdated institution that is disrespectful to the woman and bundles people together, the man dominant, so that when it's time to leave, the women feel they can't, that they're beholden to society, to other people's opinions. "People should be free to do what they want," Mom had always said. She used to say it every time one of her friends sent her one of those fancy cards for a wedding. Yet here she, Aban, is going to a wedding. She has to get off this Red Rocket; she has to go back, go back home. She can't be going to a wedding, with people she doesn't know, in this loud, stupid city!

Aban can't breathe.

Aban wiggles.

Aban opens her mouth to speak into El's left ear.

Suddenly El is touching his shoulder to hers, radiating his warmth into her. Yet he remains looking straight ahead, down the length of the streetcar out the front glass. His profile arrests her gaze and her mouth. His brown hair shines where the sunlight coming in through the window hits it. It's cut in subtle layers. Not as short as a short, back, and sides haircut, and not so long that it curls messily over his collar. But straight, layered, and tidy. His brows are neither too thick nor too thin and form pleasing straight lines over his cocoa-brown eyes, which have the longest lashes she's ever seen on a man, lashes like those of a giraffe that she saw once at a zoo cause Mom said she should see how people use and cage animals against their will. No man should have such beautiful lashes, Aban grouses to herself. His nose slopes down in a straight line toward his wide lips with a curvy bow on top, an ever-present smile slightly curling their ends. His jaw is strong, and his whole head is held up by a powerful neck rising from broad shoulders. He has no extra fat, and though the shirt covers his chest, she has a sense of crushing strength. His power quails her. She decides not to speak, and once more she watches the passing streetscape.

"This is Queen Street," El says matter-of-factly. "It's the longest east-west street in Toronto. It covers many neighbourhoods. You will like this multi-faceted street, Aban, when you get a chance to explore your new home."

She wasn't sure about that word, "home." She just came to visit. She wanted to find out about her grandmother. Home is back home, where her parents are, except . . . except Mom had said not to come back. She shoves that thought away. Home is where her parents are. Visiting Toronto is just some urge that will leave her, and then she can go back.

"Do not be too sure of where life will take you. You may say, 'I am just here to visit.' Yet you do not even know what tomorrow will bring. Keep your mind open to what is around you. That is where the surprising joy is to be found. In this moment, and all that matters is this moment. This streetcar is taking us to a wedding, a time of joy, a time to celebrate two people in love embarking on a new life together." He sighs pleasurably.

And that's the last word he utters as they ride the streetcar and then get off in what seems a weary part of town. Kitty-corner to them stands a blackened imposing church with a lawn filled with people lying on park benches. He shepherds her gently across Queen, and they walk side by side down another street for several blocks, she growing hotter and hotter. And then there they are, standing in front of a cathedral made of neat blocks of light-coloured stones that fit snugly together creating a flat surface. The walls soar up to a pointed verdigris tower and a cross on top. Wide steps rise up to an exquisite layered arch, inside which stand large closed double doors. Doubts surge into Aban's mind again, but with a hand on her sticky back, El walks her forward and through those doors into the blessedly cool and quiet interior.

8

THE LOTUS

LIGHT lifts the darkness and tickles her eyes awake. She stretches in the silence. The blind is down, though the window is open to let in the night air, which is only marginally less humid than during the day. Aban can't see outside. She's used to living out in the country, where windows are uncovered; she's used to being able to see the sky when she wakes up. She gets up off the bed and pads over to the window to raise the blind, clad only in briefs and her black T-shirt proclaiming "Power to the People." The view through the old glass of the upper pane is not prepossessing at all, nothing like her old one. A square of sky up high, trees on the right in the neighbour's yard. Aban's mouth shifts down a bit in one corner at the sight of those ratty trees with drooping branches and listless, small oval dry leaves. From what she can see beyond the tall, wood fence, the yard on the left is paved, the square concrete pavers lifting up here and there, weeds the only green in between each one. And her yard—her yard. She rolls those words silently over her tongue. They feel strange; even in her head they sound strange. Her. It's hers, and only hers. Mom and Dad own everything, even the furniture in her bedroom is theirs. They called it "communal belonging." Mom used to talk about it, communal ownership and responsibility, as being better than what others did. She'd never understood what Mom was talking about, but she wouldn't dare admit it. She just assumed it meant Mom and Dad owned it, like they owned the shop, and they made the decisions, and, the thought arrives unbidden: kept her money.

A sound below attracts her attention. A bird is hopping in the dark recesses of her yard, where brown-tipped evergreens grow. His chirps break the air. He's too small, too far away to see what kind of bird he is. She likes birds. She follows its zigzagging path as it draws closer to the house. She leans forward as it disappears underneath her.

And that's when she sees him, sees El sitting on the brown lawn, if you could call it a lawn, more like unmown weeds with brown grass struggling here and there and soil showing off its grittiness.

On that inhospitable ground El sits, lotus fashion. His back is to her, but she knows the position. Mom and Dad practice yoga every Monday, Wednesday, and Friday, after the shop is closed and before dinner. They drive home in their Toyota hybrid and change into their Lululemon yoga clothes. Mom invariably wears her Push Ur Limits tank, in green of course, 'cause green is good, and the Still Pant*Br*R in black. When Mom puts them on, and only when she puts those clothes on, she stands in front of the long mirror at the end of the upstairs hall, her hands on her thighs and hips, turning this way and that, checking out how they cling to her tight muscles and slim torso. When satisfied, she calls to Dad to carry the mats out to the front lawn in full sight of the road and cars passing by, green mat for her, blue for him.

So embarrassing.

Even now, as she thinks about it, Aban puts her finger inside her open mouth and gags. In the winter they set up in the glassed-in front porch. They light candles and burn incense;

they play CDs of nature sounds with chanting instruments. When Aban sees them coming down the stairs in their skin-tight yoga outfits, carrying their yoga gear, about to exhort her to join them or join the Baksha yoga class in town—so good for her Mom tells Aban—she sidles away in the other direction and out the back to read or, in the winter, to walk through the woods along the trails. Who wants to look at Dad's skinny legs or Mom's big boobs? Gross. Plus Aban is always hungry, and yoga makes her hungrier. They never let her eat until they're done.

Watching El sit so still makes Aban squirm. Sitting still repels her. The first time she'd said no to Mom about the yoga, Mom had gotten angry. But Aban couldn't do it, and she'd braved Mom's wrath, the only time she ever did. She continued to refuse. The memory of that months-long battle makes the bile rise in her throat, and she crosses her arms over her chest. She hates it. Hates it. Hates it. Hates it.

She wants to puke.

She swallows, in the way she's learnt to swallow.

Her face rearranges itself into its habitual non-expression.

She thinks: birds don't puke. But then they don't need to sit in pretzel positions to achieve Zen. She searches for the bird but can't find him.

She swallows again and feels better.

As she's about to step back, something or rather a lack of something stops her. She looks down again, really looks this time. El's sitting there without candles. She hears no music, no gongs or chants, deep flutes or water running. No telltale streams of smoke emerge from anywhere around him. And his clothes look different.

She strains to see. He's wearing a red tunic. It's not form fitting, but nevertheless that sense of strength still flows from him and through the cotton fabric. She sees hints of white cloth covering his legs, and a blue shawl with tassels hangs over the back of his head.

He must be boiling.

She watches him silently. His head is bent in intense concentration. She cannot see his hands. Suddenly, El morphs in front of her eyes from a man in clothes to a living, wafting entity. The blue shawl covering his head waves in an invisible breeze, draping not just over his head but over his entire being, the fringes lifting up and settling down with a happy sigh. The red tunic bursts into flame around and under the shawl, holding it up, yet being kept in place by that all-consuming blue. The white, although hardly visible, expands beyond the shape of just pants and strengthens; it holds the whole up, as if without the white, there is no foundation, no meaning, no life.

Aban shakes her head clear of that disturbing delusion. "I am not losing my mind," she says out loud as she presses her hands against her eyes. Releasing them, she bends forward and yells down on his head, "You look like a flag!"

El raises his head, twists around, and grins back up at her. "Even a flag has meaning."

"Whatever," she mutters and slams down the window. El returns to his previous position, and her chest burns while sourness overcomes her face as she remains staring at him, can't help staring down at him. Who cares what he's wearing. He does look like a flag, gaudy, screaming at everyone to look at him, just like Mom. A bird flutters down to land beside him and begins to peck at the dried-out soil. Another larger one lands further away and runs forward. A robin. His orangey-red chest flashes as he runs forward out of the shadows. "Stupid birds," Aban grouses at them.

She swallows. Again. And harder.

Her stomach grumbles.

She rips her eyes away from the sights outside and steps away from the window. She trips over her suitcase and the clothes spilling out of it onto the floor. She'd better unpack before breakfast. She may be here only a month, but she doesn't want to live out of her suitcase. As Aban steps toward the dresser, she sees herself in the mirror. Her eyes skip over her pallid face and curly brown hair to check out her T-shirt. Though backward, the words reassure her. "Power to the People." It's the people who matter; it's their actions that matter. Sitting around does nothing. The truth is reality, and sometimes reality gets violent and messy. That's what they say.

She yanks open the top drawer and busies herself emptying the suitcase and filling the dresser drawer with her briefs and tube socks. It's hotter in Toronto; she wonders if she'll wear the socks. But she's always worn her plain white sneakers with socks, just as Mom had taught her. She can't imagine not. She shuts the drawer hard and opens the one under it, to fill it with her T-shirts. She puts all her brown and khaki ones on the left side; she piles in her white and black ones on the right. And in the drawer underneath, the bottom drawer, she tosses in her assortment of khaki and camouflage army pants. She slams home the drawer with her foot, and in that moment, she remembers again that she'd packed no towels or facecloths, not even her toothbrush, when she left home yesterday. Whose towel had she used then when El had her clean up for the wedding? Was that, like, a guest towel or something? Well, if it's in her bathroom, it's hers now. Besides it's her house. She grabs a change of underwear and a fresh pair of socks, a red T-shirt—her only brightly coloured T-shirt—showing off Che Guevara's face, and a pair of camouflage pants. She trots out of her room. She jogs faster and faster down the hall and down the stairs to a cold shower.

9

WITHOUT FAMILY

ABAN is hot again, only five minutes after her cold shower. And hungry. She peeks down the main stairs to the bottom floor. Tentatively, she takes a step down. And then another. And another, until she is near the bottom. Using the newel post as a pivot, Aban swings 180 degrees so that instead of facing the front door, she's facing the rear toward the open door to El's kitchen, which is located directly underneath her own kitchen on the second floor. She halts, uncertain.

The back door swings open, and El walks through it, his shawl draped over his shoulders. He continues through the kitchen, past the first door on his right, and disappears into the second door. He shuts it. The door near her, opposite to the newel post, is also shut.

Aban rubs one foot against one calf. She pushes her hands into her pockets. She looks back up the stairs then back down the hallway to where El has disappeared. She takes her hands out and lets them dangle by her side.

That far door opens silently, and El emerges. He turns his head toward her and smiles, leaving the door ajar. He looks cool in his short-sleeved soft lemon-yellow shirt, the top button unbuttoned, and the tail hanging over his faded blue jeans. She shoves her hands in her pockets and slouches toward him. She's the homeowner, but she feels like the child who has wandered into a stranger's house.

"Have you had breakfast?" El asks Aban.

She shakes her head no.

"Come, join me."

She follows him. He gestures her to sit at his table. It's small and sits near the back door.

"What do you have for breakfast?" he asks her.

"I always have toast. With jam."

"I am out of bread today. But I have oatmeal, cooked slowly, letting the milk soak into the oats first, adding fresh figs, honey, and walnuts near the end."

"Oh." Aban doesn't know about oatmeal. She continues, "I always have toast."

"Maybe another day," he smiles at her to soften his words and turns to take two steps toward the far end of the kitchen. El uncovers a large pot that is sitting on top of the stove and ladles out a bowl of oatmeal into one of two bowls sitting on the counter next to the stove. He sprinkles over some bran and places the first bowl in front of Aban. He repeats his action with the second bowl and places it opposite her. Then he pours out two glasses of water and sets them down before sitting down in the chair that faces her. Slowly she brings her hands out of her pockets and up to the table.

"Um, I have chicory."

"Is that so?" he says as he cocks an eyebrow, his eyes bright with humour but with a hint of steel in their depths. She blinks rapidly. He releases her gaze and digs into the soft, rich oatmeal with his spoon. He eats in silence, and after hesitating, Aban picks up her spoon and scoops up a couple of creamy oats. She tentatively licks it. Her eyebrows rise, and she sinks the spoon deeper into the oatmeal to scoop up a larger portion.

After an interval of contented eating, Aban feels in need of liquid. But water? She gingerly picks up the glass of water and takes a tiny sip. But thirst overcomes her uncertainty about drinking water from the tap of a dirty city, and she drinks half of it. She bangs the glass down and doesn't pick it up again. Meanwhile, El has downed his entire glass in one swallow and refilled it. Twice. He sips his third glass slowly at the end of his meal. When he sees that Aban has finished her oatmeal, he picks up their bowls and glasses, puts them in the sink, and suggests they move into the living room where it's cooler. She follows him to the door he had vanished through earlier.

The room is sparsely furnished: a small, cushy chair stands next to the window on the back wall, the one that looks down the alley beside the kitchen wall; a sofa sits perpendicular to the outside wall and next to a Victorian fireplace; a leggy chair sits opposite to the sofa with a low, long wood coffee table in between on which are strewn magazines and papers; and behind the sofa in front of the big street-facing window with its stained glass top, sits a plain pine dining room table and pine chairs all around, glowing a honey colour in the sun lighting up the eastern sky. El sits cross-legged on the sofa and indicates the leggy chair to her. She sits down and wiggles back, then wiggles forward, then squirms to the side.

El ignores her futile movements to get comfortable and asks her, "How do you like Atasgah?"

"Huh?" Aban answers as she shifts into a position not as bad as the others.

"Atasgah. Here, where you are. Your own house."

"Oh. Yeah. It's okay."

"Your grandmother chose it. She said that it had called to her. The day she got it, she saw me walking by and called out to me to join her. She told me that she wanted to share her life with others—a tenant, mothers and fathers, and brothers and sisters, people who wanted to hear the word—in this place she named 'Atasgah.'"

"Mom and Dad moved to the country cause it was safer. They opened up their shop to sell stuff, you know, crystals rocks, spiritual books, stuff like that." Aban says.

El nods his head, "Who is your Mom and Dad?"

"Um, Mom and Dad. Like who else?"

Aban leans forward to rifle through the magazines as El contemplates her bent head with concern. "Mom wouldn't count these worthwhile," Aban sniffs.

"What is worth your while?" he asks her, with an emphasis on "your."

She looks up at him, "Huh?"

"Are your Mom and Dad worth your while? Was your grandmother worth your while?"

She stares at him for a moment and then picks up the magazine under her hand: *Maclean's*. "Mom and Dad didn't read magazines like *Maclean's*. They said it was too sensa-sensa-sens . . . stupid. It was a right-wing rag, they said. Only unthinkers got it. Guess that's why Grandma did." She flips the cover over, leaving the magazine on the table while she riffles through its pages.

"Tell me, how did you learn what your grandmother was like? Who told you about her?"

"Mom and Dad," she says absently as she continues to scan the magazine unseeingly.

"You believe they speak truth?" His voice is even, gentle, becoming softer with each question.

She jerks her head up, her hand pausing in mid-flick, and frowns. "Like, yeah." She looks back down and flicks the page.

"What is truth?"

She slams the magazine shut and pushes it away. "Huh?" she says to the table.

El doesn't answer, and Aban pulls out another magazine from the pile: *Canadian Gardens*. She stares at the cover, which features a bushy red rose.

"I adore roses." El says, "How about you?"

She shrugs one shoulder.

"What do you seek, Aban?"

She opens the magazine to the table of contents page. "I don't like roses, you know. They're thorny, and they expect you to do all this work for them just to flower. Mom liked useful plants. Mom said a plant has to have a purpose, you know."

"Roses don't have a purpose?"

"No."

"What about you? What is your purpose?"

Aban shrugs and squints down at the page she's flipped to. "They say to plant rosemary beside roses. Rosemary has a purpose. Mom cooks with it."

"Do you cook?" he queries, each word soaked in his interest in her.

"Mom makes a great potato thing with rosemary. We don't have it in summer cause it's too hot, but sometimes she'll add rosemary to fresh strawberries or something like that."

"What about you? Do you cook?"

Aban shrugs, "Mom didn't want me to have to work like her. She said I should enjoy my childhood. Grandma used to get me to cook." Aban stops abruptly, surprised at what she's said, surprised that she remembers that.

"What did she and you do?"

"Huh? Oh. I don't know," she shrugs, "I don't remember. I told you, I thought she was dead, like, when I was two or something."

Quiet descends. She slouches back in her chair, reading the article on roses and companion plants. Companion, she likes the sound of that word. El watches her until she tosses *Canadian Gardens* on the table and stares at the variety of magazines from her uncomfortable position.

"Why did you come?"

She shrugs, not looking at him. "Mom and Dad didn't want me to."

El is patient.

She shifts her stare to the ceiling. She can feel his eyes on her; she lowers her eyes to look at the cold fireplace. Her hands drift into their familiar places in her pockets, and her body slouches down further. She swivels her eyes downward to examine the tips of her sneakers peeking out from the baggy ends of her pants. Her face slowly morphs from expressionless to anger.

Aban spurts out in a harsh voice to the toes of her sneakers, "They didn't want me to come, you know. They said it was too dangerous, that Grandma had always upset me and coming here would do the same. They said they knew what was best. They said they took me out of Toronto for my own good. They said Grandma always interfered, like, she didn't listen to them and made me upset. So they sent her away. They told me she was dead. They said they didn't. But they did. I wouldn't've thought she was dead if they didn't say it. It's not fair, you know. I don't remember her. I don't remember her at all!

"It was just me and them. I always thought there was no one else. Mom never said Grandma was alive. But Mom knows best, you know. So she must've been right, right? She took care of me, made sure I was safe and all. Mom wanted me to have a life, not be upset all the time. She enrolled me in tennis lessons. She'd come with me, you know. She wasn t like other parents who d just drop their kids off. Mom took care of me. She wanted me to be active. Active. What does that mean, active? I didn't like basketball or baseball. I wanted to run on the high school cross-country team. I used to jog with Dad. But Mom said tennis was better, taught you discipline and stuff. Cross-country didn't count cause it was, like, a team, and teens are always giggling and stuff instead of working and practicing, like Mom wanted me to. They'd just distract me, she said. Dad didn't say nothing. He never says nothing.

"Sometimes, you know, he'd take me jogging with him anyway before he and Mom took up yoga, when Mom stayed late at the store. Mom said yoga was better for his knees. She wanted me to do that too. No way. I had to play baseball in grade nine, but I wasn't doing yoga. She couldn't make me do that. I went into the woods instead. I—," Aban falls silent abruptly.

She looks sideways at the wall. "I liked looking for mushrooms, you know. But I never got to eat them. Mom wouldn't cook what I picked and wouldn't let Dad neither. She said you never knew what was poisonous. But I got good at it. I read lots of books, and, like, my biology teacher, he knew mushrooms and sometimes he'd take me with him, mushroom hunting, you know, during my spare. Other kids would come too, but we never talked. Mom never found out. I don't know why cause, like, she knew everything I did, my whole schedule and stuff. Anyway, I learnt good. I knew my mushrooms. I think Dad would've let me eat them. But Mom and Dad are, like, the same. He never goes anywhere without her, and he does what she says, except for his crystals. He likes his crystals and stuff. He spends a lot of time picking them out on his trips. I went with him once. But I was bored, and Mom got mad when she heard that and wouldn't let me go again. They trust me, you know, to cash out the customers."

Aban pauses, "Well, they let me do it. That's what I do, cash out the sales. I don't really know computers, but I'm good with numbers. I can add them up in my head real fast, you know.

"They don't like that I'm here. Mom said I wasn't part of the family anymore if I came. But I had to come. I don't know why. I just had to."

Water films El's eyes. A teardrop appears, grows, clings to El's lower left eyelid, then its cousin joins it in his right eye. He remains still as one does around a skittish fawn, and he says gently, "I know." Then asks, "What is your name?"

Aban looks at him, like he just uttered the most stupid thing ever. "Huh?" She cringes into herself when she suddenly sees his silent weeping for her. It makes her feel awkward and stupid and something else that makes her uncomfortable. She shoves it away and averts her eyes from his face.

El answers softly, "Who is your Mom and Dad?"

"You asked that already, and I told you—Mom and Dad. Are you, like, deaf or something?" she demands of the fireplace.

"Who is your grandmother?"

She can't help it; her eyes are drawn to him in that question. He makes it sound as if her grandmother is still alive. She won't think about that. She won't meet his empathetic gaze but stares at his chin for a moment. Then she speaks slowly as to a moron, "I. Don't. Know."

El looks away as if to gather his thoughts. He turns back to her and explains, "Your Mom and Dad created you. Your grandmother loved you into beginning. Through the word, you received your name, as did all your ancestors before you. All who came before you live through you, and all who come after will live because of you."

Her eyes leap up to his. She stares at him as if he's grown three heads. "My parents named me," she says flatly. She takes her hands out of her pockets, leans forward, and starts rifling through the magazines again, hunching her shoulders. She picks up a University of Toronto Continuing Studies catalogue. "What's this?"

El's voice regains normal volume as he answers, "It was one of your grandmother's favourite places because, as she used to tell me often, there she fed her mind's endless curiosity and met other people who liked to discuss new ideas and think of old ideas in new ways."

"Oh," Aban says as she leafs through the catalogue slowly.

"Yes, oh," El smiles. Then turning serious, he says, "Your grandmother said that she liked to refresh her mind every year. She took her time going through the catalogue you hold, deciding which course she'd take. Sometimes, she'd study Canadian authors; other times new methods of business. One year, she took a philosophy course, but she angered the professor when she challenged his assumptions and arguments continually. She told me that perhaps she should avoid philosophy in the future. But just before she died, she was contemplating it again. She said that engaging with life meant confronting rigid people and afflicting comfortable ideas, ideas that resided in heads like familiar 'security blankies' that hid the reality in front of them. Your grandmother often rose up and confronted fear, for fear is at the root of all evil."

"Oh yeah? There's no such thing as evil. The devil is a fabrication of superstitious people's imagination, Mom said. It's a cop out. She always said all that stuff is an excuse not to, not to feel pity for our planet and the poor. We're spiritual you know, and when we're in harmony with other people, we do good. We know what action to take. That's what Mom always told me. But if we're out of sync, that's when we're bad."

El's mouth twitches into an upward curve. "Are you in harmony?"

"I do good, yeah. I have a section in the store for the people and things doing good in their world. Someone has to. While politicians talk and other people spend lots on each other during the holidays, Mom taught me to do stuff. Action is the only thing that will change the world. Wasting time on this artsy-fartsy stuff won't change the world. We gotta work together you know, not jaw away in classes." She looks back down at the catalogue and flips to another page.

"School was hard for you?"

She shrugs, "I did okay. Mom said I wasn't cut out for university. She let me look after the garden out back but said it'd be better for me working in the shop with her and Dad."

El brushes his eyes and reveals, "When we first met, your grandmother told me about how she spent years going from one career to another before she went to university. She wasn't sure what she wanted to study, but she knew she was seeking something and that spending time in a university instead of flitting about, as she put it, would show her the way. She said she never regretted her decision to spend four years on her undergraduate degree and then another three on her Master's when she was in her thirties. She got married during that time. That's when your Dad was born. She devoted herself to him but also to her studies, to her husband, and then to her new life post-graduation. She was grateful that she took the time to learn. She was grateful for what that time gave her."

"Yeah, well, wasting time is what school is. The world needs help now. That's why I raise money."

Aban throws the catalogue on the chaotic heap she's created, and it slides off the slippery covers of the rest of the magazines and disappears over the other side of the table and smacks onto the floor. She lets it lie, stands up, and heads to the door.

10

THE WOMAN WHO RESTED

"ABAN." El's suddenly firm voice arrests her as she reaches the doorway. He asks, "Whom do you seek?"

She keeps her back to him.

"Aban, what do you want to ask?"

Aban turns around and sees him unfolding himself, standing up, looking at her. She cannot read his expression, but then she can't read people anyway.

"Aban, what do you want to ask?"

"Nothing."

"Are you sure?"

"Yeah. I know what I'm supposed to be doing. I don't know why I came here. Life with Mom and Dad was fine, you know. I was doing stuff," she says, putting the emphasis on "doing."

"Yet you came."

"I had to."

"Why did you have to?"

"I don't know," she whines. "What are you, a cop or something, asking all these questions. Who made you judge? I don't have to tell you nothing, you know. I didn't even tell Mom everything."

He awaits her in silence as she frowns at the floor, rubbing the old wood with the toe of her right sneaker. She asks sideways, "So what do you do around here? They used to brag there was more to do in the big city than in the country, but so far all it got me is a fancy wedding and hot air. And useless university magazines."

El sits down and gestures with an open palm for her to join him. He waits until she can no longer resist the pull. She doesn't want to sit. She doesn't want to stay. She wants to go . . . to go . . . well, she doesn't know where. Not here. Not home. She perches at the very edge of the chair, hands between her knees, staring at the floor.

"There was a CEO in charge of a large software company," El begins, leaning toward her, his eyes upon her bent head. "He had many employees in his care, and his company produced software that most of the world had grown to depend on. He was successful. But he had a rival. His rival owned a small software company. It had few employees, and it sold its software only in Canada. The CEO looked upon his rival with contempt. She was small. She didn't threaten his large company. Yet he felt uneasy. He would work harder he decided.

"So one day, he told his managers, 'I want you to produce the best, most radical software the world has ever seen, one that will run on PCs, Macs, iPads, and Blackberries. Even on Linux computers. I will invest every penny in it. And I want it done in time for the Christmas sales.' His managers looked at each other and said, 'But sir. That has never been done before in so short a time.' He got angry at them. 'Do you not work for me? I hired you to be better than everyone else. Are you not the best, the brightest of all software designers?' They answered him, 'Yes.' 'Then do it,' he told them.

"He went away and funnelled all the company's funds toward developing their design. He came back in three months and asked them if they were done. The managers looked afraid. They said they had a radical idea but they needed more time, for current hardware would not run their new software. The CEO again got angry. 'Why are you creating problems,' he asked them. 'I told you what I wanted, now do it. If you work night and day, if you stopped wasting time sleeping so much, you'd have your time.' The managers scurried away and finished writing the software. When Christmas sales time came upon them, the CEO was pleased to see he had beaten his rival to the punch and put on a flashy presentation streamed to the whole world, and people flocked to all the stores to buy the best, most radical software ever made as gifts for themselves and their families. But within hours, they became angry. The software didn't work. It crashed constantly. On the best computers, the iPad, or Blackberries, it crashed. The people demanded refunds, and the company demanded the CEO's resignation. He never worked again.

"Meanwhile, a year earlier, his rival had asked her chief designer what he was working on. Her chief designer said he had been thinking about a new idea for the last couple of years and had run into the problem that no hardware out there would run his software. The rival asked her designer, 'What do you need?' The designer told her. She went away and set the problem aside for a month. The designer continued to refine his software idea. When the CEO's rival came back to her designer, she asked him again, 'What do you need?' He told her. She went away to take courses on hardware design, for up till now she knew software but not the details of hardware design. Then she passed on some ideas to her designer and left him to work it out. A month later, she went back to her designer and asked him what he needed. He shook his head; it was not going well. She went away for another month to think. When she came back, she said she had an idea. She spoke to a company that specialized in hardware. They worked together and designed the hardware that her designer needed. When

Christmas sales time came upon them, together the CEO's rival and the hardware company put out a few ads and put up a website to tell out the news about their new device with its radical software. No one paid much attention to it, and the big company scoffed before putting on their flashy presentation.

"But slowly people found out about it. As the big company's software crashed, the rival s rose into public view. People tweeted about it, Facebooked one another, and talked about it on their blogs. Soon newspaper reporters heard and wrote articles, and magazines featured it in their what-to-buy-now stories. People outside of Canada wanted this new device too. As the CEO's company plunged into the red, the rival's grew into the blackest of black."

Aban stares at him. What is he yammering on about now? Worse, he'd used words she'd never heard before. She feels stupid. Unfamiliar anger makes her splutter, "Seriously, what're you talking about?"

El shakes his head, "It's a simple story, Aban. Let it sink in; savour it; don't be afraid of the words."

"I'm not afraid," she retorts. Who is he to say that? She barks at him, "Like Mom says, the world needs doers not slackers."

"Yet you picked up the university course catalogue."

"So? It was sitting there."

"Many other magazines were sitting there too."

El gazes empathetically upon her face; she stares woodenly at him.

"What is your name?" he asks.

She walks out.

11

THE WILD TORONTO

"WAKE up, Aban!"

El's booming voice shoots her heart into pounding, and she almost chokes on the toothpaste foaming in her mouth. She grabs the bathroom sink to steady herself. She spits toothpaste into it, rinses her mouth, and slouches out the bathroom and down the stairs to where El is waiting.

"Come on, Aban. Let us go into the backbones of Toronto," he grins at her with the hearty air of boundless energy and joy.

"Whatever," she mumbles.

El and Aban leave the stuffy house and wade into the muggy city air. They walk up Greenwood, toward the railway bridge. Aban looks up from the sidewalk and into the underside of the old bridge as it shakes under the moving weight of a train. As they walk uphill past the bridge, a large concrete yard criss-crossed with rails and holding a silent, still, silvery engineless train or two, rises on their left. She mindlessly looks through the heavy chain-link fence toward the train as her feet scuff along and as El keeps an eye on her for a moment and then continues on. She falls further and further behind. A lazy click-clack . . . click-clack soothes with its familiarity, and a train comes into view. She halts to watch idly for a while, edging unthinkingly up to the fence. After a longer while, she turns her head to look along the sidewalk in the direction they had been walking. El is disappearing. Against her will, Aban begins to walk again. But El continues to disappear. She trots to catch up, the hot air stifling her breathing. She falls reluctantly into the faster rhythm of his walk.

The hill levels out, two-storey houses rise on each side of the four-lane road, and they reach the lights at a main intersection. Affixed to a post, a large rectangular blue sign with white letters declares that they've reached Danforth Ave.

Whatever.

They cross the wide road, walking up the hidden slope in the road that crests along the yellow centreline then down the slope toward the opposite sidewalk.

They continue on.

A large pointed grey-banded white sign declares that they are at Danforth Collegiate and Technical Institute. High school. She swallows and averts her gaze. El moves closer to her. Her gaze lands on the two-storey houses across the road. They sit silently with mere strips of brown lawn in front; the original front porches sit empty; and wide parched grass verges separate sidewalk and road. Trees grow everywhere, some young sticks, some reaching the sky and sheltering roofs from behind. Aban knows their names, and they idly scroll through her mind without effort: elm, maple, and chestnut.

Beside her, El keeps walking.

They reach a busy road. Two lanes of cars zip toward them, in her direction. Aban cringes toward the neat bungalows behind their hedges and fences. El keeps walking.

Soon they're at another major intersection. On one corner tall bright blue hoarding surrounds an angled crane with a wire hanging from its tip. "Coxwell Trunk Sewer Project," the sign reads. She takes in the words, but they mean nothing to her.

El crosses the road first east and then north, and suddenly there is no traffic noise. They're walking along a quiet street lined with brick bungalows with bow windows underscored by stonework, their roofs angling down to cover small enclosed garages. Two-storey houses punctuate the neat line of one-storey houses. Clipped green lawns edge up to the sidewalk, and majestic trees overhang the street here and there.

The road ends in a T-junction, and El and Aban step off the end of the sidewalk, cross the road, and enter a park. The screams of children erupt from the playground on the far right. The grass is brown and crisp; soil emerges here and there. Weeds creep a dark green pattern in the dead grass. Pine trees have let go of their needles, and the fallen needles scent the still, humid air. Aban's T-shirt proclaiming "I Love Nature" sticks to her back; the same camouflage army pants she wore the day before cling to her thighs and drape over her smudged sneakers. Aban wants a drink, but she has no water, and her mouth doesn't open to ask. El hands her a bottle from the bag slung over his shoulder. She grasps it, unscrews the cap, and gulps down the warm water. She screws the cap back on and hands it back to him. He regards her for a moment, but she continues to hold out the bottle, and he takes it.

El and Aban cross the expanse of stiff grass, passing by a solitary mature chestnut tree, and enter into the ring of trees and brush that edge the park on three sides. A sign, looking a bit lopsided, stands beside a set of stairs.

El pauses and explains, "We're almost there, Aban. Come, follow me."

"What do you think I've been doing," she mutters under her breath. It's hot and this city stinks, but here we are walking forever when normal people would be inside. Aban follows him anyway as he trots lightly down the concrete steps, not holding the double metal handrail on his right. The steps disappear steeply into a left-hand curve. The hill seems to be endless. Aban steps heavily down on each step, her hand sliding along the hot top rail next to her, down, down, down. A path of dried grey scree greets them at the bottom. Curved handles for another set of steps sit weirdly at the top of another hill seeming to lead a person into a forest canopy. Sumachs and brush surround and dominate the steps. Tall, wide grass bends toward them. Aban relaxes. It's not her woods, but it's not the dusty city either.

El does not continue down. Instead he turns right toward a beaten path of soil and thirsty grass. Rushes, cracking without moisture, grow at the beginning of the path. A tall tower with three rows of outstretched metal arms holding long lines and with cross braces rising up into its head, waits for them in the distance. Telephone poles, with their little crosses at the top and three strings of line, seem to march alongside the path they're on.

El gestures for her to come up alongside him and waits for her until she does. He and she walk in silence, El slowing down to her pace. It is hushed in this space. No other person is in sight. It's the two of them alone in the wild bones of Toronto.

El begins to speak. "When Toronto was formed, glaciers came along here. They packed the land and created Lake Algonquin, and great rivers sprung up to feed this giant lake. As the ice receded, the rocks and stones underneath the ice gouged out the land or dropped to form hills that sit here and there like strangers in the field. The land sprang back up after the weight of the glaciers had left. The great rivers shrank, leaving behind the steep hills of their banks, their fertile floors, and creeks and slim rivers as a remembrance of what they once were. These old river valleys are called 'ravines.' Pockets of them rise up at the ends of streets as dark woods or parks where dogs can sniff and run around and the people can find respite. But the main ones run north and south from Lake Ontario into the country, branching off into neighbourhoods and disappearing under the streets.

"At one time, politicians kept these ravines tidy. Their idea of nature was to groom it. But a few years ago, people called upon the politicians to let their ravines be. Clipped grass gave way to nature growing as she saw fit. The Carolinian forest used to inhabit southern Ontario, even Toronto. Most of it is gone, but the people and the politicians decided to find out more about Toronto's native plants, and they planted them. Slowly, the earth has rebounded and brought forth an abundance of growth. In the Fall, these native plants and trees will spring into their colours of red and purple and gold."

Aban says, "I joined Greenpeace cause they really care about the environment, you know. I raised funds for when they attacked the Japanese for killing whales under that bogus science stuff. Humans are the worst species on earth. The earth can live better without us. Farley Mowat said so." Aban falls silent.

El bends toward her, attentive, clasping his hands behind his back.

Aban says, "We need to live in harmony, but we just kill the planet, you know. I mean, we all know climate change is gonna kill us. But the politicians, they think it's not happening. They say they need more proof. Yeah, proof, like it hasn't rained all summer. That's proof, you know. Then there's our boreal forest. Greenpeace is helping keep that, you know. They're the only ones that care. If we cut down those trees, like, they won't grow again."

Aban speaks faster, "It's time for politicians to recognize what's happening, do what Greenpeace says, and set aside intact areas of the boreal forest so our planet can breathe and our native people can live in harmony with the land." She falls silent again.

El turns his head to look full into her eyes and asks, "What about your own garden?"

She averts her gaze to the ground, "My garden?"

"Yes. Yours."

Aban shrugs. She doesn't know what he's talking about. Yeah, she gardens, but it isn't hers. It's Mom's.

El contemplates the back of her lowered head and continues to walk beside her, bent toward her, as she slouches along. Aban sees only the ground, while El hears her heart and listens to the sounds of the woods around them, locating without seeing them the noisy sparrows or shy blue jays in the trees, the squirrels in the dried-up bushes, the humming cicadas. Aban scuffs her feet along the path, hands jammed in her pockets, her head down.

El straightens up, letting his arms move loosely in rhythm with his languid steps. He speaks again. "Listen to what I say, Aban."

Aban hunches her shoulders.

"One day there was a gardener. It was springtime. It was time to plant. The gardener took his bucket, filled it with seeds, and slung it over his shoulder. As he walked, he sowed the land. Some of the seed landed on the path and lay there. Soon birds came and pecked at this bounty, digesting the seed for their nourishment. Some landed where the soil sat shallowly amongst the sharp stones. The seed spread its roots out horizontally looking for water, but the sun came out and parched the thin soil and shallow roots. The young shoots withered and died. Some landed in the weeds, weeds like creeping charlie, purslane, lady's thumb, green pigweed, garlic mustard, bird rape, and white clover. They crowded out the seeds, their roots and stems entwining and choking off the seed's shoots. But some landed on good soil. This soil had been enriched by the death of old plants. These plants when young and fruitful had fed the creatures of the earth and had in turn been nourished by plant-eating animals and by hidden sources of water. The seed grew up into grain in this good soil, feeding the people and feeding the land after harvest."

El finishes. Silence stretches. He bends down and asks her gently, "Do you have ears to hear, Aban, the stories that I tell you?"

"Yeah." Aban replies derisively. "But what's that got to do with anything? Like, you know, conventional farmers have to use chemicals for anything to grow. They grow only one crop, and big chemical companies are taking over our food. The seed is all the same. The soil is all the same. Farmers are all the same. Mom has us buy organic food cause then we know how they were grown. It's real food. It's better for us and for the environment. Better than those mushy tomatoes they truck in from California. You know they had to divert a river to grow things down there. It's all artificial, and animals don't get the water they need anymore from that river."

El sighs at her obtuseness, "Can you hear me, Aban?"

"Yeah. I heard you. We're losing diversity in our seeds, that s what the environmentalists say. It's like those bananas. You know that if a disease gets in them, we won't have any bananas to eat, cause like they're all clones. They have no seeds. They're gonna die out soon, you know. And like carrots all look the same. You know at one time they were like purple and yellow and stuff. Mom suggested we buy those kinds of organic carrot seed from this grower so we could have them in our vegetable garden, but the summer has been so hot and the township said we had to ration our water, so they kind of died. Politicians who say there's no climate change should come out to our place. Like, hardly any vegetables grew this summer. The tomatoes are doing okay cause I've been babying them." Aban frowns. "I hope Mom will look after them. They'll die if she doesn't. Anyway, I won't be here long, so, like, they should be okay. Besides it's really Mom's garden.

"I like tomatoes from our garden or even the local farmer. As Mom said, if you can't grow vegetables, then you gotta buy them from your local farmer. Support our farmers and save the environment."

El shakes his head sadly and turns around. Aban keeps walking, having spoken to the beaten path all this time, not realizing for a minute or two that El is no longer beside her. She stops, looks up, searches around until she spots him going in the opposite direction.

"Hey!" Aban calls out, "We going back now? About time. I'm thirsty."

He halts, pulls the bottle of water out of his bag, and waits until she catches up to hand it to her. She finishes it and holds it out to him, her eyes sliding away from his and down toward the brush. But he doesn't take it. She keeps holding it out. He still doesn't take it.

She lifts her chin at him, "You want I should throw it on the ground?"

His eyes darken as he looks upon her, "Pay attention to what you hear, Aban, for what you give is what you will get. It is yours. I gave it to you."

Aban shrugs but lowers her arm and holds on to the empty bottle. El's anger vanishes as swiftly as it rose, and he guides her back to the steps they'd passed by earlier. But instead of going down them, they follow a path along its side. Tough black netting holds the scree in place, and they duck past a cloud of silent tiny insects zipping tiny distances then hovering in the air. They arrive onto a paved path. They can hear the constant hum of distant traffic here. Ahead, between the wilted trees a small creek meanders, its bank held in place with wooden slats. He turns right and takes Aban up to where the path crosses the creek. She slows, and her head droops under the suffocating heat. The path is barely wet. Although rocks churn the water on one side, the other side is sluggish and laps the edge of the path with little energy.

Aban doesn't notice; she's busy scuffing her sneaker on the grey concrete path, watching small stones roll away from her toes.

El speaks loudly to her hidden face, "There are many that are thirsty but don't know it; there are many that are thirsty and look for water but cannot find it; and there are many whose thirst is quenched, for they can name it, the source. Which are you, Aban?"

She shrugs at the path.

"Aban?"

"Whatever! I'm hot. Can we go somewhere where they have, like, juice?"

12

THE SEED SOWER

THE room lightens as the sun rises in the east, awakening Aban. She's getting used to the semi-darkness that the artificial light outside creates in her bedroom even in the deepest hours of the night. She hasn't pulled the blind down since that first night. She wants to see the sun when it rises, like at home.

Aban's muscles are sore in unexpected places from yesterday's long walk in that . . . in that . . . what did he call it? She mentally shrugs. A deep, leafy pit. Oh yeah, he called it the backbone of Toronto, whatever that means. Not her woods anyway. The memory of her place brings with it the memory of her parents' yoga sessions. She sits up abruptly without the aid of her hands, swings her legs over the sheets twisted on the edge of the bed, stands, and pads to the window. She lets her eyes drift to the sky, but the ground pulls her gaze inexorably down.

El is there, his back to her, sitting on the ground, meditating, like her parents. Aban's mouth distorts, and then she sweeps her mind free. Her mouth straightens back to neutral, and Aban simply looks at El.

And she sees that El is not in the lotus position.

He's sitting on his knees, arms upraised, head up. He doesn't move; he doesn't sway. He is still. She watches for a while, crosses her arms, scratches one leg with the other foot, until the call of the bathroom is too much for her to ignore.

Dressed in a grey T-shirt proclaiming "I Have the Power" and a fresh pair of khaki pants, she goes back to the window. El's arms are down and out of her line of sight; his head is bowed. Shrugging, she makes her way down the dark stairs to the second floor. Opening the stairway door, she blinks at the sun streaming in through the uncovered living room windows across the large room at the front of the house and right into the hall. Attracted by the light, she walks into the room and crosses to one of the windows. She looks down at the cars passing by. She hears the labour of a big engine as it accelerates to her right, out of her sight. Her stomach rumbles. She looks around the empty room. Well, not totally empty. In the far corner, next to the other front window is a single green-fabric covered chair with a semicircular back and four stick metal legs splayed out underneath. Beside it sits a tiny round silver-metal table with a flaring pedestal leg. A large round what-looks-like-a-paper ball hangs over the table from a thin metal arm sticking out from a tall pole. That's it? She turns slowly around three hundred and sixty degrees to see if she missed anything. She didn't. She walks over to the ball and touches it. It swings gently, and she notices the lamp cord that snakes out from its bottom to a plug behind it.

Mom would have a lot to say about this.

Aban is glad she isn't here.

She stares at the chair, and that lawyer's words return to her—or was it El who said them, about how Grandma said she wanted Aban to get her own furniture. But . . . she's never bought furniture. Aban hoofs it out of the room and down the hall to the kitchen, her sneakered feet squeaking on the wooden floor.

She stops in her kitchen doorway, heart pumping.

How will she make breakfast?

She always has toast. But where's the bread? How does she get it? Back home, Mom makes out the list; Mom drops her off at Bernie's Grocers while she goes off to do whatever she does; Bernie helps her get everything on the list; and then Mom picks her up. Sometimes she gets Eddie the cabbie to drive her.

She looks at the tiny empty table against the narrow window with a black phone its only occupant.

She has no bread. What will she do?

She scans the rest of her kitchen and looks back at the table.

A loaf of bread is sitting on top of a round wooden plate on the tiny table. A bread knife lies next to it. Confusion screws up her face. Did she buy this and forget? No, it wasn't there a moment ago. She knows it wasn't. Doesn't she?

Aban rubs her eyes. The loaf is still sitting there. She stares at it long, without blinking, in case it goes poof. But it doesn't. It continues to sit there. She rubs her eyes harder, then her face. She drags her hands down her cheeks, dragging down her lower eyelids. The loaf remains, though looking a little blurry. Aban drops her hands and steps slowly into her kitchen up to the table, up to where the loaf sits to look at it without expression. Lifting her head, she takes a few steps to the left, past the avocado-coloured fridge toward the dark faux-wood cabinets near the stove at the end. She randomly opens a cabinet door. Empty. She opens another, leaving the first door wide open. Empty. She yanks on the cabinet door near the fridge. A single plate lies there next to a single glass and a single mug. She grabs the plate, and leaving that cabinet door partially open as she had the other two, Aban grasps the knob of the drawer in front of her. Her eyes glaze over the honey-blond faux-wood counter as she struggles to open the humidity-soaked drawer. Mom's kitchen works. She uses real wood. Mom's doors and drawers don't stick, Aban grumbles as she grasps the knob harder and jerks it. The drawer screams out, and she stumbles backward, almost dropping the plate. She automatically suppresses her frustration and steps back toward the counter to look in the drawer. It has one knife, one fork, one spoon, one teaspoon, a kind of small, flat knife, one pair of scissors, and a cutting knife. Everything is only in ones around here. Weird. She takes out the normal knife and carries the plate and knife to the table. Aban sets them down and looks around for the jam. It's not in the cabinets; she frowns at the open doors. Mom would hate those. Why are they open? She shrugs, goes to close them, and then sees the pukey-coloured fridge. Maybe the jam is in there.

Aban grasps the fridge handle, but the door doesn't open. She yanks at it, and she and the door fly to the left. Only her grasp on the handle keeps her upright. What kind of kitchen is this? Slower this time, but once again she automatically shoves her frustration down. She takes back her footing and pokes her head around the door.

A fresh litre of organic skim milk and a jar of jam await her. She grimaces at the skim, shuts the fridge door hard, and starts banging open and closed all the cabinet doors, all the stiff drawers, in search of the chicory Mom makes. Nothing. Only a jar of instant coffee and a box of Darjeeling tea. She returns to the fridge, takes out the jam, and heaving a sigh takes out the milk too.

Soon jam is on a slice of bread—she's too tired to look for a toaster—and milk fills that single glass, and she's eating. Finished, she dumps the plate and glass in the sink near the fridge, leaves the bread cut side to the air on the wooden plate, and leans over the table to look outside.

El is rising from his knees, easily, smoothly, without aid of hands or arms.

Spooky.

He's been sitting on his knees all this time, yet he moves without stiffness. Mom and Dad can't do that.

El disappears underneath her and reappears with a canvas bag slung over his left shoulder. He buries his hand in it and throws out something from it. She wonders what it is. She squints as he repeats the motion. It can't be. It's summer time, and the whole of Ontario's in a drought. They won't grow. There's no water. Even Toronto has been put on water rationing, or so Mom said on Canada Day. Mom and Dad thought it was hilarious. Snooty Toronto having to live like the rest of Ontario.

He's still at it though. He had begun from where he was sitting in the horizontal middle of the backyard, close to the small deck at the back door, and is now crossing from side to side moving to the back row of brown-tipped evergreens, throwing out seed from his satchel. His stupidity insults her.

Aban runs out her kitchen, down the stairs, jumping the last two steps, skids around the newel post, runs the length of the house, and bangs open the back door.

"What are you doing?" she yells at him as she leaps down the back deck steps.

El doesn't pause.

His natural, swinging movement is his only answer. Birds land behind him and hop and peck the seed that lies where the grass has withered into the ground and the soil has been packed and hardened down near the deck.

"What are you doing, I said?"

El answers, "I'm sowing the garden."

"That's dumb. It's too hot, and we're in a drought, you know. Didn't you hear you can't use water for gardening?"

"True," El says as he continues to spread the seed onto the packed soil and dead grass, onto the thriving weeds and patches of struggling grass.

"Everyone knows seeds don't grow in drought. You need the proper balance of light and water and the proper nourishment for them to grow. That's what Mom says. Now is the time to conserve. I use Mom's special mixture of compost and manure with some peat moss to prepare the soil before I even plant anything. And that's in the Spring. Also, with a lawn you hafta poke holes in the grass first before putting on a thin layer of top soil and organic fertilizer. Then you can throw seed on it. Mom says so."

"Yes, everyone does it that way."

"Well, everyone knows what's right. What makes you so different?"

El glances up at her with a friendly smile and continues throwing the seed out of his bag. He is off the packed soil and into the weeds now. And the seed thrown from his hand nestles in amongst the creeping charlie and clover that somehow have found water to remain green.

"Okay, this is stupid. Mom's been gardening for, like, a gazillion years, you know. I've been gardening my whole life. And this year we only planted on the two-four weekend, you know. It was useless after that, everyone saw that. First, we had, like, no snow, and you need snow for plants to, you know, like, grow. Crops—seeds—need snow cause the melting gives seeds enough water to grow. And then we got no rain for, like, months. If we planted anything, they'd've died, and the township told us, like, in June, we couldn't use water to garden anymore, not even vegetables. Mom believes in natural plants, you know, plants that used to grow in Ontario, not those fussy imports like roses, but they didn't do too well neither. Seeds aren't going to grow now. Everyone knows that! Why do you think you're so different? This is stupid," she exclaims, stamping her foot on the last word.

"An abundance of words does not equal an abundance of wisdom."

Aban almost screams, she's so frustrated with his puzzling words. "What do you mean? You're always talking in riddles and saying weird things. Can't you just talk English already?"

El bends to throw a handful or three of seed amongst the fallen pine needles at the back fence. Then he straightens and goes to one side of the yard to ensure even the furthest edges have been seeded.

"Aren't you listening to me? You have to stop! They won't grow! It isn't raining! You're wasting seed, and the birds are eating them all!!"

"Not all, just the seed on the packed earth."

Her mouth drops open, "You know that? So why'd you put seed there?"

"It is not enough to talk; it is not enough to feed with bread; and it is not enough to rely on human dogma."

"Dogma?" Aban juts out her lower lip to send air up her forehead in exasperation. "Whatchya talking about? Can't you use real words?"

"You have the power," he says.

"Huh?"

He looks pointedly at her chest. Aban looks down and reads it too. Oh yeah, she'd forgotten she'd put on this shirt. She stares down at it while El returns to seeding the edges of the yard where the full heat of the sun never hits, where blades of grass struggle, their bottoms brown and their tips still green. Aban watches him, breathing heavily. Why can't she get through to him? Why can't she stop him? She's so uncomfortable. She doesn't like what he makes her f—

El replies, "Your grandmother tended this garden. After her death and the drought, the weeds took over, the grass withered, and the trees turned brown. A garden needs a gardener. Seeds and plants need someone to care for them even when all seems futile, when there is no water and no food. The gardener must plant in faith and wait for the growth."

"I bet Grandma wouldn't have been planting seeds this summer."

"Your grandmother was zealous for the vulnerable, the oppressed, the trusting, and those whose children faced the hardest hunger, the harshest conditions in which to grow. She would have been beside me, sowing the seed with me, her whole heart with them."

"Well, that's just stupid. Mom wouldn't have. Mom understands Nature better. Yeah, I'm with Mom if Grandma was like that. She was always getting me to think wrong so I argued with Mom, you know. It's stupid."

El snaps, "The measure you give will be the measure you get. Nothing is stupid that is thought out beforehand and walks forward in the strength of those thoughts. But when you confuse good thoughts with bad, when you rationalize bad thinking into good, then your garden will die."

"Well, I think your garden will die. You're not growing anything from that seed. It's not gonna rain, you know. And it's too hot here."

"It isn't raining—now. But see the shelter the trees behind provide? See how they keep the sun off the grass when it is at its hottest? See that not all is brown? See the green here and there? There is water where you cannot see it. So do not worry about the future, Aban, about what the weather will or will not do tomorrow. Be concerned only about today, of being the good gardener. For only the nations strive without ceasing, only the people who cannot see and cannot hear busy their minds with revolving thoughts, only those without questions have no thought for today and tomorrow."

"Well, today is hot and sticky, and there's no water. And those seeds need water when you plant them, you know. They're not, like, weeds. They suck nutrients from other plants. You can't just get around that."

"No. You're right, Aban," El says as he crosses to the other side, the north side, where the weeds are and finishes seeding at the edge of the rickety peeling painted fence with its close-together vertical boards.

Aban stuffs her hands in her pockets and looks down at the ground where she's standing, absent-mindedly scraping it with the toe of her shoe, dirtying her shoe more if possible. No matter what she says, it doesn't seem to move him. It's like he doesn't care what she thinks. He doesn't listen! She doesn't see that he pauses and turns around to study her, that he draws his brows down and shakes his head sadly. She sees only what's under her feet: weeds and seeds. She stops her foot as she realizes what she's scraping into the hard dirt. She feels bad for the seeds, not having a chance.

El lifts the bag off himself and turns it upside down to shake it out, ensuring every seed hits the ground and doesn't stay in the canvas. He tucks it under his arm, rubs his hands together to clean off errant seed shells, walks back to the porch and the house, and pauses inside the door, holding it open for her. Aban follows reluctantly then brushes past him, her feet quickening, taking her upstairs and into her own living room, slamming the door behind her.

13

THE FRAY

"ABAN?" El knocks on her closed living room door. He'd given her a couple of hours after he'd heard the door slam shut before following her up. He knocks again, "Aban?"

She opens it a crack and peers out with one eye, "What do you want?"

"Aban, may I speak with you?"

Her eye swivels to the right, to look away from him and back into the room; the visible portion of her face starts to shrink.

El stops her from closing the door with the kindness in his words, "Why did you come here?"

Her shrug is barely discernible. El waits. She breathes out, "Grandma left me it in her will. I wanted to see."

"To see what?"

She disappears but leaves the door ajar. El stretches out an arm and pushes it gently open. Aban is at the window directly across from the door and staring down. Her shoulders are hunched, her hands are in their comforting pockets, her fingers playing with the seams and shredded tissues inside.

"Aban," El says quietly. "Come, listen. I will tell you what you want to hear." She doesn't move. After a moment, he walks over to stand beside her.

"I met your grandmother many years ago on the day she moved in to Atasgah," El begins. "She had had a good life. She had volunteered in her community. She had raised funds for the United Way every year. Then one day her husband died, and her son married a wife who did not want to know her."

"Mom wanted to know her. She did. But Grandma . . . ," Aban's voice peters out. She hunches further into herself, and El's eyes mist but his voice remains strong like a rock that one can lean on.

"Your grandmother missed her husband. She missed her newly-married son. One day, she wandered the streets and found this house, lying empty. She bought it. I came to her on the day she moved in. She was lonely and invited me in for tea. It was the first of many conversations. She told me of her life. And I told her my stories. Your grandmother was a good listener. She chose the one thing that mattered and named this place 'Atasgah.' She planted a garden in Atasgah's rough soil and went back to school to get her teacher's degree. She was a keen student and not only at university. Then she began her purpose."

El pauses, but Aban says nothing. She has grown very still. El continues, "You were born, and your parents named you 'Aban,' after your grandmother's grandmother. For generations, it had been a treasured family name, given to the first-born daughter in each generation. But after your great-great-grandmother's generation, it was no longer given. Your grandmother took the giving of your name as a sign that peace would come. She believed that you would bring her and her son and daughter-in-law together. But I warned her that 'no prophet is accepted in the prophet's hometown.' She did not listen then. And when trouble returned to the relationship, she despaired.

"We had many talks. And she tried different ways, even suppressing her own self when in their company so that she would make herself pleasing in their eyes. But instead of pleasing them, she angered them more, and her friends became unhappy with her."

"Well, she should've tried harder."

"Perhaps. But what about your parents? Should they have tried?"

"It wasn't their fault. It was her problem, not theirs."

"As was you moving here? Is it only you who is the problem, or your mother also?"

Aban shrugs.

El picks up his tale, "Like you, your grandmother did not hear my words. She did not listen to me when I warned her that when she chose service over the world, that her chosen life would divide her daughter-in-law and son from herself. She strived ceaselessly to mend that relationship.

"But the truth cannot hide; it cannot deceive itself. The truth of who you are or the truth of who others are will reveal itself. No matter how she tried to cover it up, the truth of your grandmother's passion, her new joy for teaching the lessons she had learned, revealed itself to her son and daughter-in-law. And it did not sit well with them. The day her son and his wife moved out of Toronto, taking you with them, she turned to me and asked me why. I asked her again a question she had refused to hear before."

El pauses. The silence grows long. At last, Aban asks the window, "What question?"

"Who is your brother? Who is your sister? Who is your mother?"

Her hands fly out of her pockets to hide under her crossed arms, up under her armpits. "Mother is Mom. You know that! Mom."

El regards her for minutes. But she says nothing as she continues to stare at the passing cars, their engine noise muffled by the heavy air and the window pane.

At last, El forges ahead, speaking to her profile, "After your parents left with you, each sunrise your grandmother and I sat outside in her backyard when it was hot and inside when it was cold. In the summer, the roses gave off their fragrance, and the grass bent under our knees. The evergreens protected the back fence, and the dogwood and lilacs leafed out sheltering shade. Your grandmother nourished each plant, each flower, each blade of grass as if they were her children. She gave them water. But not too much. She spread food on their roots, each according to its kind. But not too much. She let them struggle to reach the light and spoke to them encouraging words. Some of her friends laughed at her for talking to her plants. But she would reply that they heard and understood her words. 'Unlike them,' she'd add, with that mischievous smile of her. They d laugh together. One friend, a male friend younger than her, rebuked her for spending too much time in the garden and not enough time on the street. He told her no one cared about her garden while people were living on the street. His contemptuous words were meant to hurt, though he denied it and said that they were for her own good. But as he was about to leave her and Atasgah after one final argument, he looked back and saw her standing there. He remembered the words, 'When you go with your adversary to the magistrate, make every effort along the way to settle with him, lest he drag you to the judge, the judge deliver you to the officer, and the officer throw you into prison. You shall not depart from there till you have paid the very last penny.'

"Your grandmother was fervent for her garden and the growth within. She spoke matter-of-factly about her garden and its lessons, debated, argued, cajoled, and always underneath her words lay her laughter. Her wit was dry and often misunderstood. Your mother chose to misunderstand her and would often allow herself to be offended. Your grandmother made an effort to hide her wit when with her. Yet at times, her ire rose up, and she would make her wit drier just to watch your mother's outrage. Your grandmother would regret it immediately and apologize at once. But apologies were never enough for your mother. Once offended, always offended."

"Yeah, Mom gets her back up, like, real fast. You can't tell her different, not even if, like, you don't mean it," Aban says to the closed window. "You hafta agree with Mom. Anyway, Mom is always right, you know."

El continues. "Each time she apologized, your grandmother would vow to me that she would control her mouth. Yet she often failed. And so she tried to see her son without his wife. But her son told her that as long as she could not get along with his wife, he would not see her. This became an impossible condition, for his wife remained determined not to get along. Your mother shifted the bar for peace after each transgression and each request for mercy. Your grandmother's apologies would be forgotten. Your mother would say she had never apologized and would demand an apology. Being caught up in these manipulations, your grandmother once again forgot my question and my words and despaired.

"One day, I told her about a family feud in which two sisters-in-law did not get along. One made a disparaging remark about the other; the other took her to court and won. The fine was a public apology, printed in the national paper where all saw it. But that was not enough for the victor. No, the victor clipped out the printed apology and every time she saw her sister-in-law brought it out to shame her."

"Mom wouldn't do that!"

"That's what your grandmother said. But one day, she had had enough. She decided that she wanted to be true to herself and to what she had learned."

El's voice stops, and his sigh is heavy. The room grows quiet. A board cracks under Aban's shifting weight. The air crackles with the tension of Aban trying not to think, not to feel, not to want to know. But she blurts out, "What's that?"

El replies, "When you hear, you will know. As your grandmother did. As your father and mother did not. That day, she went to see you and your mother and father. After she arrived, you and your grandmother went for a walk through the woods behind your house, as you both did every time she visited. It was a treasured time for you both. It was the only time your mother was not present and could not be, for she would be working in her store. And though your father would be at home, since your mother didn't like leaving you alone with your grandmother, he would not come into the woods with you but remain behind. When your mother questioned him about the day, he found it easier to let her believe that he had joined you in your walk.

"That day, your grandmother, walking again in the truth, told you all about Atasgah and the friends she'd made, the students who came to hear her teach, the lessons that had grown into conversations as the people sought understanding. Aban, you became excited. You asked her many questions. And you wanted to visit her and to meet her friends during the holidays. When your mother got home, you jumped up and down all around her telling her about what you'd learned and about going to Atasgah. Your mother was upset and after dinner when you had gone to bed, she became angry with your grandmother and with her husband, calling her husband a traitor to her, his wife. She didn't want your grandmother talking to you about Atasgah, about me, about her friends, and about her teachings. But your grandmother had become zealous for what she had learned, whom she had met, and she no longer wanted to deny it.

"The next day, again your mother was forced to go to the store, but she admonished your father not to let you be alone with your grandmother, to guard against filling your head with her superstitions and her lies. But your father was afraid of offending both his wife and his mother. And so when you dragged your grandmother into the woods, he did not follow in his agony of indecision. Your grandmother told you more tales about the people she met and about Atasgah. And she told you a story. You were sharp back then, you listened well, and you suddenly realized what she was saying. You became angry; you rebuked your grandmother. She took it but debated with you. For she wanted to make you think. She did not want you to be afraid of new ideas or of challenges. Then you became worried that she thought you were stupid for not believing her. Your grandmother laughed—I can still hear her bold laugh—and told you emphatically that she never thought you stupid, that not wanting to hear didn't make you stupid, but refusing to hear, refusing to learn, refusing to challenge did. Sometimes your grandmother could be too zealous." El shakes his head sorrowfully.

"I don't remember that."

El has been looking at her the whole time they've been talking. Now he pauses, "No," he says thoughtfully. "Your grandmother had wondered, but I knew. You had to forget."

"Why? Anyway, it's not good to upset children."

"Why not?"

"Because. Mom said so. She spent her life protecting me, making sure I was not upset."

"And what have you learned from that?"

"I got to be a child."

"Did you? Aren't you still a child?"

"I'm twenty!"

"In years only."

They stand together in the hush that descends, El biding the minutes patiently for her to speak.

She shrugs, "Maybe."

El draws in a breath and says, "When your mother returned that night, you told her what your grandmother had told you.

You were still upset, but you were seeking reassurance and more importantly understanding. You were a child, so you didn't know how to think deeply about things. Your grandmother felt that you were such a curious, engaged child that you could handle it and that already you were seeking because you did not stop asking questions. She wanted to fill you up. But no matter a person's age, it is not easy to challenge one's comfortable ideas. But she knew that time and guidance would help you think through these ideas and that you would calm down and seek even more.

"But your mother was furious. She was too afraid to answer your questions, and she rose up in anger against your grandmother."

"Mom? Afraid?" Aban interrupts, astonished.

"Yes. She feared judgement where none was being given. For she judged everyone herself. She also felt inadequate in not knowing how to answer your questions. Yet no one human being can know everything. It is said that Samuel Coleridge was the last person who lived who knew everything, yet everything that needs to be known can be learned by those who want to. All the rest are facts and details."

"Huh?"

"All your mother understood was that your grandmother was upsetting her world, and she didn't like it. She thought she needed her treasured ideas, needed others to think the same as herself. She had a desire for others to prove their worth to her. It was familiar and comforting to be that way."

"Mom's not like that. I don't hafta prove nothing."

"Don't you? When you said you were coming here, what did she say?"

"She didn't want me to come."

El waits. And waits. And waits. Finally Aban whispers, "She said if I left, I was no longer part of the family."

El moves imperceptibly closer to her, his slight touch a comforting one that doesn't scare her like an overpowering arm around her shoulders would have. He asks, "Why did she say that if your disobedience to her will didn't threaten herself? Why did she say that if she was confident in your love? Why did she say that if she did not need her desires, her ideas to be yours? Your grandmother threatened your mother's very sense of self. Your mother saw you, Aban, as hers, as a furniture maker sees a chair as his creation, his possession alone. Yet your grandmother stirred you up and made you hungry for more. Possessions don't do that. And yes, your grandmother upset you. But this life is not all about superficial getting on, about relationships that skate over the surface of each other's lives. Mother and daughter, sister and sister, son and father will be set against each other, yes, even against their own life. For without setting against, without rising up your thoughts and questioning your assumptions, without challenging what you know so as to open yourselves up, you cannot clear the soil of rocks and stones and till the dead vegetation into the ground. You cannot set a fresh foundation for new growth. Your mother wanted her soil to be undisturbed, and she wanted yours undisturbed too in case it disturbed hers. Your grandmother's spirited desire to share threatened her, and your grandmother knew you no more."

"She didn't hafta do that, you know. If she'd, like, kept her mouth shut, I could've known her. Why didn't she keep her mouth shut? Like, that's all Mom wanted. It's not hard to do, you know," Aban ends on a whisper.

"Though it saddened her and though she knew what the consequences might be before she went up that weekend, she also knew that she must speak" El's voice rises gradually and becomes vigorous. "To hide her tiller in the barn, doors closed and locked, no longer worked. She understood at last that allowing another to keep you quiet allows bad thoughts to flourish, good thoughts to die, injustice to ascend, and real peace to wither away. Isn't it better Aban to have confrontation than a false peace that masks hostility and is possible only because one person has denied themself in order to satiate another? That kind of peace cannot be without the death of one soul and the corruption of another.

"Your grandmother hoped that her words would resonate in you and sink deep into your mind until one day you sought her out."

Tears stroll down Aban's face. El puts a warm hand on her shoulder. She lets it lie there. El's comforting spirit and succour flow through her shoulder awakening her weeping heart, and she hugs herself and bows her head almost into her chest, choking the sobs back until she can no longer. His hand remains on her shoulder.

El speaks, trying to alleviate her anger at her mother and her grief at not knowing her grandmother, "You can know her again. You can continue on from that day when she was sent away."

Aban says nothing but holds her breath as she thinks, "I can?"

14

THE DINNER

ABAN wakes up restless. She had slept in the guest room on the second floor, shedding only her pants as she fell onto the bed in the wee hours. She wanders into the kitchen in her bare feet and damp, wrinkled T-shirt, looks around at the cupboards, stares at the bare table, glances up at the window, and sees dried-out trees. Sighing loudly, she pads out, down the hall, and into her empty living room. She stands inside the open door. She just stands there, her eyes not focusing on anything. She blinks rapidly three times and sees the lonely chair, sitting there, waiting, empty. She pads over to the window and looks at the sky. Her head droops down, and the road comes into her view. Cars slide by in both directions, grey, silver, taupe, all the different shades of grey that clog the highways, even the small one near her home. Occasionally, a burgundy one punctures the sameness.

An ambulance wails by. She jumps. She hadn't heard the siren till the wide, white van-truck was in her sight; the flashing lights startle her. A small sedan driving in the opposite direction screeches into the curb as the ambulance swings out into the left lane of the oncoming traffic to fly past the oblivious cars in its lane.

Aban reaches down deep into her lungs for air and blows it out.

She wanders out of the room and hesitates at the bottom of the stairs that go to the third floor. It's hot up there. She climbs into the heat, and standing at the edge of the landing looks around. She leans into the wall for long minutes.

Clink; chop, chop, chop; water gush: the sounds vibrate her sharp ears and percolate into her mind. She frowns and twists her head round to look down the stairs, as if the dark tunnel will tell her what she's hearing. Letting the wall support her, she turns her body round to follow her head and steps down the stairs, one step at a time. At the bottom, she stops.

Bottles rattle together in the distance. El's opened the fridge.

She takes a step forward, feels the wall brush her bare leg, and glances down at herself. She stands there for long minutes, contemplating her bare legs and the shortness of her T-shirt, the hot, humid air oppressing her. She climbs the stairs back up slowly, pads into her room, picks up a pair of pants on the floor, and fights to put them on as the fabric sticks to her moist legs. With a grunt, she pulls the waistband into place and buttons and zips her pants closed.

Many minutes later after a pause on her bed, Aban is standing in the doorway of El's kitchen.

"What're you doing?" Aban asks eventually.

"I'm making dinner," he answers.

"Oh."

"My friends are coming over. Would you like to join us?" She shrugs.

He picks up a saucepan from the stove, carries it over to the sink, lifts its lid, and pours out water. She takes a step in, another step, until she can see that there are whole eggs in the saucepan.

"I'm making Salad Niçoise, a pasta salad with fresh vegetables, and fresh bread to be dipped in olive oil or eaten with cheese."

"Oh." She watches him as he pours the eggs carefully into a bowl of ice water and begins shelling them.

He tells her, "Dinner is at six."

At six o'clock, Aban comes downstairs dressed in her plainest white T-shirt and khaki pants, her hair still wet from the cold shower she had taken after spending long hours splayed on her bed, her chest weighed down by the heat and an unwanted emotion that she cannot identify. She wears bare feet; it's even hotter than this morning. The humidex has risen all day.

She arrives first. When she sees the empty hall and notices the lack of voices, she hesitates at the bottom of the stairs.

El calls her to come into the living room. She drags her feet on the old, wood floors and enters. The rooms are filled with hazy sunlight. The two chairs have been moved so that they're against the wall and underneath the narrow window. The dining room table is under the main front window. The lower pane has been raised, and damp sheets are tacked over the opening with bowls of ice standing in front of them. Three dinner-plate-sized platters of food and sliced bread line up slantwise on a wooden board on the table.

The front door bangs open, and a voice rings out, "Hello, El!"

El turns to Aban, "In the latter days, your grandmother would send me to greet the guests. But this is your home now. I am sure my friends would like to meet you." He ends with an encouraging smile.

She slouches out into the hall.

"Hi," the stranger says. "Who're you?"

"Aban. I own this place."

"Oh! You're Aban! It's great to meet you," the stranger exclaims. "Lucky you, to be right here, living in this gorgeous home your grandmother made, seeing El every day. El's the kind of guy everyone wants for a friend but don't know it till they meet him."

"Really?"

"Definitely." The stranger steps forward as the door opens behind her. Another two walk in, a man and a woman. They greet each other like old friends, are introduced to Aban, and begin chatting as they walk down the hall and disappear into the living room. The front door opens again. This time a group bustle in, shouting and cracking up at each other. They giggle hello to Aban as they pass her by. She stands there as more people open and close the front door, stream past her on their way to say "Hi!" to El, to each other, and to dig into the fresh food. She frowns after them: there're so many coming and not enough food. They begin to spill into the hall, into the kitchen, and out the back door. Maybe they eat less here in Toronto at dinner than in the country. Suddenly, she misses her mother's cooking. She shoves that thought down automatically.

It's so hot. She fans her face with her hand. It's useless, like moving stalled water-laden clouds with her pinky.

She takes a step toward the living room door when she hears the knob click, feels the outside air moisten her back, and a bigger group jostles in. They are all in a hurry, in such a hurry that they almost trip over each other, but the yakking crowd in the hall slows them down. This group doesn't see her; she creeps back toward the wall at the bottom of the stairs, hiding in the shadows.

"I can't wait to see what El's cooked up," says one.

"Cook? How can you think of hot food in heat like this?"

"Hey, even cold food has to be cooked first. And what diff would it make anyway?"

"You gotta say hi to El first."

"Sure, sure. But the food is probably half gone by now."

"You're such a pessimist. You know El always makes enough for everyone."

"Yeah, but you say hi to him and next thing you know, an hour's gone. I'm going for the food first this time." The group's laughter fades as they wade through the crowd into the living room.

For the next half hour, she watches groups and couples and singles come in, knocking and immediately opening the door, expecting they are welcome to enter. All are eager to see El. She doesn't get it. He's so hard to understand, how can they be so eager? Now if it was Deepak Chopra, she'd get that. She'd be the first in line to meet her hero. She'd wait all day if she had to! And she'd take all her books to get him to sign them. Mom never let her come to Toronto when he was doing that renewal weekend and he was gonna teach the secrets of healing too. It was the biggest disappointment of her life. And she'd forgotten until now.

These people are like Chopra fans.

But they don't have to pay, she suddenly realizes.

Voices rise, clash, pile on top of one another, echo off the plaster walls, spill out into the hallway. People follow the cacophony out into the hall and flow into the kitchen and out through the open back door into the back yard. The voices have more space in the open air, but the humidity is like a wall, and the noise builds on itself there too. It's like the party back in high school, the one which she'd snuck out to attend, where she d felt alone while everyone else got drunk to have a good time, and she'd dared not. Mom forbade alcohol. She could smell it a mile away, Dad would joke. If she'd smelled it on Aban's breath . . .

Aban shivers.

The walls feel like they re closing in. She shoves the feelings down and stays in her place. Conversations pierce her consciousness.

"Did you see what the TSX did today?"

"Yeah, my stock tanked. The solid one, the one that was supposed to be safe."

"Oh no. How much you'd lose?"

"Too much."

"Did you tell El?"

"No. Why would I? He's not a banker!"

"Or an investor, though maybe he'd be smarter than my financial planner."

"I can't believe it. I could kick myself. My budget's shot to pieces. I don't know what I'd do if I didn't have you guys."

"El can help."

"How? He doesn't do anything but listen. How's that help?"

A throat is cleared.

"Hey, don't spout medical science to me. I know all about how sharing and being heard makes your stress hormones go down, for women anyway. But I need money. El's not going to loan me money. He won't pay my bills. He won't put food on my table. He doesn't even have enough for himself!"

"Yeah, but he's never in want, you notice that?"

"Yeah . . ."

"Well, since you know so much, you know I'm right. And besides, you know that being with El makes you feel stronger, like you can face the most impossible situation and find solutions. I did when my wife left and cleaned out my accounts. I'm doing fine now."

The door opens, and traffic and new voices drown out his answer. Aban makes a face.

Another conversation floats up from the centre of the crowd to grab her attention.

"I have to see the doctor again."

"The tests came back positive?"

"I don't know. He just said, come back in."

"I'm sorry. Maybe El can help?"

"Yeah, I talked to El. He listened. He made a couple of suggestions, but no one can help me really. Not even him. And I wonder if he wanted to anyway . . ."

"Of course he does!"

"Does he?"

"Yes!"

"So why didn't he do more? Listening isn't enough when your life—"

The words choke off, and an older man crashing through the front door distracts Aban from hearing any more.

After it seems like no more are coming, she leaves it and manoeuvres through the crowd. She searches for El but is waylaid by the first stranger, who speaks into her face.

"Hello, Aban. How're you liking Toronto?"

She shrugs, leaning back.

"Your grandmother loved this city and her friends. There's nothing she wouldn't have done for us. After she passed away, El kept up this tradition she started."

Silence stretches. "Tradition?"

"Yeah, tradition. The tradition of this dinner. Didn't El tell you?"

She shakes her head slowly from side to side.

"Typical. He tells no more than he thinks one needs to hear. It's maddening, eh? Anyway, your grandmother, bless her. I still miss her. We all do. Well, what was I saying? Oh yes. Your grandmother started this tradition of having a meal for all her friends, all her students, and her neighbours, although I don't see the new neighbours. But they didn't know her, and people are more comfortable keeping to themselves. It's safer."

"Safer?"

"Yeah, it's safer not to meet people because then you'll have to talk to them when you see them, then that leads to coffee, and before you know it, you'll be in a relationship with all those obligations," he stresses and lengthens the word "those" as he leans in. "And you know where thinking of another leads you. But I was glad to be friends with your grandmother. Being around her, I don't know, life was more . . . life! El's like that too. They remind you how rewarding friendships are, how buoyant they make you feel."

Aban scans this stranger. It's so hot, so sticky, but her clothes are dry, even her hair is dry and clean. Not one hair sticks to her forehead.

"Aren't you hot?"

"Sure. But when you get to share time with people who like you and want to be with you, who feels the heat?"

Aban stares, disbelieving.

"Your grandmother fed us, she said, in the heat of the summer so we'd take memories of each other with us when vacations and trips temporarily parted us. She used to say memories of each other would feed us, bring us home again, and keep at bay the natural resentment of no longer being on vacation because we always had each other no matter how hard the job became or what crises we faced. She used to talk first, feed our stomachs second."

"Talk?"

"Yes, talking and listening fed our spirits. We'd sit outside in the back yard on her lawn of thyme and grass, it smelled so good. And she'd sit underneath her evergreens—back then they were ever green, if you know what I mean, not brown and dry like this summer. Anyway, she'd sit there, and when we all had gathered, she'd talk. And we'd listen. And then when she was done, she'd listen, and we'd talk. We had these most amazing conversations."

"Oh."

The stranger smiles at her.

"About what?" Aban asks reluctantly.

"Oh, about the ways of life, of being, of who we are and who we are meant to become."

Aban frowns. More meaningless words. Doesn't anyone in Toronto speak English?

"The cicadas would sing around us. Even after the sun went down, we kept on talking in the darkness with only the kitchen light on. After the sun had set and the mosquitoes had gone to bed, she'd tell us it was time to eat. It was always too soon for us. But she'd say that we needed food bread too, not just mind bread." She chortles. "Also, it was usually cool enough by then to go in."

The stranger pauses as she lingers in the past. "Your grandmother believed in the old methods of keeping a house cool. But between you and me, I like air conditioning, but we wouldn't miss her supper for anything. Spending time with her was like sitting with good, you know as in the opposite of vampires."

Aban blinks. This person believes fantasy is real?

The woman laughs on seeing Aban's expression. "You know, vampires, people who suck the energy out of you."

"Oh. Mom and Dad don't believe in air conditioning either," Aban says. She looks down at the floor, stuffs her hands in her comfortable pockets, and watches her fingers play inside their hiding place, wondering if Grandma made as little food as El has done. She looks up to see the stranger has gone. She lurches forward as someone bumps into her from behind. She walks into the living room, searching for El.

"Hi! You must be Aban. You look just like her, you know."

"Uh, yeah," she replies, wondering who "her" is.

"Your grandmother was the best person ever. She saved me. I was a telemarketer, you know, one of those people who calls you up at dinner hour and bugs you to buy something. Anyway, it's a boring job, and people are awful to you. Geez, I was just trying to make a buck, to eat, you know. One day after work, I was wandering the mall. I couldn't go home. Well, to be honest, I didn't want to go home. I didn't make enough to live on my own, and I couldn't find a better job or a second one. I was still living with my folks. I hated it. Every night, they'd tell me what a failure I was, not finding a real job, a disgrace to the family, they said. God! They didn't get it. I went to college and everything, and I tried everything. I sent out hundreds of résumés. But no one was hiring, even the temp agencies said I was too inexperienced. I was a lousy typist anyway. So anyway, I was wandering through the Eaton Centre when your grandmother came up to me and said, 'you look like you could use a cup of tea.' I thought who is this old bat, something out of one of those PBS specials? But, you know, I went with her. She and El gave me courage. And the rest as they say is history. I work for Parks and Rec now. I look after the parks, and I love it. Not many women do my job, and I'm hoping to inspire more women to do the heavy manual work. It makes you feel good, using your muscles to create beautiful spaces, and as your grandmother always said, being a gardener is the best job in the world," she finishes on a chirp.

Aban finds herself alone amongst the crowd once more. The people swirl around her as she digests the fact that everyone is here because of her grandmother. But as she looks around, she realizes that although it's her grandmother—Grandma—who brought them here, it's El they want to see. It's El who attracts them in that annoying way of his. He stands there, holding a large wine glass half-filled with ruby liquid, sipping and laughing and chatting, surrounded by people, young and old, women and men, all listening, all questioning in turns, all conversing. His mouth moves, but she doesn't hear his words. She can see the faces of his listeners. They're soaking in what he's saying and being stimulated into more conversation. They cannot get enough. Yet after a bit, the closest ones leave for the dining room table to join other circles of conversation so that the ones behind can move in closer and the ones outside can become part of the circle. But with all these people, how can there be enough food?

Suddenly, her chest grows hot, her teeth clench, her forehead hardens, her eyes sharpen.

She's being told how wonderful Grandma is, a grandmother Mom and Dad had let her believe was dead, a grandmother they didn't like, whom they'd said outright was a disturbing presence not good for her. She was a child! And they'd lied to her! Instead, strangers got to meet her. She gets to hear from strangers all about her grandmother, how they're missing her, grateful they knew her, making it worse. That just proves Mom was right, there is no God. A real God would ve made sure she d met Grandma. If Mom was right about that, maybe she was better off not knowing Grandma. Maybe these strangers are the liars.

Mom and Dad took care of her, protected her, knew what was best for her, gave her the best things in life. They taught her the truth. They were right. But . . . but . . . she doesn't know her own grandmother. All these strangers do.

Who is right?

She searches the people's open faces, seeing their eyes crinkling happily, their bodies leaning into each other, seeing a careless pleasure in life, something she hadn't seen in her home, something she doesn't know. Yeah, she felt good about contributing to her causes, but was it pleasure? It was not this . . . this . . . thing that seems to be rising from . . . from deep within all these people. It wasn't these friendly smiles she sees here. It wasn't light like this.

What is she supposed to do?

She hugs herself. It's not like Grandma will rise from the dead, and she'll have a second chance at getting to know her. And why did El make so little food? She's hungry, and there won't be any left.

She shoves her way through the crowd, unheeding of people blurting, "Hey!"

El looks her way. "It's time, Aban."

"Time for what?" she yells over the heads of the people in front of her.

He doesn't answer. The crowd parts and melts away, leaving Aban and El staring at each other almost nose to nose as El moves toward her.

"Why?" she yells at him.

"I cannot answer that. Only they can tell you why they made the choices they made."

"You act like you know everything!"

"People have to speak for themselves. I will not substitute myself for their misdeeds, and I cannot make things all better with a bandage."

"Why not?!"

"That is not my way."

"It should be."

El shakes his head with regret, "Though it may seem like it should be, in this world people have free will to think the things they do, to say the things they want to say, to act out their thoughts. They have the ability to control them, to channel them into better thoughts and actions. They have the ability to think about how their actions will affect another. People can reflect on their real motives, and they can see consequences. Many choose not to. Your parents chose not to; they liked being right." El's voice hardens, rises, "And no one, no being, can save them from themselves and the rightness of their ways. But their unpleasantness, their bad choices, and the hurt they cause another, will not go away. They will ripple out from them and be reflected back to them. They cannot skirt their own accountability." El pauses. "But with your complicity and ignorance, they have succeeded up until now."

"It's not my fault! It s not fair!"

"No. It isn't. But they chose to listen to their own voices, their own ideas of what is right, feeling righteous in their choices. They chose to ignore a wiser voice. Their own voices became louder to drown the voices of your grandmother and whom she listened to, and they stopped seeing anyone else's perspective, including yours. They saw only their own point of view."

"Who'd she listen to?"

"The gardener in the garden." El pauses for Aban to ask who that is, but she doesn't. He suddenly grows impatient and exclaims, "Listen, Aban! Listen well! The gardener waits for those who knock on the gate. Many see the wide front gate, but few are they who enter the garden by the vine-covered narrow back gate close to where the gardener stands patiently. Many want to plant the easy impatiens and marigolds. Fewer want to plant demanding thorny roses and vines, apple trees and cedars. Fewer still submit their roses and vines to hard pruning to produce good fruit. You will know these few by their fruit. Fruit reflects that which grows it. Diseased trees, trees with growing rot in the middle, dead trees cannot grow good fruit. Those who refuse to see and hang onto the diseased trees, waiting for a miracle, saying that the disease does not exist, saying it's God's fault, or their neighbour's fault, will produce bad fruit. Those who refute the wise advice of the gardener will produce bad fruit and not even what's left will be saved for carpentry wood but must be burnt. Those who walk away abandon the garden to certain death.

"But your grandmother, she heard; she obeyed; and she was ruthless. She pruned hard. Yet she pruned only what was rotten, bringing light and air to the healthy branches. And she produced good fruit. Look around you at the transformed lives you see—they are but a small planter of what she wrought. Can you say the same?"

"I'm only twenty, you know."

"Yes. I know. But there are people here younger than you, older than you, who met your grandmother early in her life and in her dying days, heard and acted on her words. Whose words have you acted upon? Whose words have you listened to? And whose words are the truth? You ask for fairness, but you haven't asked the ones who harmed you to justify themselves. You want another—you want me— to speak to you for them, to make it better. But I cannot. They must speak to you for themselves."

Aban sends her eyes in every direction but El's. She glimpses the table between the backs of the people standing talking in front of it and faces El abruptly. "Why did you make so little food? I thought you were going to have a dinner party. There won't be any left."

"Is anyone hungry?"

"I am."

"Then eat."

She stomps to the table. El is so . . . so . . . talking in stupid words that make no sense. The people part, not wanting to be knocked about. Aban glares down at the table. There is plenty of food left. How can that be? All these people have gone up to the table; even now several are helping themselves to salad or bread, holding glasses filled with lemon-coloured liquid, clear water, ruby wine, or tea-coloured drinks. Ice clinks in their glasses as they gesture animatedly. She frowns. Where did they get the glasses from? She's so thirsty, and the cold drinks look good. Not the wine though.

"Good iced tea," the one next to her smiles at her. "I got it from the kitchen. El puts pitchers in the fridge so they'll stay cold. And the ice is in the freezer. I can get you some if you want. You must be Aban. I'd recognize you anywhere even though the picture she had of you was when you were a little girl. She saved my life, you know, then introduced me to El. I knew him right away when we first met. I mean, he was like a familiar, old friend as soon as we met, one who expects a lot from you but gives so much in love and trust. She was like that too, but more like a grandmother." Aban swallows hard, but the woman carries on unnoticing. "I can tell you stories about her you wouldn't believe. Grab some food and come with me out back where it's cooler and quieter, relatively speaking, that is," she chuckles. "C mon, let's talk."

15

EXPLORATION

ABAN looks out her bedroom window the next morning and sees El meditating, standing up, arms flung out, neck stretched to the sky. She snatches up her wallet and stuffs it down her front pocket. Today her T-shirt proclaims "I can be anything." She runs down the two flights of stairs and out the front door, shutting it behind her. The morning sun barely cuts through the haze and barely fills the little front garden with light. She turns right and heads to the crosswalk. El had explained on her first day, when they were returning from the wedding, that it's a place where pedestrians can cross busy roads and how to make the traffic stop. She follows his instructions to press the button on the pole nearby to make the crosswalk lights flash, but cars don't stop. Tentatively, she steps onto the road, and the car nearest her flies through the crosswalk, but the one behind brakes. She crosses safely to the other side and walks over to the bus stop. And waits.

And waits.

A bus roars up to the curb. The brakes squeal. She gets on and asks the driver how to pay; she can't remember how El paid because she wasn't used to paying attention to what her parents or any adult did unless they told her to. And even then, not always, with Mom normally doing everything for her anyway. He gestures with his head; she doesn't understand and asks again.

"Girl, can't you read?" he growls at her.

"Um, sure."

"Put the money in that box in front of you," shouts a middle-aged woman from the back. Aban looks for the voice, past the yellow rails near her, past the boxed-up compartment behind the driver and a fat black platform, past a stroller filling the aisle, and down to the far end of the black-sided corridor. The woman nods. Aban fishes out her wallet, digs out loonies and toonies, is about to drop them all in when the woman shouts, "No, not that much, man." The woman trundles up to the front, sorts through the change in Aban's hand, takes out a few coins, and drops them in to the box. They clank into the bottom, the driver depresses a lever letting the coins disappear, and accelerates away from the curb. Aban is thrown against the black wall of metal behind the driver, but the woman has already expertly snagged back her seat. Aban staggers toward the seats, grabbing rails and poles to steady herself. She sucks in her nonexistent gut to squeeze past the stroller. A diaper bag sits on top of the platform next to the seat where a young woman holds onto the stroller. Passengers sit and watch her or read.

With a whoosh, she's past the stroller. The bus brakes; Aban stumbles forward and lands in an empty seat. The passengers on either side of her seem oblivious. She wonders now if this was a good idea, going out into Toronto on her own. But she needs to be by herself. Last night's dinner was so weird. Weird is a safe word, safer than voicing how she really felt, the emotions it stirred up. All those people; all those stories about Grandma; and El in the middle of it. Weirdest of all, no one was hungry when they left. They said they were stuffed. They said they had a good dinner. Weirder, no one left drunk, drunk on alcohol that is. But they sure were drunk on something.

All the passengers are getting off, and the driver is following them. Aban hurries off herself. She looks around and wonders which way to go. Then she realizes that there is only one way, down. Down, down she goes and ends up on a platform. Whichever way this platform goes, she hopes it's the right way.

El had given her maps at the end of the wedding. On their way home, when she was woozy and tired, he'd shown her the TTC and how to get downtown. She'd forgotten to bring her map. All she remembers is west. She looks around the platform for a sign. Suddenly the air blows her curls across her face; a silver train whooshes in, a sign on its front declaring Kipling. Was that west? She gets on anyway and sits down on a red fabric seat. It's hard. The people's faces on the train are hard. She looks around surreptitiously and sees some sleeping. She mimics them and tucks her head down, staring at her lap. Three chimes sound, a hiss of air escapes, and the doors zip together, hesitate, shut. A whine fills the air, a knock sounds as if the two cars are pulling apart, and the train pushes itself forward, pushing her into the seat back. She begins to fidget and, unable to help herself, looks up. She sees the same weary, hard people. She shifts her eyes to the right toward the window and watches as the black tunnel swallows the lighted train, hears the wheels click clack under her. The whine lowers in pitch as the whole train vibrates and smooths out into a constant forward motion.

The train slows down; Aban's body leans forward as if pulled by an outside force. The whine gets lower in tone. The train judders into a greyish kind of station with maroon letters. Donlands. That sounds familiar. She thinks. The train stops hard, three chimes sound, the doors whoosh open as the brakes let out air explosively.

Another station goes by, yellow this time, and another, pukey green. The stations and tunnels become a shifting blur of light and darkness. The train fills up; people begin to stand. A fat woman sits next to her and lets her purse strap fall onto Aban's shoulder. Aban pulls her left side in, squeezes into the train wall as much as she can. She looks around for a map and sees one above the door on the opposite side of the train. She has excellent sight, but she can't quite make out what the words say. She feels pinned in and unable to move. She stares and stares at the sign until finally she makes out that she's going in the right direction. The train pulls into a dingy yellow station; its platform is on the other side of the train from the previous platforms. Passengers crowd around every door. This must be where she's supposed to go. She gets up, and as she waits for the passengers to funnel through the doors and through the people on the platform trying to push in, she looks at the map again. She finds Yonge, scans down the yellow line, and the name "Dundas" leaps out at her. That's where she wants to go. Downtown. Where the cool kids hang out. Where everyone goes to see Toronto. Or so she'd heard from her classmates who went visiting and told everyone about it back in school.

She files out behind the crowd and is almost pushed back in by the oncoming passengers. She shoves her way out, putting her head down like a bull. She pops out and almost smacks into the tiled wall. Hugging the wall, she follows the biggest group of people as they head toward stairs that go up, stairs that have a big S next to them. Upstairs, the station flares out, columns separate the platform into two. As she follows the crowd, the columns disappear and the platform becomes one. It's so spacious; she doesn't feel like she'll become part of the wall or fall onto the tracks as she did in the one below, especially after the train had left the station on a big wind. She walks aimlessly down the wide platform until a train stops beside her. She gets on behind a young couple, he with long brown hair and baggy jeans. She with a motorcycle jacket. He's white; she's black. They're holding hands. Aban looks around at the faces in this train and suddenly notices all the different colours sitting next to each other, talking with each other like they're not different or anything. Some even read next to each other, with their bags lying loosely on their laps as if they're safe.

Her hometown is not like this; the variety both fascinates Aban in a zoo-like way and repels her. She feels uneasy. The boy in front of her—he looks her age. She can't imagine any of the boys back home dating a black girl or one as dark as that one sitting on the three-seater in front of her, with straight, light-sucking black hair. She looks different though from the other black girl. It's like she's black but not black. And then there's the Oriental next to her. Mom says we don't call them Oriental anymore. But Aban doesn't know what she is. Chinese? Japanese? What's that other one . . . ? She frowns then shakes her head. How can you tell them apart? They're so different from her. It's like she's ended up on a hospitable, alien planet. And they're talking to each other. The words the boy is saying to his girlfriend filter through into her brain.

"He says some guy is controlling him."

"What?" the girl says.

"He says someone is telling him what to do."

"Who?"

"I don't know. He says someone is taking his brain cells and dissolving them."

The girl laughs, "Oh God. Who?"

"I don't know."

Aban edges away, trying to avoid the long, thin puddle from a rolling coffee cup and the newspapers flattened on the floor, until she's at the end of the car, her back against the door that goes to the next car, her palms flattened on its cold surface.

She hears that pleasant woman's voice announce, "Next station is Dundas, Dundas station." She pushes herself away and creeps toward the door, hanging onto the pole. The train brakes, swinging her around, banging into a man holding a briefcase, wearing a suit. "Sorry," she mutters. He ignores her like he's used to this sort of thing. He hasn't budged at all, yet he's not holding on to anything. Most of the passengers surge out when the doors chime open, and Aban is carried along.

She follows them through a turnstile and through strong doors. But then she stops. Ahead, she sees a mall. She doesn't want to go into a mall. Everyone has malls. She wants to see Toronto. She sees a sign that indicates a set of steps that will take her up to the street. She follows it. And climbs the steps behind other people going the same way, while many more jog down them in the opposite direction. Everyone stays on their own sides on this stairway. But she can't avoid the newspapers, cigarette butts, used Kleenexes, flattened coffee cups, footprint-covered papers, and other unidentifiable garbage. The others don't seem to notice it all. Aban's grossed out. Home was not dirty like this.

Up top, she feels freed and stops. The people behind her bump into her, swear under their breath, and go around her. She takes a few steps forward and looks around. Next to her is a stone building with trendy clothes in the windows. They draw her close. The mannequins look so cool. Taking her eyes away, she turns around and regards an aloof white metal tubing and glass structure. Is that the Eaton Centre her classmates raved about? It doesn't look like a mall. Mom always said malls are a waste of money. Malls aren't for her. She turns slowly to her left. Across from the white building is a concrete square, with small fountains and other stuff. It looks like a mess of people and things. She grimaces. Across from it is the ugliest thing she's ever seen: a grey building covered in flashy and flashing signs. The hazy, humid air dampens her curls and makes them stick to her forehead. Aban's T-shirt grows suspiciously wet under her arms. Her pants stick to her thighs. She wants to go home.

"You look lost. Do you need some help?"

Aban looks around and sees a kind face.

"Is this your first time visiting Toronto?"

Somewhere in her mind she thinks she's not supposed to admit to that, but she does. "Yeah."

"Where do you want to go?"

Aban shrugs.

"No prob. Thinking is hard in this heat, eh?" The woman with the kind face pauses to give Aban a chance to say what she needs help with. Aban says nothing; continues feeling lost. "Hey! How about some ice cream? It helps me think, and it's the best way to cool down on a day like this." She smiles.

Aban says nothing.

"I'm Zenobia," she says as she holds out her hand.

Aban wipes her hand down her pants leg and takes it, "Aban."

"Welcome to Toronto, Aban."

Aban smiles tentatively. Zenobia looks delighted and leads her through the press of people at the corner and away from the Eaton Centre, the concrete square, and the ugly, flashing building. They walk up a sidewalk strewn with black flattened gum and punctured with large metal grates. They cross a small street. They stop in front of a thin storefront with big windows and a pink and white confection of a sign on top: *Marble Slab*.

"Here we are," Zenobia says as she opens the door and cold air blows into them. She holds the door open for Aban to enter. Aban loves the air conditioned cool. She'd never thought she'd like this artificial cold—Mom always said it wasn't for them. "It's a waste of energy and a pall on the environment," she said. But suddenly Aban doesn't care. Today, she likes it. She likes it a lot. She stops inside the door and waits for Zenobia to lead. They walk toward a line of people standing between two ropes, like the kind you see when waiting for a movie.

"What would you like?" Zenobia asks her.

"What can I have?"

"Anything you want! It's a free country, eh? You choose the ice cream flavour or flavours you want, how big you want it, what cone you want it in, and what to put in it. They mix it all together, and you have your own unique ice cream cone. Cool, eh?"

Aban feels a knot form in her stomach. How can she choose? Mom always knows what's best. She swallows. "Um . . ."

"It's easy, really."

"But . . . how do you know what flavours are good? What are they anyway?"

"There," Zenobia points to a slanted-glass case on their right with little signs on it inside saying which tubs of the good cold stuff are what flavours. Aban's mind boggles. So much choice. And there's chocolate. But not just one kind of chocolate, all kinds of chocolate. Her mouth moistens.

"Can I have chocolate?"

"Of course." Zenobia laughs with her. "No rules here. Only choice. But you know, sometimes your choice mayn't be what you wanted after all. Sometimes, I find I order chocolate when I really wanted strawberry. So choose carefully."

Aban barely hears her, she's latched onto the tub of chocolate nearest her. She stares at the most chocolatey, dense one as the line moves forward. And then it's her turn to give her order. She suddenly realizes she can choose. No one will choose for her. Excitement mingles with fear, and she goes all out like a starving person unleashed. She asks if she can have her ice cream in a chocolate-dipped cone. "Of course," the server replies, and to Aban's amazement, immediately goes to get one. She asks if she can have chocolate sauce and those shiny candies. The server complies. She watches fascinated as the server folds the ice cream over and over the toppings and sauce and then scoops it into the large cone. She pays at the cash and takes her cone carefully before looking around for her new friend. Somehow Zenobia has moved behind her and is now following her. Aban isn't sure when that happened.

They walk out into the heat together, Aban licking her cone, enjoying the coldness hitting her tongue, zinging her teeth, cooling the top of her mouth. "This is good," Aban smiles, her face relaxing.

"That's a lot of chocolate," Zenobia laughs.

"I'm not allowed to have chocolate. Mom says it's bad for you," Aban says as she licks greedily.

"In excess perhaps. But chocolate is amazing and amazingly good for you."

"It's good," Aban gasps between rapid licks. "Um . . . ," lick, "too much chocolate," lick, "but," slurp, "good." Suddenly the bustle around her is not so overwhelming; the people around her with their different faces and different dress not so daunting; the city not so filthy and not dangerous.

"Thanks," Aban says to her rapidly disappearing ice cream cone. Zenobia grins in response.

They arrive back at the intersection.

"Enjoy your day, Aban."

Aban nods absently, for her attention has been caught mid-lick. Across the street, kids are jumping through the fountains as the water rises up into the air in rectangular sprays with rounded tops. A young boy weaves his bike in and out through the cool-looking spray. Aban s mouth twitches upward slightly. She follows hungrily with her eyes the people walking their dogs on the edges of the fountain splash. She wants to join them. She wants to enjoy the day like they are. She turns to tell Zenobia. But she's gone. Aban blinks and frowns, turns slowly around to scan the throngs for her new friend. And then the light changes, and people are crossing the intersection in three different directions, even diagonally. She follows the diagonal crossers, feeling bold walking in front of four sides of stopped cars, biting off pieces of her chocolate-dipped cone, heading toward the fountains.

16

THE MARKET

"LET us go to the market," El says to Aban from her bedroom doorway.

Aban opens her gluey eyes, seeing him with blurred edges. "Wha?" she mumbles.

"Let us go to the market. Come on, Aban, get dressed, get ready quickly, for I am waiting." And he's gone.

Aban wonders if she was dreaming. She falls back asleep.

"Wake up, Aban. Time for the market," El barks from her doorway.

She sits up startled, drawing air in sharply, her heart beating rapidly.

"It's time for you to be ready," he says and disappears, leaving her mouth open with her retort unsaid.

Glaring at the empty doorway, she stretches and scratches. She lets her body fall back down; the bed bounces softly to her weight. She had her day out already. It's too hot to move; the heat is like a woolen blanket just out of boiling water, heavy and wet. Who can move? A crash smacks her awake. "All right, all right," she mumbles. "I'm coming. What's the rush anyway?"

Moving slowly, she pulls on her white T-shirt proclaiming
"Everything is Possible" in purple letters then her camouflage
army pants and sneakers. No socks. Maybe her feet won't broil
if she wears them with no socks. She should've taken Mom's
Birkenstocks. Why didn't she?

Because you're afraid.

"Oh, shut up," she mumbles and lurches down the stairs to
end up in front of El, who is standing by the front door.

"There you are," El says, nodding. He strides out, leaving her
to shut and lock the door. But she's forgotten her keys and
stumbles upstairs in the cloying heat to get them. Getting
hotter, she attempts but fails to pick up her pace going back
down to lock up. She totters to the sidewalk, veers toward the
bus stop, and finds that he's not there. She stops and
unnoticing chokes on the textural air as through the
sideways-dawn she looks down the street toward Lake Ontario
then up toward the bridge and the Danforth. Aban spots him
disappearing up the hill almost underneath the railway bridge.
Aban stumble-runs after him. Sweat pops out on her face, soaks
her back and under her arms, and makes her curls lank. "Why
the hurry?" she mutters to herself, gasping on the dust and
particles in the air. He could've waited.

"Why didn't you wait?" she yells at him, her throat raspy.

"Why were you not ready?" he replies.

"I didn't know we're going to the market. You never said."

"Why do I have to say for you to be ready?"

"What do you mean why? Talk English already."

"I am. But you do not listen. Open your ears. Do not be like
the well-off and complacent, those who see no troubles, who
say 'I'm all right, Jack' and so do not use their ears, do not use
their eyes, hear only what they want to, see only what they want
to but not what is in front of them."

"I'm—"

El picks up speed as if it's a cool, Spring day to be enjoyed, leaving Aban talking to nothing. She hesitates in shock, but her anger ripens, driving her legs forward. She catches up, barely. He hikes silently uphill, while she puffs noisily beside him. Finally, she has enough breath to retort, "You keep talking about hearing. But it's not fair to wake me up at—. What time is it anyway? You're not Mom, you know. I don't hafta get up this early. On a Saturday too. I bet the birds aren't awake neither, like, who would? No one! You keep talking about being ready. Well, I would've been if you'd told me."

El snorts with impatience, "Have I not told you to be ready for all things? How long must I instruct you before you will listen?"

"Instruct me? Who told you to instruct me? I don't need no instruction. That's what Mom is for, and I left her. She can't get at me now."

"Is that why you came?"

Aban shrugs, suddenly not having enough breath to reply.

"Aban, you came for a reason. Do you not even know your own mind? Do you not even know why you came?"

"I came for my inheritance."

"Did you?"

"Yeah," Aban hesitates. "Yeah, I did. I did!"

El shakes his head and speeds up. Aban strives to keep up with his brutal pace.

He enters the still air of Greenwood subway station, and Aban follows about a minute later in silence. Its maroon-and-mucky-yellow tiles echo the sound of El's token falling into the stile as he walks through it once he sees Aban entering the station. The stile's metal arms turn and smack to a stop as Aban fumbles with her wallet, her change clanging into the fare box while the guy behind the booth's thick glass watches her under half-closed lids.

"Have you not yet bought tokens?" El asks her when she catches up to him at the top of the stairs. "You went downtown yesterday, yet you're so unprepared you paid cash there and back and you're still paying cash today?"

"Yeah, so what," she mutters back. "I don't got enough money to buy tokens anyway."

"You have no money, no tokens because you put no forethought into it." His eyes bore into her as they stand at the top of the stairs. Her eyes drop after a few futile moments of trying to hold his gaze. He turns away and leaps down the grey-tiled steps, his arms pumping in tune with his legs, while Aban follows at a run, her hand sliding along the metal rail, picking up black gummy brake dust that lies like a fine cloak all over TTC subway stations. She doesn't notice. The train blows in as they arrive on the platform, lifting for a brief, refreshing moment her damp curls.

They sit across from each other in the almost-empty train. He looks at her chest and reads out loud, "Everything is possible."

"Yeah."

"What if one day you are hit by a bus. Will it be possible for you to stand up?"

"Depends."

"Depends how?"

"Well, if it like hit hit or just, you know, tapped."

"You prevaricate like a lawyer."

"Fine. Whatever that means. But you don't get it anyway. It's about . . . about . . . you know, you. Your spirit. What you can do with your life. Not about getting hit with a bus."

"If everything is possible, why didn't you leave your mother's house in the last twenty years?"

"I was a kid!"

"Not for five years. Many leave home years before you did, knowing it's time."

"You don't get it."

El contemplates her. She turns her head away.

They conduct the rest of the trip down to Front Street in stony silence until they get off the bus El had led her onto after the subway. Aban doesn't know where they are and scans the buildings around her to get her bearings. The early morning light outlines the structures nearby and the haze obscures the tops of the further-away tall office buildings and hides the CN Tower's tip, but she thinks she recognizes them and takes a step in their direction. But El moves off in the opposite direction. She swivels to follow and almost twists her foot. She grimaces and yells, "Ow!" but El keeps walking. She glares at his back as she limps to catch up.

The darkened buildings across the road remind Aban of some of the older buildings in the touristy towns near where she lives, but the one on their side of the street is like some boring thing someone plopped down. They come upon an open area. Tables covered by tent-type roofs line up along the sidewalk. A squat, rectangular building rises up behind the tables furthest away from where they are, its concrete façade painted blue with a happy market scene, light spilling out from its centre. She forgets to limp as she stares at the mural then wanders closer to browse the tables. But El has other ideas. He keeps going. She hurries to catch up.

As she passes the end of the last table, just before the building has a cut-out in it where doors are inset, she sees the old, imposing building across the street for the first time with people laden with packages streaming out of the bustling light of its three doors and people streaming in with empty bags. It reminds her of nineteenth century sketches of port buildings sitting on docks, except there's no water here. Weird. Who'd build a port and a dock in the middle of land? A few people are sitting on the pier part eating. Her stomach gurgles. She wonders what they're eating but suddenly realizes El is once

again way ahead of her, has already passed the cut-out, and is
about to disappear around the corner. She rushes forward.

As she rounds the corner, she almost bumps into a table
laden with herbs. Their freshness scents the air, and her
stomach rumbles louder. She had no breakfast; even fresh herbs
by themselves seem good to her. She looks around for El,
wondering whether she's supposed to buy food. She doesn't
cook. She doesn't know how. She wouldn't know what to do
with the herbs. Mom cooked dinner on Sundays and Dad the
rest of the meals.

Aban can't see El, and she steps away from the table and
toward the corner of the intersection. The closest lane is lined
with trucks, and the sidewalk is buzzing with people. Where is
she? She looks up. "Jarvis," the blue rectangular sign declares
the street's name. The one perpendicular to it says, "Front." She
lowers her head and looks around again for El. A group are
clustered at the corner, gazing at the other side, kitty-corner to
where they are. The dawn has lifted the dark, and she can
follow their gaze easily. El is near a brick wall with a yellow and
red sign blaring "Convenience" overhead. He's bending over a
crumpled heap of clothes while people hurry past, laden with
paper bags, plastic bags, Whole Foods bags, Big Carrot bags,
Loblaws bags. Everyone wants their name on a bag. Her parents
don't put their shop name on their bags, she thinks smugly.
Mom had always said that plain brown paper bags were best.
They were good for the environment, and they don't need to
trumpet who they are to get people to shop at their store.

"It was his fault. I saw the whole thing." A voice next to her
interrupts Aban's reverie.

"Yeah? What happened?"

Aban listens to the voices around her and watches El across
the intersection at the same time. El places a hand on the man.

"The homeless guy just wanted some money, you know. Like
would it have killed him to give him a loonie? I know him, you
know."

"Yeah?" comes the breathless reply near Aban.

"Yeah. He's the CEO of the insurance company I work at. He's always sending memos out telling us how to do our job better, how we have to make the company more money and spend less on claims. Last month he said we'd paid out too much in claims, and he wanted to see a ten percent reduction this month. Bastard."

"I know. Our management is the same. Always asking for the impossible, like our bosses do any work, those rich bastards."

"Yeah, well look at him now," the woman says with a laugh. The other laughs with her. A man near them interrupts them, "But wasn't he robbed?"

"Yeah, but it was his own fault," replies the first woman. "I saw it all. He just walked by the homeless man, even shoved him away. I saw it."

"Tut," the man utters. "At least give the poor guy a loonie. But those rich guys they live in a world of their own, got no time for us ordinary folk."

"That's what I say," the second woman replies.

El sits the man up and pulls something out of his own pocket. Aban squints to see better and realizes it's a large white piece of cloth. El dabs the man's forehead with it. Redness stains the man's face and soon stains the cloth. Gross.

"Well, he's bloodied now," the man says dispassionately before turning to resume his shopping.

"Serves him right," the first woman says viciously. "Now maybe we won't be getting those ten-percent memos."

"I doubt it," the second says. "Nothing but death stops those CEOs from always wanting to cut, cut, cut, take more money for themselves away from people who deserve it."

"Yeah, don't I know it." Aban finally gets the courage to see who's talking. She slants her eyes sideways. The two women are staring at the spectacle across the intersection. They watch contentedly for a moment more until an ambulance draws up, blocking their view of their show.

"Well, did you get that pig shoulder you were going to make for dinner?" the first woman asks the second as they turn back to the market and their shopping.

"Not yet. Is your husband coming or does he still have to work late?"

"Men and their work. I talked to him again . . ." The two women drift off.

"Why would El want to help a man like that?" Aban grumbles to herself. Mom always said those corporate types were no good. "Psychopaths," she had called them. He should be locked up not helped. The heat of her anger steams into the heat of the air, and redness suffuses her face. She wipes the sweat off her cheeks and rubs her hands down her sticky pants, over and over. First El pulls her out of bed, saying they had to get going, like, now. Then instead of shopping like normal people, he's over there getting his hands bloodied and gross, leaving her over here by herself, in a strange place. And for what? Some guy who deserved what he got!

"Why'd you leave me?" she demands of him as he returns to her, still wiping his hands on another white square handkerchief. She hopes that's not the same one he used on the man.

"The paramedics are looking after him," El replies wearily. "They're taking him to St. Mike's to bandage up his wounds. I must go to the washroom to wash my hands. I'll be back, Aban." And he leaves her standing there, mouth agape. She hurries after him, almost hitting the washroom door as it closes on her. She wants to enter but conditioning keeps her outside the door, her right foot tapping as she stands in the way of men coming out, who blush or mutter as they almost run her over.

"Well?" she demands as El swings the door open and stops in front of her, nose to nose.

"My neighbour needed help," he explains.

"Your neighbour? I never saw him on Greenwood."

"You wouldn't have seen him, for he doesn't live there. He lives in the Bridlewood Path area."

"So why'd you call him your neighbour? That's stupid."

"A man robbed him."

"Yeah, I heard. It was his own fault for not giving that homeless guy a loonie. We should always help the homeless. Mom said it's cause our community takes care of each other, we don't have no homeless like here. But in the city no one cares. Would it've killed him to help? A rich guy like him can afford a loonie. He could've given him a hundred dollar bill. I bet he has stacks of em. I bet that's like a cent to the rest of us."

"His attacker was homeless, yes. A homeless man plagued by demons who came down from your small town to find help here but found only a concrete bed and all but missions not wanting to know him. But he didn't attack because the man refused him a loonie. He attacked because for the last several weekends, he's taken to cursing the man out, telling him to empty his wallet or else, telling him the aliens are demanding his pound of flesh. The man attempted to have the police do something, but they told him to cross the road and refused to help them both. He attempted to have the city's social workers do something, but they said since he wasn't harming anyone, since he hadn't physically hit anyone or harmed himself yet, they couldn't. He had the right to decide if he wanted help or not. And whenever they asked, he always replied, 'I'm fine.' Even when he suddenly went on his own to see a psychiatrist, the doctor told him to go to the ER but didn't lift a finger to make sure he got there. The homeless man had the right to go insane on the streets, unclean, unfed, and uncared for. The man realized giving him a loonie would not help him; the problem was bigger than that. And he didn't want to think about it either because then he would have to act, and he didn't want to leave the comfort of his life, to change his life that much. Today, the man tried to go another way to his car in order to avoid the homeless man. But the homeless man had targeted him and jaywalked to catch him. He said that this time he was going to take the man's wallet, because he had tried to avoid him. The homeless man punched him and took his wallet, his watch, his gold wedding ring, and his keys. I found the keys a metre away from him. The rest is gone. Because he'd reported him before, they know who he is. So who is to blame? The man? The homeless man for being insane? The city? The police? Or the social workers and nurses and psychiatrists who knew about his growing insanity?"

Aban doesn't answer.

"If the rich man is to blame, doesn't he still deserve succour?"

"Huh?"

"Aid, help, comfort."

"It was his fault," she mutters.

"Does he not deserve mercy?"

"You don't know what kind of man he is. He harms people. I heard, you know."

El bursts out, "Why do you listen to the evil speakers? Are their words not like choice morsels that slide down happily into your heart, causing you to see what is not there even as you watched me clean his wounds? Are the evil speakers you listened to so blameless that they can judge another fairly, that they can say he deserved it no matter what his sins? Are you so blameless that refusing your neighbour aid makes you better than he? You hypocrite!"

Aban reels. Her mouth hangs open. She snaps her teeth shut and narrows her eyes. "Well, he did too deserve it," she spits out. "He deserved being beaten up. That woman said! And she knows cause she works for him. 'It's hell working for him,' she said. She knows. He beats up on people all the time, just not physically so that's, like, okay? Corporate people are like psychopaths, they don't care about us ordinary folk, Mom said so. It's time someone gave him payback. A man like him doesn't deserve to exist."

"Though he may be lost, yet still he deserves to be saved. He is our neighbour, our brother, and our family. We don't abandon them."

17

RALLY SATURDAY

WITH a huff of contempt, Aban swivels round on the ball of her left foot, turns her back on El, and stalks off. Arms swinging hard, legs pumping furiously, she doesn't notice the condos and historic structures she's passing, the people strolling along, or the empty section where the office buildings preside. When she slows down to heave a sigh and wearily slouch against a hard, hot wall, she doesn't know where she is. She looks around and feels like she's in a cold echoing canyon. A car drives past. A person across the street dashes in the opposite direction.

She's alone.

She wanders aimlessly for some time, trying to find a street that's familiar, not that any of this useless city is familiar to her, she thinks, trying to push her fear under a mask of sourness. The revealing morning light morphs into Toronto's daily mustardy haze. She finds herself near the lake. She's never seen Lake Ontario before. She stands across from land covered in trees, a ferry puffing silently toward it, sailboats bobbing on the surface, their white sails at times flapping, the entire scene filtered in yellow. Aban shifts her gaze to her side of the lake;

the lake looks flat and dark grey-blue. Her stomach growls; she looks up and around for food. Spotting a hot dog cart, she heads toward it. She orders a hot dog and a bottle of water. The man tells her an outrageous price; that's when she realizes she doesn't have much money. She digs into her pocket, draws out her wallet, and checks its contents. She's down to her last $10. But it's enough.

Aban sits down on the edge of the waterfront, dangling her legs near where boats moor, and gulps down her dog and the water. Afterward, she sits there for a while, holding the garbage in her hands until something moves her to stand up and go in search of a recycling bin.

She stuffs her now-empty hands into her pockets, and she shrugs along, her head downcast, her feet kicking errant stones in her path, unnoticing of the people she bumps into and their "I'm sorrys." Every now and then Aban lifts her head as a pigeon flaps past or a sparrow lands to peck at bread on the stone walk. She crosses a street, almost tripping over the tracks and doesn't notice the annoyed streetcar dinging like crazy. She keeps scuffing along, away from the lake, away from the waters and into the confining heat of the city. She struggles uphill, crosses bigger roads blindly, and finds herself in front of an enormous round and tiered fountain. Metal salmon leap in the air, away from her, while others below swim exposed, toward the etched charcoal stone walls. There is no water. As she stares at the frozen, parched salmon, she gradually hears the sounds of a crowd cheering and chanting.

She lifts her head. Her feet turn.

Following the sound, Aban approaches an enormous concrete structure near the dry fountain. It has blank walls. The sound seems to be coming out of its top, and her eyes follow the walls upward. The side nearest her has no roof, the other end is covered by a semi-circular dome. Keeping her eyes aimed upward toward the empty roof, except when she trips on cracks in the walk, she circles the structure. As she rounds a corner, another source of chanting, in sync with the first, hits her ears. She lowers her gaze and stumbles to a stop to figure out where to go. Anonymous windows face her, and the chanting ahead soars in volume before falling back again. Aban begins to walk again; she rounds another corner and another until she emerges on the opposite side of where she was, and chanting explodes in her ears.

People are everywhere in a square beside the concrete structure.

And barely visible underneath their feet and packed bodies, square stones pave the ground and trees struggle to grow in the humid air.

Large screens loom over compacted congregations, which have their collective heads raised and voices repeating in time to repeating images of a man appearing on one screen after another. The man is animated, walking back and forth, dressed in a blue suit and tie, barely discernible against the blackness of the screen from where she's standing. Aban inches closer, squeezing around and between enraptured people until she can see him.

She lifts her head to the screen.

She's mesmerized.

He's so energetic. So full of life. His confidence flows out of the screen, over the people, and into her. His words become discernible in her ears, and her lips start to move in unison, just like everyone else's, even though she has no idea who he is. It doesn't occur to her to ask the girl beside her who he is.

He says, "I am!"

The crowd inside and outside the giant structure replies, "I am!"

"I am!"

The crowd replies, "I am!"

"I am!" the man exclaims, punching the air.

The crowd and Aban punch the air in reply, "I am!!"

"Somebody."

"Somebody," the crowd chants.

"Somebody!"

"Somebody!" the crowd and Aban chant.

"Somebody!!"

"Somebody!!" the crowd and Aban exclaim louder, punching the air.

"Respect me," the man says quietly.

"Respect me," the crowd and Aban reply, equally quietly.

"Respect me," the man says with emphasis.

"Respect me," the crowd and Aban reply.

"Respect me!" the man lunges forward on the last word.

"Respect me!" the crowd and Aban yell but have no room to move.

The man walks forward two steps. "We are," he says to the screen.

"We are," the crowd and Aban reply.

"We are," the man says louder.

"We are," the crowd and Aban reply louder.

"We are!" the man shouts.

"We are!" the crowd and Aban shout.

"The present!" the man shouts, raising his arms in emphasis.

"The present!" the crowd and Aban shout back, raising their arms.

"The present!" the man shouts again, not a hair on his coiffed head moving.

"The present!" the crowd and Aban shout back.

"The present!"

"The present!"

"I am!" the man shouts.

"I am!" the crowd and Aban shout in reply, punching the air, their mouths splitting into grins of mob joy.

"I am!"

"I am!"

"I am!"

"I am!"

The man's voice drops, "Hope."

"Hope," the people reply.

"Hope," he says.

"Hope," they reply.

"Hope!" he exclaims.

"Hope!" they exclaim back.

"We have the power!"

"We have the power!"

"We have the power!"

"We have the power!"

"We. Have. The. Power!"

"We. Have. The. Power!" the people mimic almost jumping in their enthusiasm.

"Listen to us," the man says, hitting his chest with his hand on each word.

"Listen to us," the people say punching the air with their right fists on each word.

"Listen to us!"

"Listen to us!"

"Listen. To. Us!" the man says, almost screaming in his zeal.

"Listen. To. Us!" the people scream back.

Beams stream out of the top of the open dome up to the light-swallowing sky; red, blue, white they circle in rhythm to the chant. Aban watches the rotating beams transfixed.

"Good night, everybody!" the man waves at the people inside and outside.

The crowd roars and claps and stamps their feet, their thunder rising inside and outside, echoing all around Aban. The man's eyes flash in the lights as he turns and jogs off his stage.

The screen goes black.

Aban wants more. And for a while, Aban and the people around her continue to clap and dance their feet on the spot, trying to keep the feeling going. But one by one, they stop, look back down to eye level, look for a way to move on out. They turn their feet away. The doors open, and thousands stream out of the massive concrete basilica, joining the crowds outside. People congregate in small groups as one of their members steps back and flashes their photo against the grey-beige concrete walls to commemorate this moment. Many wear brand-new black T-shirts proclaiming "We have the power" in big white letters. Aban wants one but cannot find where to buy them.

Soon, it's just her and a few stragglers. Quiet descends. She fishes her wallet out of her pocket and finds only a few coins. She'll have to walk back to Greenwood, but she doesn't know in which direction that is or how to get there. She stops a young woman at the edge of a laughing, buzzing group.

"Um, how do you get to Greenwood?"

"We have the power!" the woman replies, and she pumps her fist in one accord with her group. Aban wants to join in, but they stop the chant as abruptly as they'd begun, and the woman turns to Aban. "Oh yeah, Greenwood. You go that way," and she points toward the dome.

"The building?" Aban asks.

"The SkyDome? No, of course not. Past it. Way past it." The group skips off, parallel to the concrete walls of what the woman called the "SkyDome," though Aban doesn't remember seeing that name anywhere; it's like not knowing who that man was leading them all when everybody else did. She shrugs and sets off too.

Aban follows the happy group until they reach a large street. As they cross the road, she turns to look behind her to check which side of her this SkyDome is on and sees the strangest creatures hanging off its walls laughing at her. Aban rears back and, after hesitating, walks along the sidewalk parallel to the

SkyDome's frontage. Her arms move freely in rhythm to her legs. She crosses street after street. As the excitement wears off, she feels the heat, the closed clingy air again. It's like walking in a sauna. Her feet become sluggish. She passes an imposing stone structure with fat columns and crowds moving in and out in ones and twos and families. She passes a theatre with a sophisticated flat, angled awning, its underside lined with lit bulbs overlooking black limos at rest. She passes the market again. She hesitates at the closed main doors, remembering the smells of fruit and meat. But she has no money. She hurries past the corner where the man was beaten up. She slows down as the crowds grow sparse, where the road has grown cracks and bumps and cars hurry past. She walks and walks until she gets to a bridge, and from what she can see, pedestrians are not welcome.

She stops.

As she's gaping at the strangest house she's ever seen, its first floor a fat square pole, with three squares angled on top, covered in posters, looking forlorn, a voice interrupts her.

"You look lost."

Aban yanks her head around. The kind face looks familiar.

"Is this your first time in this part of Toronto?"

Aban's jaw drops. It's her.

Smiling widely, Zenobia says, "Don't worry, Aban, you're not alone. Greenwood is this way. Let me show you."

Aban follows Zenobia, not noticing in which direction they're going, not caring which streets they're taking, oblivious to the bridge they're crossing with the verdigris sign that says "this river I step in is not the river I stand in," just trying to comprehend how Zenobia had found her and why she's here.

"There you go," Zenobia points. "We're on Queen. We've crossed the bridge, and now it's a straight walk until you get to Greenwood. There's only one way to go, north, because Greenwood ends at Queen. You'll find your way home, Aban. No worries."

Aban looks in the direction of her finger, then back at Zenobia, except she's gone. Aban blinks, rubs her eyes, peeks, shakes her head and squints her eyes shut. She opens them cautiously. Zenobia is still gone. Aban revolves slowly scanning the street, the sidewalks, the small street in front of her, but she cannot see even a fleeting glimpse of Zenobia's hand or her skirt. She shrugs and crams her hands in her pockets, and with head down once more, Aban walks.

18

THE DREAM II

THE formless deep waits. She is dangling over it. She looks down; the tips of her toes are touching it, disappearing into it, yet she feels nothing. A flicking motion to her left grabs her attention away from her toes. She moves her eyeballs left and sees two squishy, ribbed-white bodies undulating toward her along the crests of black silk waves that swirl in rhythm with their movement. Their blurred triangular shapes swim in a straight line toward her, in front of her, the waves moving ahead of them, surrounding her. A second couple hoves into view. Two by two they come. Maggots. She kicks her massless feet, trying to rise, to get out of their way and out of the waves that hide the formless deep, but she's stuck, gripped by an unknown force and the niggling thought: does she really want to move? "Aren't they fascinating, these effervescent couples with their soft bodies and hypnotic movement," a crepuscular wisp whispers into her ear. She stops struggling.

The soft white bodies have now formed a long line of pairs in front of her, the line separating the deep from the unseen fog-like space above them and her. The line of bodies stretches as far back as her eyes can see and keeps growing. Her eyes watch while her mind disengages. It is so easy to disengage, to see them as having nothing to do with her. They're just maggots swimming by. That void beneath her feet, the one sucking at her toes, does not exist.

They turn.

The front of the line is now way past her on her right, so when they turn, they fence her in on her front and right flanks. She tenses, but as her mind is about to re-engage, the end of the line appears, space opens up behind them. She relaxes. They can't harm her.

Pause.

Another creature materializes. Long and slender and s-shaped, it too is white. But its ribs are black bands, and translucent spikes stick out of each rib in all directions, their tips quivering with drops of venom. She doesn't like that. It doesn't swim in a slow rhythm like the maggots, instead it has many, many tiny feet on the end of many, many tiny straight legs that hustle fast. Toward her. It keeps an even distance from the end of the last maggot, but its eyes, its entire being is focused on her. She shivers. She can no longer pretend that these creatures have nothing to do with her. She wiggles hard, harder. She thrashes, harder and harder, but her feet only treadmill the black silk. The tiny waves she's creating attract the maggots' attention. The millipede's eyes gleam. Fear rises in her throat as the millipede draws near, so near she can see its grinning maw opening for her.

Aban wakes up.

The sheet beneath her is wet. Her teeth are chattering; her breathing is ragged. She sits up suddenly, hits the floor running, and races downstairs. She skids around the newel post, her right hand acting as a pivot, and stops. She pants, and dizziness draws her head down. Gaining her breath and standing up carefully, she pulls down her grey T-shirt that asks on the front "You want a scripture you can believe in?" sort of aware that she's wearing only purple boxers underneath. The back of her T-shirt answers, "Read your dog's eyes."

Light flickers into the dark hall from the living room.

"Come in, Aban," El says to her out of the light.

Aban walks down the hallway and into the lit living room slowly. El is sitting on the floor in the lotus position in front of the low coffee table; a clay oil lamp sits on top of the table burning a flame that surrounds him with light, throwing the rest of the room in shadow. Abruptly, Aban feels the heat of the night. The oil fills the cloistered air with a sweet scent that sort of smells like the balsam pines near her home. She lowers herself to the floor gingerly at the end of the coffee table. El doesn't stir. They sit together in the quiet, eyes toward the steady flame, inhaling the intense fragrance, her T-shirt becoming a part of her skin.

"I had a bad dream," Aban blurts out.

"Tell me about it," El encourages.

"I can't."

"Telling out the bad makes it lose its intensity. You will not be so afraid, Aban. I promise."

"I . . . It . . . It was . . ." She hugs herself and drops her head. The skin under her chin and the skin of her neck soon cling together.

"You don't need to be afraid, Aban; you're here with me. The nightmare cannot harm you in the telling."

Aban shakes her head, her skin rubbing against itself.

"Aban, you must," he urges.

"No!" she shoots up. "It's too hot. How can you burn anything? It makes it hotter. It makes everything hotter!" She flees back into the darkness of her space.

19

THE BLIND

THE next morning, Aban wakes up soaked. She takes a cold shower and has barely dried off when the heat once again begins to build up layers of moisture on her skin. Her thighs stick together before she has a chance to pull on her pants. Her forearm sticks to her upper arm when she bends her arm to comb her hair. Her feet peel off the sticky floor when she walks through the bathroom's humid air into the hallway's dampness. Damp damp damp. Hot hot hot. Aban hates it, hates it, hates it.

She yells, "I hate this heat!"

She doesn't feel better.

She feels restless. She wants to go away. She wants to go home. She doesn't want to go home. She wants to find El, she doesn't know why. Aban acts on the latter impulse and heads downstairs where she hears murmurings—gentle words with overtones of firmness—filtering out of the living room. Aban follows the words and peeks through the living room door.

El is sitting on his sofa. The coffee table has been moved toward the fireplace. Facing him, sitting cross-legged on the floor, are seven men and women, faces upturned to El. Between them and El, a man sits cross-legged, facing El yet not quite looking at him. It's as if the seven have the man's back, but the man is nervous anyway.

El asks, "Why are you here?"

The man answers, "I'm blind."

Aban sidles into the room as El asks, "How did you get that way?"

"Does it matter?"

"Why do I ask?"

"I don't tell people. They know I'm blind; they don't want to hear why, because then it could happen to them. They're afraid."

"Because they can't do anything about it?"

"Exactly."

"How did you become blind?"

"Why does it matter?"

El doesn't answer. The man jerks his head side to side as if searching. El waits. The man fidgets with his hands and mutters, "It was an accident." El murmurs encouragingly. The group wait in a way that seems to hold the man up. The man inhales raggedly, "I was, you know, in charge of the fireworks for Canada Day a few years ago. I always did it. Me and my son, we went to get them, the fireworks. We got all the favourites and some new ones. I followed the rules, you know. Had a hose nearby, stuck them in sand in a bucket. But we don't have a large backyard. It's Toronto, you know," he pauses. "Anyway, I set them off like always and like always one doesn't go off. And like always, I go over to see if I can get it to go. But it explodes. Right into my face. The pain was awful, like thousands of fires landing on my face and my eyes. My eyes! My eyes . . . ," he peters off in anguish. Everyone holds their breath. The man sniffs, wipes his marked face with the back of his hands, his head downcast, hiding his face from El's gaze. He begins to speak again. "The fireworks went into both eyes. The doctors said I closed them quickly. It's instinctive. But . . . Anyway, I got help. It was superficial, the doctors said, just to the corneas, not the whole eyes. They said they could treat the injury. My face healed, but my eyes never did." He stops talking. His story seems to be over, yet El continues to sit in anticipation. The group look at him puzzled, then at their friend.

His voice pierces the quiet as he takes up his tale again. "I have nightmares. I see the flash. I can't hear. And then I can't see. Little fires are all over my face, and my eyes are burning so much. I thrash about trying to put them out. I sleep separate from my wife so she doesn't have to know about my nightmares. I don't want her to know. My son, he wakes up screaming most nights. He thinks it's his fault. I tell him not to talk about it; it's best to forget it, to put it behind him. It's not his fault anyway. I tell him that every night. I'm past it myself."

"Has not talking about that night helped him? Stopped the nightmares?"

"No."

"Are you really past it? And what does that mean, past it?"

"I want my sight back."

"I know."

The man whispers low, "No. I'm not past it. The pain is deep inside, and it's too hard to let out. I feel like I'm a downer when I do talk about it. People get bored; they've heard it so many times. Others get restless; I can hear them fidget, wanting to be anywhere but with me. So I pretend. I pretend it's no big deal so that everyone else can be happy. But everyone still suffers because of it, because my pain comes out in other ways. That's what my wife tells me. I want to see."

El asks, "Can you see anything?"

The man raises his head quickly and lets it drop again. He says, "Only light and dark, vague shapes. I cannot distinguish your face."

"What do you want me to do for you?"

"These people told me about you, said that you could give me sight."

"Do you believe that I am able to do this?"

"I have nowhere else to turn. The doctors cannot restore my sight though they've tried. I've been to doctors in Mexico and India, even China. No one can help. They don't know why I can't see better. I have nowhere left to go."

Moved with compassion, El tilts the man's head up gently with a hand under his chin. He lays his hands on his eyes and speaks silently. El removes his hands and asks, "What do you want me to do for you?"

"I want to see."

"Can you see anything yet?"

He shakes his head no. El again places his hands on his eyes and moves his lips silently. The group bow their heads and move their lips in attempted unison. El removes his hands and asks, "What do you see?"

He opens his eyes wide, cocks his head, and tells El, "I've never spoken of that day before . . . after I no longer had to tell the doctors about it. I just say I had an accident and most people sound relieved they don't have to hear the details. But you, I can feel you looking at me—.

"I can't see you, but I knew you looked at me with compassion, not sympathy, not pity, but like you knew what it's really like, like you know my pain. It's a relief to speak of it to someone who listens, who isn't judging how I'm doing or the accident itself, who isn't telling me to get over it or feeling awkward . . . you . . . I . . . I can feel your compassion for me." He thumps his chest. "In here. I can feel you in here, in my heart." He shakes his head, puzzled.

El places his hands on the man's eyes and bows his head as he speaks silently. The man sinks into the floor as if tension is fleeing his muscles. His shoulders drop; his hands fall off his lap to lie on the floor; his breathing steadies to a slow, deep rhythm.

El removes his hands.

His face revealed, the man smiles, his eyes opening wide, crinkling at the edges, the muscles soft with peace. "I am not alone," he says wonderingly.

"No," El replies. "You are never alone."

"There is one person in this world who isn't judging or pitying or avoiding me, who . . . who likes me just as I am, with all my complaints and pain and . . . and the good stuff too. I can tell you wouldn't be jealous of my successes either, as meagre as they are. Everything will work out. It isn't what I expected, but it will be okay." He pauses. "I am not alone," he whispers. "Thank you."

El says, "Go to your home. And tell your son too so that he can speak his heart out to you as you have done here."

The group stands up as the man does. He reaches back, and one of the group picks up his cane from the floor and hands it to him. He expertly unfolds it, taps the floor to assess where he is, and surrounded by the men and women, leaves, moving his cane side to side rhythmically, the taps echoing down the hall, its tone changing as it hits the porch floor. Aban doesn't move for long minutes after the door has closed on them.

"Sit with me, Aban. I know you have questions."

"You didn't heal that man," she accuses as she walks toward him.

"What did he ask for?"

"His sight," she replies derisively. "You know, so he could, like, see." She draws out the last word.

El sighs with resignation, "You did not use your own eyes. Sit down and listen. Use your ears to hear."

Aban flops into the chair near the window, sighing dramatically, her arms dropping over the chair's arms.

"Is it easier to give sight or to give peace?"

"Who wants peace? I want to see, so did that man."

"Have you ever had peace?"

155

"No."

"So how do you know what it's like if you've never had it? How do you know if you don't want it if you've never had it?"

"Yeah but it's hard to live without sight."

"Yes. It is." El scrutinizes her for long moments, as Aban swings her legs back and forth. Her eyes drop from his.

"What was it he was looking for?" El asks Aban.

"You know, being able to, like, see," she says, her voice becoming hard and deep on the last word.

"But the doctors cannot restore his sight. He has seen many specialists, many alternative healers. And no one can restore his sight. What now?"

"Well, he came to you, didn't he? Those people thought you could, like, heal him."

"Do you think that I am able to do that?"

"They thought so."

"That is not what I asked."

Aban shifts her head away. She looks past him, out the side window to a wall and the alley in deep shadow. She stares at the walls, inside and out, and mutters, "No one can do that. It's all . . ."

Mom's voice is in her head; she can hear her dismissing healers as fraud artists, scammers of the religious right. But somehow Mom's words seem all so jaded, so put on, and so fake. She doesn't believe anyone can heal . . . does she? She wonders. Just because she hasn't met anyone who can heal, does that mean those kind of people don't exist? El didn't! But that man left as if he had. Why? These questions hurt her head. It's like an old muscle being demanded to work again. She rubs her forehead hard. "I don't know," she blurts.

El nods.

"Why didn't you heal him?" she cries.

"Because the people who brought him didn't need proof."

Aban blinks at him, not understanding him at all. "Huh?"

"Their eyes are opened already. They brought him so that he may see like them too."

"God! Can't you speak English? Like, does everything have to be so, so hard with you? It's stupid!"

"It is not hard or stupid. I speak in your tongue. It is you who choose not to hear and see. I am telling you I gave him the sight that he needed. Did you not see how he left?"

"Yeah. With his cane."

"I am here for the sick, and I made him well."

"No. You. Did. Not."

"Listen, Aban! Look, Aban!"

"I saw!"

"What did you see?" he huffs in exasperation.

"I saw that guy get up and walk out with his cane, as blind as ever."

"What else did you see?" El slaps his thighs, "Do you not use the eyes that were given to you? Do you willfully ignore what is in front of you so you do not have to think? Do you not use the brain that was given to you? Do you willfully shut it down so you do not have to see?"

"You can't talk to me like that!"

El's face suddenly softens, his eyes grow tender, "How hard it is for you to observe and think for yourself."

Aban frowns and drives her hands into her pockets, slouching deeper into her chair. She watches her feet, then suddenly pulls them in under the chair, sits up, and takes her hands out. "Okay, since you know everything, tell me."

"What have I been doing if not telling you?"

"In English!"

"What did you see when I took my hands off the blind man's eyes?"

Aban pauses for five seconds, "I don't know." El stares at her intently. His gaze drags her out of her safe cocoon. Aban cannot resist, and suddenly she tastes the freedom outside the cocoon.

157

It's faint yet attractive. She looks away, not to escape but to let herself think. Her heart beats fast, her breaths come shallowly. "I . . . I . . . saw his face."

"And what did you see on his face?"

"I don't know . . . I don't know what to call it."

"Try, Aban. It is time for you to think," El says, emphasizing the last word. "Did he look sicker?"

"No," she turns her gaze back to him, her eyes opening in shock as her mind's eye remembers. "He looked . . . happy. No! Not happy, like better, like, like . . ."

El waits. The minutes tick by slowly. Tick. Tick. Tick. Aban deflates. El encourages her, "Is that peace? Is that what you saw?"

Aban sits back up and thinks. In her mind, she asks herself the question again. "Yes . . . but . . . but there was more."

El nods.

"Like he was real happy?"

"Yes, joy," El affirms. He regards her as if expecting her next question.

"What will he do with it?"

"What did he say?"

Aban answers immediately, "I am not alone." She thinks for a bit. "But all those people were with him anyway."

"He wasn't talking about them, was he?"

"Noooo . . . ," Aban hesitates. "Was he talking about you? But how could you be with him when he is at home and you're here?" Aban furrows her brow; she rubs her forehead with her right hand. She drops her hand, her head falling against the chair back, and sighs, her eyes closing, then snapping open at him, "I don't get it."

El smiles and stands, "It is enough for now. Let us eat."

20

THE BREAD

A BAN follows El into his kitchen, where he gathers together fresh yeast, sugar, a cup of water, flour, butter, eggs, and salt on his counter. He begins.

"Have you baked bread before, Aban?" he asks, as he heats up the water briefly in the microwave.

"No."

"Today, you will learn. Pay attention."

"Why? I don't wanna learn."

El begins teaching. "I will make it easy for you. I often make bread using my mother dough, but today, for you, I will use a basic recipe. First you must proof the yeast. Do you know what yeast is?"

"No." Aban doesn't know what mother dough is either. But she doesn't ask him.

El clicks his tongue. He removes the cup of water from the microwave, pours it into a bowl, and crumbles the block of yeast into it. He says, "It is a life form."

"Ewww."

El stops and looks at her, "There's no ewww about it. You eat life forms when you eat meat. You eat life forms when you eat cheese. You even eat life forms when you eat vegetables."

"I don't eat that kind of cheese, and vegetables are plants, you know."

El sets the bowl aside and turns fully toward her, "Your ignorance is astounding."

"I'm not ignorant."

"No, you won't be after I finish teaching you."

"I don't need any teaching. I went to school, you know. And I graduated."

El doesn't reply but resumes, "The yeast likes to grow—"

"Plants aren't animals."

"No, they are not, Aban, but animals aren't just the ones you can see. Animals include life that you cannot see. Bacteria and smaller organisms live in the soil and in the growing season crawl into some vegetables. You cannot get them out of the vegetables' crannies when washing the soil off. Even a scrubbing may not be enough. And so whether you know it or not—and you have not until today— you eat them when you eat some plant life."

El laughs as a look of revulsion grows on Aban's face. Her mouth opens. "Don't laugh at me!"

"No, never at you. Humour lightens life, Aban." El grins then returns to his work. "Yeast is a micro-organism. It is life, and it feeds on sugar and likes warmth, just as we like warmth and feed on it. You must give it what it needs for it to grow else it will remain as a cake, useless to anyone even to itself. You want the yeast to grow so that it will leaven the whole bread and will be in every morsel you eat. But beware: you must have good yeast. You can try and try, but you will not have perfectly leavened bread if you use bad yeast. And if you overfeed it, the bread will grow so much it will be yeasty in flavour and again be bad." El pauses and asks, "Are you listening?"

"Yeah," Aban replies.

El nods and continues, "Handling the yeast takes patience, knowledge, and experience to ensure it leavens the bread well. Bread-making takes practice. You cannot have a good loaf every time if you make bread only here and there. Sometimes you will use too much yeast; sometimes not enough; and sometimes if you wait too long before you bake the risen loaf, your yeast will become useless even with sugar and warmth."

"Okay," Aban says.

"Okay?"

Aban shrugs, her eyes sliding away from his.

"You measure out one-quarter cup of water, warm it till your finger feels the warmth but does not burn, and stir in the yeast. We will wait now while it grows until it puffs up into a milky, sweet mixture."

El leans against the counter, his hands loose by his side, contemplating Aban. Aban glances up then swiftly back down to her feet. She shifts from side to side; she looks up and around the kitchen, avoiding El; she slides toward the back door, and she looks out.

"Come over here, Aban and look at what the yeast has done." El's voice recalls her to their task. Grudgingly, she saunters over and leans forward to look inside the bowl. She shrugs and takes a couple of steps backward to lean against the fridge.

"We must make the loose part of the dough now, adding eggs and sugar and the first cup of flour." El adds in each ingredient to the yeast mixture as he speaks and mixes it by hand with a wooden spoon. Aban notices the wood of the spoon is smooth, like Dad's favourite maple spoon. The realization brings on a pang of homesickness. She shifts her position.

"The yeast doesn't care where the sugar comes from or the water. It cares only for the nourishment and warmth they bring. But we care. Good sugar and good water make a difference to the final flavour. They also make a difference to the earth and to the people who work it to bring us these products. Being able to dominate the earth is not permission to use it as we like but to use it with care, to nurture it, and to allow all of it, including ourselves, to grow into the beings we were meant to be. Home is not where we grew up but where we find the food and water we need and, like the yeast, where we flourish best."

"Is that why the sugar is that colour?"

"Tawny?"

"Yeah. Mom uses that same kind, but no one else does. The diner, theirs is white, really, really white. They said it's normal."

"No. This sugar and this flour are as they were meant to be. Come and see."

Aban leans forward as far as she can, but it's not far enough, and she must take a few steps forward to see into the bowl. A loose dough sits in there, its edges clinging to the sides, its smoothness appealing. "Oh." It smells attractively sweet.

"This is good," El says. "But it is only part of the beginning. Now the work gets harder. We will add the rest of the flour and the salt. We must not add too much flour, for then the dough will be hard, and if we add too little, it will be too soft to work with. We must take into account the humidity, for the more humidity there is in the air, the more flour we will need. We must also take into account the kind of flour that we have. I am using bread flour. It is made so that there is enough gluten in it to make a good dough, and the bread will rise. But though the flour is the largest ingredient in weight and volume, the salt is the more important one."

El pauses to see if he has her attention. Aban is still looking at the dough and watching his hands as he measures out the flour. He reaches for the pot of salt, but her eyes remain on the bowl.

"See this salt, Aban?"

She doesn't answer. He arrests his hand.

Aban takes a few minutes to notice. She looks up. "Um, yeah?"

"Did you see, Aban?"

"Um . . ." She sees his hand is empty and examines the counter.

Suddenly impatient, El barks, "Pay attention, Aban! See the salt? In the pot?"

"Yeah. I see it."

"Listen! Salt flavours the whole world."

"So?"

El vents his frustration out his mouth and nose, "Salt flavours the whole world, Aban, but only in the right amount. Too much will retard the yeast. The yeast will not grow. Too little, and the sugar will feed endlessly. The yeast will feast and feast, and the bread will become yeasty. You must measure out the salt precisely so that it will flavour the whole bread, retard the yeast just enough, and grow you good bread."

"Yeah, okay."

"Listen, Aban! A good baker does not over-salt the dough, for she does not want to retard the yeast. A lazy baker, a well-meaning baker, a mean baker, a baker that wants to tell the yeast how to rise and when, all these bakers will be either stingy or put too much salt in. The yeast will not grow properly, while too much salt will dominate the flavour of the bread, losing its value."

"Okay, okay."

"Do you understand, Aban?" he asks with urgency in his voice.

"Yeah. Too much, it's a hockey puck. Too little, it's a sponge."

El smiles in relief at her understanding the bread part at least. "Yes. You have it." He finishes mixing the bread. He flours the counter and puts the dough on top of the flour sheet. He kneads, adding in a bit of flour here and there as his hands rhythmically pull and push and fold the dough until it is smooth all over and doesn't stick to the counter. He oils a clean bowl, gathers up the dough, puts it in the bowl, turns it oiled side up, and covers the bowl with a tea cloth.

"We wait."

"How long?"

"Until it doubles in size."

"How long's that?"

"As long as it needs."

"How long's that?" Aban asks exasperatedly.

"Until it reaches to the top of the bowl."

Aban rolls her eyes, "Fine." She huffs to his table and slumps down in a chair. He makes a pot of tea and joins her, pouring out a cup for her. She takes a gingerly sip, "Ow. It's hot."

"Tea is meant to be hot. You should have waited for it to cool a little bit."

Aban glares at him. "In this heat, it should be iced tea."

"Did you know that in India where it is hot, they drink hot tea? It helps them sweat out the heat."

Aban continues to glare at him and blow on her tea vigorously, creating waves that almost slop out of her cup. El's mouth twitches upward. She squints at him suspiciously. He straightens his mouth hurriedly.

They sit for a while, the heat making Aban sluggish while the yeast eats happily in the dough and grows and grows, pushing the flour and egg and sugar and salt molecules apart, making the whole bigger.

El suddenly sits up. "Wake up, Aban, the dough has doubled."

Aban snorts awake, sits up, stretches, and looks over at him as he lifts the cloth, "How'd you know?" she mumbles.

"I told you. A baker who is patient, learns, and practices consistently and regularly is aware of his dough, even when it is ready for the next phase."

The cloth is off, and El waits for Aban to join him. Suddenly, El punches it down. Aban gasps. The dough releases gas and deflates sharply.

"Why'd you do that?" she exclaims. "Now it's all flat and stuff."

"It is necessary for the dough to be punched down so that it has a chance to rise again, making a more stable structure."

"Huh?"

"I did not kill the yeast, merely restructured its home."

"Oh."

"Do you still not perceive or understand? Is your heart so dead? Do you have eyes yet fail to see? Do you have ears yet fail to hear? Do you not remember anything I have told you, anything you have seen, even this morning?"

"Yeah, I remember. I'm paying attention, you know."

"Then why do you not yet understand?"

"I'm trying, you know."

"Are you? You said you did not want to learn. If you do not want to learn, how can you try?"

"I'm here, aren't I, watching this boring thing." Aban glowers at him. He stares steadily back at her. "We're talking about the same thing, right?" she finally asks.

"There is much going on under your nose, but you do not see, for you want it to happen as you watch, like a movie in fast forward. That is not bread. It is not life. It is not reality. As long as you do not live in the present, as long as you do not live in what is the truth, you will not see, perceive, or hear. Attention, Aban! Opportunities don't come when you are ready for them but when they are ready for you."

El returns to work. He beats up an egg in a small cup and sets it aside. He flours the counter, places the dough on top, and quickly and confidently cuts it with his knife into six pieces. Each piece he rapidly rolls into a length of rope. He braids the long, bigger ropes into a big braid. He braids the three, smaller ropes into another braid and places it on top, melding the two with the aid of some water and his hand. He covers the braid with the cloth.

"We must wait again while it rises. I will turn the oven on in an hour so that when the bread is ready, the oven will be too. Planning ahead is part of the baker's art. But wise planning only comes with experience, knowledge, and practice. With learning, Aban."

Aban says nothing, but wanders out of the room to sit outside on the deck and watch the grass not grow. There is no sign of the seeds El had planted. The birds had pecked every last one that had landed on the hard earth. She sinks into a funk until El calls her back in. Wearily, she pushes her hands against her thighs to stand up and almost falls over. She pauses. She pushes the damp curls off her forehead and rubs her eyes until they stop drooping half-closed. She shuffles into El's kitchen, letting the screen door bang behind her.

"Yeah," she says to announce she's inside.

"Come and see, Aban."

Aban goes to look.

"It's ready; it is exactly the right size," El tells her.

The bread is beautiful. The braids hold their shape yet have risen into one. El paints on the beaten egg with a beige bristle brush, and the braids shine like a beacon of good things to come. She can smell it already. Aban inhales deeply, and pleasure lights up her glistening face. He lifts the bread onto a sheet and pushes it onto the middle rack of the oven. He sets the timer.

"Note, Aban, that baking time must be precise. Five minutes here or there may not make much of a difference when the dough is rising, but in the oven, it will mean a bread that's either over-baked or under. As always, Aban, we are looking for the perfect bread, the best we can make it. Understand?"

"That's why you're here, you know. I can't do this. I don't know how. But you do. You know what you're doing, so why do I need to learn? I have you."

"I will not always be with you to bake bread. Then what will you do?"

Aban shrugs. She blinks her eyes rapidly and turns her back on him to hide her face. His hand touches her shoulder. "You will learn, Aban. Before I go, you will be ready." She lifts her shoulder and walks out.

But when the scent of bread wafts out of the kitchen, down the hallway, ascends the steps, and meanders into her living room, Aban cannot resist. It smells so heavenly. It's been a long time since fresh bread filled her with such a desire to eat. A memory surfaces of Grandma pulling out a just-baked loaf from Mom's oven. That's all she remembers, but she sits with the pleasant memory until the present reasserts itself as she hears the faint ping of a timer. She gets up quickly and races to the stairs. She forces herself to slow down and walk sedately down the steps. But the scent of the bread beckoning her is irresistible and unconsciously she speeds up as she motors down the hallway to El's kitchen.

"Is it ready?" She hurries over to look at it, its top shining in the sunlight coming in through the window, its shape and size beautiful.

"It is. But first we must wait for it to cool a little bit." El smiles to soften his words, and Aban goes to sit at the table, to wait patiently yet with her mouth watering in anticipation.

21

THE PRUNING

ABAN sits up, stretches her arms wide, yawns, and swings her legs to the floor. She's feeling good, still savouring the memory of the bread from the day before. She pads over to the window to see what position El is meditating in this morning. But he's not there. She furrows her eyebrows in puzzlement at the unexpectedly empty spot; she leans forward to take a harder look. No, still not there. Aban moves her head this way and that, hunting to the far-off sides of the yard, close to the house, and finally toward the back where the evergreens are. She spots a ladder leaning against a straggly tree she hadn't noticed before. She squints and finds El hidden in its shade, his arms disappearing into the shadows of the branches, pruning the tree with long-handled pruners.

"Wha—!" It's the heat of the summer. He can't prune at this time. The tree will die. It's already half-dead. Doesn't he know this? First the seeds, and now this. And he thinks he's so smart.

Memory of the sweet bread banished by her anger, Aban turns to her dresser and scrabbles around for a clean T-shirt and a fresh pair of camouflage army pants. "He should've pruned that tree in the spring," she snarls as she pulls on her blue T-shirt with the saying running down the middle, one word per line, "Body-Centered Listening Resolves Conflicts". The sticky air doesn't slow her down in her rush to the back deck in her bare feet.

"What are you doing?" Aban yells at El as she slams open the back door.

Clip. A large branch flops down, bouncing gently once before its parched leaves sigh into the ground.

"You can't prune now! Don't you know anything!"

Clip. Another branch falls.

Aban puts her hands on her hips and frowns. This must be another of his confusing things. And he's rude, not answering her.

Aban stomps down the steps to see better. El has started at the top where the new growth is. He's chopped almost all of the new growth there, what little there was in this drought. He's now pruning the previous year's growth where leaves are growing and not as limp or shrivelled as on the new growth. But he isn't being gentle; he's pruning hard, right back to where a branch has branched out from the trunk in some cases. The pile on the ground swells as thin branch, small branch, long branch, main branch get clipped and fall down onto it.

Aban shrugs. It's his tree. Suddenly, she realizes it's her tree. Her tree. Given to her by her grandmother. How could he prune her tree? What kind of tree is it anyway? Maybe it should come down. All of it. Aban strides across the hard ground toward his ladder, but stops far enough away so that the pruned branches won't hit her. El has climbed down a few rungs since she first saw him. She hopes he knows she's standing there. He's acting as if he doesn't. Yet that man has eyes in the back of his head and around corners too. And he always seems to know what she's thinking . . . or feeling . . . in a way Mom and Dad never did, her classmates didn't, or that girl in grade ten, or her teachers. And El seems to know who is where. All the time.

She's never seen him surprised or startled by a person creeping up on him. She shivers suddenly and steps back.

"Why are you afraid?"

She jumps. "I'm not."

"Why do you persist in denying the obvious? You shivered with fear."

"How did you see that? You didn't even know I was here."

"I always know where you are, Aban."

Aban shivers again in fear of him, in fear of what he knows about her, about how somehow, in ways she doesn't understand, he knows the real her, and she's afraid to tell him all that. And so she says instead, "You didn't answer my question. Why are you pruning this tree? You should've done it in the spring or before it budded late last winter. What kind of tree is it anyway?"

"An apple tree."

"Not like any apple tree I've seen," Aban mutters.

"This is an old, old apple tree and has been neglected many years. Your grandmother left it to its own devices, pruning only a little here and there in the spring. She claimed that it was well experienced in the ways of growth. It never disappointed her in the fruit it bore. But today I came out to scrutinize its growth and saw no signs of fruit. Its blossoms did not become fruit. It's all leaves. No good for anyone."

"Yeah, but you can't prune it now. It's too hot."

"When a tree bears no fruit, it is time to cut off every branch that is not fruitful. And those that show promise I must prune so that it will become more fruitful. No branch that is not close to the trunk can bear good fruit. If all the branches in between are lazy, then the furthest branch will be anemic. And so the whole must be cut off. Far away from the trunk, the main source of water and nutrients, the branches can do nothing but bear leaves. And those branches that are close to the trunk yet bear no fruit but are content to grow only leaves, which serve to create food for itself alone and not to share with others, also must be cut off. This tree must be pruned hard so that next year it will bear fruit."

El's words make Aban's head spin. "That's like, abuse."

"It is not abusive when it means growth in the future. To not prune is abusive, for that means the gardener is not paying attention and is not interested in her garden. Overgrowth that is unchecked and wild is as unwanted as those plants and trees that are hacked without thought or left to die from lack of water and food. With fewer branches and the remaining branches closer in, the trunk is not overtaxed and can send more nutrients to those that will bear good fruit. It may seem hard to you, but a good gardener knows it's necessary and will do it, despite any screams or grumbles or criticisms she may hear."

Aban mulls over his words for a while. This yakking on of fruit is . . . Her mind sidles to a halt. A thought enters unbidden: is he talking about the tree or something else? Or maybe somebody else? Like her. She steps back. She watches him warily. But he continues pruning as before. Clip, flop; clip, flop. Aban relaxes and looks around the garden, thinking of the seeds and wondering if they've grown in this drought. She doesn't see any growth. She snorts, "So if you're such a good gardener, why aren't the seeds growing? Why didn't you prune before, like in the spring, you know, when good gardeners do it?"

"You were not here."

"Huh?"

El doesn't reply but steps down from the bottom rung, takes one step to the left, raises his arms with his hands holding the pruner's handles firmly, and opens the handles wide so that the two blades fit around a fat branch he can reach from ground level. The branch is so fat that the blades do not have any space between them and the bark. El must push the blades forward, scratching lines into the wood, until they completely cover the width of the branch. He shuts them hard. Clop. The branch falls with a thud next to the pile of limp leaves and smaller branches. Aban looks down at this fat branch, cut off from its trunk, covered in leaves with not an apple on it. It looks forlorn, hurt, dead. She takes another step back.

"Why are you afraid?"

"I'm not."

El picks up the ladder and leans it against the fence. Sunlight filters between the newly opened spaces in the tree, casting light patterns on its trunk and on the ground, dappling El as he moves around it. But Aban is busy squishing her toes into the arid soil and watching the dry grains flow down around her digits. El returns to the piles of branches, the pruners in his right hand. He begins to chop the branches methodically and ruthlessly into a pile of tiny twigs and small branches for the compost and another one of big branches for the fire.

"Come, Aban, and help me," he calls to her.

She shakes her head. The whole thing has given her the creeps. She doesn't know why, and that creeps her out more.

El stops what he's doing, letting the pruners dangle from his hand, "Either make the tree good, and its fruit will be good, or let the tree weaken, and its fruit will be bad. This tree, like all trees, Aban, will be known by its fruit. Do not be squeamish about it. A tree cannot produce good fruit if the gardener is unwilling to prune. A tree cannot produce good fruit if it's unwilling to use all its nourishment wisely. A tree cannot produce good fruit if it's unwilling to share. Good fruit not only allows the tree to seed and multiply, but also to feed others. Good fruit is both for the tree and for others. How can you be so selfish? How can you say I do not want to prune? You want to take the easy way! You want to take the way of looking good to others so that they will like you. Yet even when no one is watching, you shy away. And always you listen to words meant to keep you down, to keep you from being who you were created to be. You coward!

"The tree is justified by its fruit; the gardener is known through her trees. If the gardener does not know when the tree needs rest, when the tree needs food and water, when it needs pruning, how to grow it so that it can live longer and longer without water, then the people will say the she is lazy, incompetent, unwise, unwilling, and full of dishonesty."

Aban's jaw hangs open. How can he speak to her like that? She feels bruised and confused. She has no words. For long minutes, she stands gawking at him as he glares at her, impatience and exasperation and frustration pouring out of his every pore. The thought niggles into her mind: is he right?

They continue to stand glaring and gawking at each other.

The thought grows in Aban's head: if he's right, who has she been listening to? Mom, comes the thought unbidden. But moms are always right, always want what's best for you. Well, maybe not moms who dominate, comes another unbidden thought. But her mom loves her. That's why she's done what she did. It was for her own good. Mom never spoke to her like El did. No, comes into her mind, no, your mom just bossed you around. Aban thrusts those thoughts away. Yeah, but El never got her pumped up and excited like that man in the dome did. That felt good. This doesn't feel good. What's wrong with feeling good? Well, what good is feeling good when that man and your mom didn't want you to think for yourself, only what they wanted you to think? comes the disturbing question.

Aban shakes herself. She doesn't like these thoughts. She moves so as to silence them. She leans down and using both hands, picks up some of the tiny branches, the ones with many limp and parched leaves on them and carries them over to the black compost bin in the opposite corner. The lid is on it, and she stands uncertain for a moment, not wanting to drop her handful of branches yet not knowing how to open the bin. Back home, they had an open pile for all their pruning and fall leaves. El is suddenly there, unlocking and lifting off the bin lid for her.

"We must keep the bin locked so that the raccoons and squirrels will not raid the compost for apple cores. They take a bite and drop them wherever they happen to be, seeding trees indiscriminately. Toronto is rife with these litterers, and it's best to lock the compost."

Wordlessly, Aban drops in her small handful and returns for another. El puts a hand on her upper arm and stops her. She halts but doesn't look at him. He awaits her. Finally she turns her head, sees his compassionate eyes, and drops her gaze.

"Who is better: the person who at first says no but then changes his mind and does it, no matter the cost? Or the person who says yes, of course, but never gets it done?"

Aban doesn't answer.

El holds out a pair of large, heavy-duty gardening gloves for her. She takes them, keeping her head down, and slips them on. With gloves on, she can pick up more of the detritus.

While she carries the twigs and leaves and small, pliable branches to the bin, El walks over to a big box at the end of the deck. It's made of old plywood and painted white. He unlocks the angled lid and lifts it to lean against the deck's rail. He returns to the pile and carries the branches meant for the fire over to the box. He tosses them in and returns for another armful. When all the wood is in it, he closes and relocks the lid. He disappears into the house and comes out again, a rake in his right hand. He walks over to where the leftover leaves and twigs cover the ground and rakes them up so that Aban can pick them up easier.

Aban continues to walk back and forth, from pile to bin back to pile, unseeing, unthinking. For the uncounted time, she returns to the pile, but the ground has been cleared of all that came from the tree. It takes her a moment to see it. She looks up at the tree, the sun in her eyes, and sees so much loss. She wipes her left cheek with the back of her gloved hand. El stands, leaning on the rake, both hands wrapped around its handle, one foot over the other, toes on the ground, attending to her.

"What do you see, Aban?"

"A dead tree."

"I see promise."

El pushes himself off from the rake onto both feet, hefts the rake into his right hand, brushes off a couple of stray leaves speared on its tines, and carries it into the house. He leaves Aban behind to follow him or not. Her choice.

22

THE RICH MAN

ABAN startles awake in blackness. The millipede had almost touched her. In. That. Dream. Her heart pounds; copious perspiration drenches her skin, her T-shirt, her sheets, the mattress. Aban folds up and hugs her knees, hiccupping a sob.

Bang.

Aban flings herself open. Her heart pounds harder, practically moving her ribs. She grabs her knees again and listens intently, eyes wide, trying to figure out what that was, but she's too scared to move off her bed to go look.

Bang.

Something hard whips at her window. Deep shadows dance across the glass, bending, bending, bending, then suddenly snapping back. The air smells electric. Her heart beats faster, her breaths come shallowly, her body quivers. Slowly she uncurls and reaches down tentatively to the floor with her toes.

Bang.

Her arms retract fast. Her chest pains from all her heart's thudding. She calls on what Mom had taught her about yogic breathing, focuses on the rhythmic movement of the shadows until her heart slows and the dream has unwrapped its last tentacles from around her mind. Sighing and with a last shudder, Aban lets go of her knees and sits up. Her eyes having adjusted to the blackness, she realizes that the shadows must be made by the trees swaying in a strong wind. The house does not move, not a thing rattles in it, only the shadows tell of the wind.

She stands up firmly this time and walks to the window.

Bang.

Aban jumps back. It's just a branch hitting the window, she scoffs at herself. She peers through the dust-covered glass, expecting, hoping to see rain. But there is no rain. No thunder or lightning either, just the wind.

Suddenly El strains into view. She recognizes him from his shape, for she cannot see details in this black night. All the lights outside are off. El is in her neighbour's yard, one arm around a man, his other hand supporting the man's arm as El helps the man up the stairs to her neighbour's back door. The man must be her neighbour. El and the man are leaning forward, legs scissored apart in sync, almost horizontal, yet they have stopped moving. The man looks drunk or stunned, the way his head is dropping in contrast to El's, which is aimed straight into the force.

Aban goes to turn on her light. But nothing happens. She flicks the switch on and off a couple of times before realizing that the power is off. Fear flutters her heart; she wants to be with El. She picks up yesterday's clothes from the floor and drags them on before racing downstairs and attempting to open the back door. But it refuses, and branches and garbage and loose bits flee past the door window and round and round into ascending verticals. She'd better put her shoes on. She runs back upstairs, taking the stairs two at a time, thrusts her feet into her shoes, hops to the top of her steps as she tries to tie the laces, finally has to stop to bend down and tie them up properly, and then leaps down the stairs, almost falling on her face at the bottom of the last flight. She steadies herself and runs to the back door. She stops. She takes a deep breath, depresses the handle, and with all her weight pulls it open.

The hot wind slams it to the wall and pushes against her. She leans into it, and the door slams against her side. She holds it away from her as best she can while forcing the screen door open and taking one slow step forward after another until she's free of both doors' trajectory. The back door smacks back into the doorway while the screen door remains flung open against the outside wall. Breathing heavily, Aban stands a moment, trying to get her bearings, deafened by the wind blowing past her ears, overwhelmed by the smell of burnt air and sewage and the leaves and small branches stinging her face. She squints her eyes. Her heart has sped up again, but now it's part of the maelstrom outside. How did El get into the neighbour's in this storm? She reaches her hands out, arms straight out, head down as the wind lashes her face. She bends an arm across her face to protect it. She can hardly see in this blackness and flying debris. She feels her way forward.

Crack.

The sound startles Aban into looking up. A pole, with snaking wires is smashing through the evergreens and down the length of the yard toward her, its top with its light still attached smacking into the earth only a metre from her. She freezes. What is she doing out in this? She wants to go back. She turns. But the wind fights her. Hard. She grits her teeth, and a branch slams into her back. Fright lends her strength. Not home; El. She runs in slow-motion round the deck toward the alley. Perhaps between the two brick houses and closer to El, she'll be safer. This wind can't pull out bricks and start hurling them. She hopes. But the wind screams between the two houses, scouring the concrete of its loose surface of dust and dirt, burning her bare arms and face, swirling her hair up, down, around, blinding her. A plastic cup comes skipping down the alley and hits her legs, changes direction, and skitters off. Aban leans against one of the brick walls, trying to hug its hotness, and, in one of the brief moments the wind releases her hair from in front of her eyes, realizes she's facing the gate into the neighbour's yard.

She strains her legs toward it, searches for the latch, and feeling it, lifts it up. The wind snatches the unlocked gate and thrusts it against the fence, letting it bounce once before slamming it again and holding it there. The wind shifts and pushes Aban through the gate, making her hair fly straight forward, stretching out her curls, giving her tunnel vision. Her feet skid forward, and she tries to grab purchase on the bricks, the fence boards, the gate posts. The wind flings her against the open gate and holds her there. Folds of tabloid and broadsheet newspapers join her, plastering the vertical boards she's mushed against. Aban turns her head to the side and eyes the gate with trepidation. Her eyes have adjusted to the darkness, and she can see better, as long as her hair stays off her face. She steadies her breath, remembering again Mom's yogic breathing. And that's when she notices El and the man are frozen in the same position in which she had first seen them in. The man is a dead weight; he's collapsed even more into himself. El still has one arm around his shoulder, his other hand holding up the man's arm closest to him. Flickering candlelight through the house's kitchen window casts their fronts into grinning Halloween shapes. The candlelight flares up, and she sees blood dripping from the man's forehead. El seems unhurt.

Taking a deep breath and twisting herself into position, Aban launches herself forward and is almost pushed into the earth. The newspapers join her, curling around her legs. When she tries to compensate, she's slammed back into the gate, and the newspapers shoot straight up and are flung over the fence, their folds rippling open and closed. How dare the wind change direction like that? She screams into the baking wind and hurls herself forward. Again, one leg loses ground, but her anger keeps her upright and moving forward. A plastic bag skips across the opposite fence, darts across the yard, and smacks into her neck, missing her mouth by centimetres. She yanks it off, breathing harder, the wind sucking the air out of her lungs, her heart leaping out of her chest. Yet this fearsome ferment is unable to stop her from going forward.

Aban wants Mom.

Aban's eyes water. She wants so badly to return to the house, that safe, solid house inside which she couldn't hear this evil thing howl. She wants home. She wants the familiarity of Mom telling her it's time to do those stupid breathing exercises, the ones she does during yoga and had made her do before every exam. Tears stream out her eyes and are whipped off her face. She turns to the side so that the wind cannot suck her breath out so easily and forces herself to inhale and exhale slowly, deeply until her heart slows down and no longer hits her ribs. Turning back, Aban takes the measure of the wind, and this time with deliberation, not anger or fright, drives forward, first one foot, then the other without stumbling.

Aban reaches El. She continues going, past him to the other side of the man, crawls her left hand across his shoulder, across El's arm, and at the same time grabs the man's right arm with her right hand, adding her weight to El's. Together, they advance, half dragging the man until the movement, slow as it is, recalls him to his consciousness, and he half stumbles. Aban and El pull him up the three steps to the back door without his help. El reaches forward and pulls the door open. He uses his body to keep it from slamming shut upon them, and they cross the threshold and fall onto the floor. The door crashes shut.

The quiet is creepy. They lie there, listening to it, the man's blood trickling onto the floor. El gets up first and lifts the man into his arms. He disappears down the hall, while Aban slowly sits up and leans against the wall. Something is hitting the door rhythmically. It reminds her of her dream. Tonight, she had heard drums drumming in time to the motion of the maggots. Drums had sped up the millipede's flight toward her. She hugs herself hard and starts to shake. El drapes a blanket around her shoulders. The air scorches, yet she is so cold.

"Come. He will be all right. You must return to the house while I seek out others injured in this storm."

Her teeth are chattering too hard for her to reply.

Somehow El has guided her back to her house safely. But before they enter the back door, he turns her around. She reaches an arm up to shield her eyes, afraid of what will hit her next. He points, and she follows his pointing finger toward the scraggly apple tree at the back. It's the only one standing strong, hardly swaying, none of its branches, not even a twig, being snapped off while all around, even the evergreens are losing bits and pieces of themselves. Satisfied that she has seen, El opens the back door and pushes her inside. She's glad she's back in Grandma's house, but she doesn't want to be alone in the dark. El places his arm over her shoulders and leads her into his living room, settles her on the sofa, snugs the blanket around her, lights one candle and then another and another until the entire room from front window to back, from wall to wall is alight with the gentle glow of the flames.

He leaves.

She doesn't know how long she's been sleeping when voices awaken her. The room is no longer filled with candlelight but sunlight, and the blanket El had put on her is crumpled at her feet. Sweat mats her curls to her forehead and wrinkles her dirty T-shirt. She brushes at her shirt absently as she tries to listen. The voices are coming from behind her, from El's dining room table. Quietly, she lifts herself up and peers over the back of the sofa. El and a man are sitting across from each other; El's back is to her. The man's suit is a lightweight blue, with a slight silky sheen; his shirt is crisp and pure white, the cuffs brought together with winking cufflinks; his tie is a subtle blend of blue on blue stripes with a sapphire tie pin nestled in the middle. Sapphire. Aban draws in her breath. A heavy gold ring decorates his pinky finger; a gold chain wraps his wrist. A watch on the other wrist reflects the sun in red, blue, green, yellow. Diamonds. She's never seen diamonds before. Her eyes widen. The man is facing her, yet he seems oblivious to her presence. He looks worried.

"I am wealthy beyond measure, yet something is missing. It was borne home to me during last night's storm when that wind took down our old oak tree in our front garden. It upset my wife seeing it fall and break apart like that, as if it was nothing. All my money couldn't stop it."

El nods.

Aban blurts out, "You should use your money for good. There are lots of good causes, you know, like the whales, and Greenpeace. And, like, people in Africa need water, and children are forced to work in India instead of getting to go to school. They need money, you know."

The man says without turning to her, "I give to many good causes here in Canada and in Africa. I support Warren Buffett's call to billionaires to spread their wealth."

"Oh."

Aban can't figure out why he's unhappy then. He has it all. He gives a lot, he says. That's what makes you happy, so they say. So what's wrong? El's back seems to be waiting for her; she doesn't know why. She sinks back down.

"What must I do?" the man continues, speaking to El.

"Have you stuck to the rules society has taught: do not murder, do not commit adultery, do not steal, do not lie, do not defraud, do not covet, honour your father and mother?"

"I have kept them all."

Aban pulls herself up again to watch.

El answers, "Have you?"

"I have worked within the bounds of business."

"And have those been within the bounds of those who came before you?"

The man whispers, "No."

"Are you keeping them now?"

"Yes. I'm trying. I am. Since I have pledged to follow Buffett's lead, I have strived to return to those ways even in my work life. But I am unhappy."

"Happiness is not the objective in life," El pauses. He continues softly, gently, "Woe to the rich. You are receiving your consolation now. Woe to the satiated. You are full now, but you will be hungry. Woe to those who laugh now. They are carefree and complacent now, but they will mourn and weep."

"I am weeping now."

"Yes." El waits a beat. "There is one thing you lack."

The man leans forward eagerly, "What is it? Tell me."

"Sell everything you have. Everything. Share your wealth with those in need; live on the generosity of others while giving of yourself; see at last that your needs are really wants; offer your time and energy and yourself to the hurting; lead by a different example; and you will have what you seek."

"I can't do that. How will I live? How will I pay for food? Food inflation is high, and I should know. I trade those commodities every day. How will I pay for my family's wants, our needs, I mean? The private education, the vacations down south, the cottage, the jewellery, the daily lattés at Starbucks. My wife will kill me if I nixed the last. And what difference would it make except take a small joy out of her life? How will I sustain our roof? And keep two cars? I won't be able to afford even one, and the kids will soon need their own cars. They have to get around on their own someday. My wife and I each need our own cars. We can't be expected to have just one between us with our busy lives. There's no TTC out to my daughter's barn or to my son's hockey games. Besides, public transit is dangerous and dirty and public schools provide inadequate education. I won't have my children be deprived. They deserve the best. That's why I make sure they get the latest iPhone or Blackberry, whatever is doing best these days. It helps them keep in touch with us and their friends. I couldn't do that if I sold everything. You can't live in this society without money. My family deserves the best. No. I can't do that. You're expecting too much." He shakes his head hard. He focuses hard on El, anticipation writ large on his face that El will change his answer, for people do with him when he puts forth a cogent argument. And this was cogent, he's sure.

But El disagrees.

El shakes his head slowly side to side, "I cannot help you. You've chosen lattés and cars as your own reward. Jobs instead of Job gives you comfort. As long as you cannot see, I cannot help you."

The man slowly stands up and leaves, arms drooping by his side. The door closes behind him.

Aban says to El's back, "He's right, you know. It's too expensive to live today. Like, he can't sell everything. That's stupid. He has to keep some of it for himself."

"How hard it is for the rich. How hard it is for you in the west to recognize your riches—and your poverty. How hard it is for those who rely solely on themselves and expect others to do the same, for when calamity befalls them, they cannot sustain the load they have told others to carry. Money distorts perspective. I tell you, no one who follows what I tell them will fail to receive a hundred times as much in return. Joy is its own reward. How hard it is for you to understand." El sighs, stands up tiredly, and makes his way to the kitchen, asking her over his shoulder, "What would you like for breakfast?"

23

THE TAXMAN

THE next day, Aban stops on the last stair, her T-shirt proclaiming "Be Present in the Now," her right hand on the newel post, not feeling the peeling painted surface of it. Instead Aban is staring at the mail on the worn wooden floor. Funny, she hadn't thought of this place as getting letters. El sees people in person, and bills aren't a part of his life, or so she had assumed. After all, she hasn't seen him handle money, other than the Metropass for the TTC. Yet here the mail is, lying on the floor, just like at home. She steps down onto the old floorboards and stoops to pick up the letters. As she straightens, she sees the mail slot in the door. She blinks at it. Was it always there? She finishes straightening up and riffles through the mail.

All of it is for her.

Who would write her? They all have her name typed on them, kind of like the ones her parents get. She wonders what she's supposed to do with these letters. She looks around for a place to toss them until she feels like opening them.

El pokes his head out his living room door, "What do you have there, Aban?"

"Mail."

"Just mail?"

"What do you mean?"

His head retreats. She stands there for a bit, then sighs. She huffs her way back upstairs and into her kitchen where she drops the mail on the tiny kitchen table as she swivels on her foot to retrace her steps. But the letters bore a hole into her back. Sighing, she returns to the table, sits down, and begins to slit them open roughly with her thumb.

One's a letter from Bell, on glossy paper, telling her about some new service. She has a phone. She must. Every house has a phone. It never rings. What else does she need? She tosses it to the side. She opens another one. This one's from Rogers selling her cable. What does she want that for? Mom didn't believe in TV, and Aban doesn't neither. She'd gotten used to not knowing what the other kids were talking about at school and not caring about it. And it doesn't matter now. She tosses that one toward the first one, not noticing how it almost slides off the Bell ad letter and skitters to the edge of the table. She scans the rest. Are they all going to be like that: stupid crap? She sighs and picks up another one. She opens it. Again from Bell. She's about to throw it toward the first one when she realizes it looks different. It has numbers on it. She reads it and gasps. So much money for a phone that never rings? She'd rather send that to Greenpeace. She goes to throw it toward the other discarded ones when the thought that maybe she should pay it halts her hand. But how? She stares at it for a while, thinking it might reveal the how. But it doesn't. She sets it carefully down to her left and picks up the next letter. It's from the City of Toronto, reminding her about Water and Solid Waste Management. She has to pay for water? Who pays for water? You turn on the tap, and water comes out. This is stupid. And what is solid . . . she squints at the top of the bill again . . . solid waste management? It must be a scam or something. But she sets it down on top of the Bell bill. She's not sure if she wants to pick up the next one; it kind of looks like the one she'd just opened. It too is from the City of Toronto, with lots of different folded pieces of paper in it. Some in languages she doesn't understand. Don't people speak English in this city? What is she supposed to do with all these? The bill falls out of the pile as she's flipping through them. She picks it up and sees that the city wants taxes, something about a final property tax bill. She flips the multi-folded bill around and around to figure out what it's about. The back is a busy page of numbers and dates. When she realizes the numbers are what she owes, she gasps. She can't pay that. She's never had that kind of money before. What has Grandma left her? How does she even pay that? She slaps the tax bill on top of the other bills and shoves the rest of the letters and inserts away from her.

Standing up, Aban goes to the fridge and reaches in for the new carton of orange juice. It reminds her of how after the storm yesterday, after she'd eaten breakfast, El had taken Aban for a walk around their neighbourhood helping to clear up the littered gardens and listening to people's stories as they tried to make sense of what had whirled through their lives. She'd kind of liked it at first; she'd gotten to meet her neighbours through El. But then he'd kept going and going, as if he'd never stop, and the stories were all the same. And her T-shirt and pants were drenched. She swore it got even hotter after that fierce storm. There was a limit. Of course, with money, you gave as much as you could afford, but as Mom said everyone's busy, everyone has their own worries, that's why you pay charities to take care of people. Enough was enough. Besides, didn't Mom always say your taxes are supposed to pay for stuff like, like after a big storm and things? And listening to the same stories over and over . . . God.

But El had ignored her hints that it was time to go home—he'd actually seemed interested in all their stories. Finally, he had finished, but instead of going home, he'd taken her to a grocery store. The air conditioning was a relief—she could get used to its coldness—but all she wanted to do was lie down while El was determined to lead her up and down the aisles, pointing out the kinds of things she should buy to feed herself and insisting that she did. Laden down with groceries in bags she had bought at the store—she liked how they were saving the environment—he had taken her to another kind of store to buy some dishes. They only had one pattern: plain white for the china, clear glass for the glasses. What a relief. She had no idea what she liked, and she was too tired to make decisions. But though she had grumbled all the way, she was secretly glad he had taken her there. Her one-dish set was annoying her.

She takes out the carton of orange juice, unscrews the cap, pulls off the plastic tab, throws the tab away, and pours the cold, mandarin-coloured juice into one of her new glasses, the cold of it condensing the water in the air on the sides of the glass. El had admonished her to wash all the glasses first, but she had been tired last night, and she can't be bothered this morning. The juice tastes funny. She makes a face and puts it down. She picks up the carton to look at the label again; it's the same one as Mom buys at home. They must sell weird stuff in Toronto and keep the good stuff for everyone else. Torontonians will eat anything; she saw that in the store yesterday.

The bills are staring at her again. She hunches her shoulders and tries to leave the kitchen. But it's like the bills have some sort of fishing line on her.

"Oh, all right," she grouses to herself. She sweeps them up and takes them downstairs. "What am I supposed to do with these?" she asks El as she tosses the letters angrily on his coffee table.

"What have I to do with bills?" El replies, not looking up from the sofa corner, where he's reading a thick book.

"Can't you help me?"

El doesn't reply.

Aban grabs the letters, crumpling them in her hot-sticky hands, and stomps out. Now what is she supposed to do? She returns to her kitchen, throws them onto the table, slams into her chair, puts her elbows on the table, leans her head on her hands, and glares at them. Tears form and drip down her face. Grandma couldn't have known how hard it would be, leaving her all this. Or maybe she did, that's why she left it to her. Mom had said Grandma liked to upset her. But Mom was wrong, wasn't she? Grandma must've known what would happen. How do people do this? Why didn't she leave her money? She has no cash left. That stupid letter; it's too bad it had found her. She shouldn't've have gone to that lawyer. It's all his fault, giving her the keys, showing her the video, making her want to see this house. And then that banker . . .

She sits up. The banker. That lady. She had said to call if she needed help. Yeah, that's right, she had said she'd help her figure it out. And she does have money. She remembers now—the lady had opened an account for her and put money in it. She wipes one cheek and then arrests her hand. How does she call her? She doesn't know her name or nothing.

The business card. She had given her a business card.

Where'd she put it? Maybe her wallet? She stretches her right leg out to reach in and pull out her wallet. She opens it and sees an unfamiliar glossy plastic card. She frowns and then her face clears as she remembers this card gets her money from that machine the lady showed her. But then confusion clouds her face again: how does she get it from that machine to these bills demanding money? The lady. She'll tell her. She yanks out the plastic card and out falls a business card. It flitters to the floor. She leans over and picks it up. Taking a deep breath, Aban reaches for the phone sitting on the far side of the table, dials, and hears a life-saving voice.

"Um, yeah, hi, this is, Aban."

"Oh yes. Hello, Aban. How are you doing? Are you settling in?"

"Yeah. Um, I have these bills and stuff."

"Of course. Why don't you come in, and I'll help you sort them out. Did you receive the cheques?"

"Cheques?"

"Yes. They'll have come in a fat envelope or small package."

Aban looks at the pile. "Um, just a sec." So many letters in that pile; she reaches a hand forward to flip the letters over one by one until she gets to a fat envelope. "Yes, there's one here."

"Why don't you open it. I'll wait."

Aban drops the phone on the table and wrenches open the envelope. Out slides a pile of cheques, with her name and address on them and everything. She hurriedly picks up the phone. "Yeah. They came."

"That's great. Bring those with you along with your bills. And we'll get it all done. Don't you worry, Aban. You'll be a whiz at this in no time. Now, let's see. Why don't we say next week, July twenty-second?"

"Uh, yeah, sure." Aban scrambles around for a pen.

"I'll call you the day before to confirm, just in case your schedule changes. I know how busy we all are."

"Yeah, sure. Great. Thanks."

"You're welcome. I look forward to seeing you next week, Aban."

Click. Aban slowly takes the phone from her ear and presses End.

"She's gonna help me," she informs El as she enters his living room later.

"That's what she's there for. Find the help you need from the right people, Aban, and you will do well." El returns to his reading.

Aban glares at him and is about to open her mouth when a knock on the door halts her words. "Are you getting that?" she demands of El.

"It's your house."

"Yeah, but they're always here for you."

El doesn't reply but continues reading.

Aban stomps out and down the hallway. She yanks the door open, and a young woman smiles at her, holding out a box with a slot on top and letters on the side: "The Feast of Madeleine."

"Hello. I'm here for the annual Madeleine donation drive," she says as if Aban will know what she's talking about.

"The what?"

"The Madeleine donation drive. It's to help provide Madeleines for the poor and needy."

"What the hell are Madeleines?"

"Madeleines are little cakes named in honour of Madeleine and to celebrate her inspiration."

"Her?"

"Oh. Uh. Madeleine was a woman who was cast out by her family, shunned by her friends, and afflicted by strange illnesses. Whoever came into contact with her was repelled, and they called her many names and accused her of being lazy, a hypocrite, a thief, and a liar. One day, she met a man who accepted her and in accepting her recalled to herself who she really was. He redeemed her. She turned her life around and became an inspiration to women everywhere. She gave comfort to the poor and needy; she taught the illiterate; she made powerful men uncomfortable until they changed and began to help the vulnerable; she empowered women and raised them to be on equal footing with their husbands through her own example and her teachings. Every city has a hospital dedicated to healing women's diseases because of her. A famous chef in the sixteenth century created these little cakes in her honour. At first, only the rich could afford them because they're hard to make, but they're so light and have this sweet orange flavour. One day, an upper class lady said we should not be the only ones to eat these cakes. She said Madeleine lived for those who couldn't afford luxuries like these. Let us make enough for everyone on Madeleine's day, and on that day we will all feast, rich and poor alike, on Madeleines and remember her. Since then every year we celebrate her memory and example by handing out these cakes to as many people as we can on the streets and at subway stations. Every city around the world celebrates on the same day."

"That's a waste of money."

The young woman rallies back, "Maybe, but it brings a tiny bit of joy to everyone, even the people who have it bad, and reminds us we are all human, together."

"I got no money, and anyway as I said, it's a waste. You should be collecting worthwhile stuff, things the homeless really need, like clothes and stuff. Not cakes."

Aban feels a presence looming up behind her. She turns sharply and sees El, the dark depth of his eyes inscrutable.

"I will donate," he says as he slots coins into the young woman's box. "Everyone needs a touch of sweetness in their life. And before you go, let me say a blessing to you for the joy you will spread next week. For even in the midst of suffering, we must feast and celebrate."

Aban spills contempt out her mouth and slams her feet on the stairs as she returns to her kitchen. She doesn't get El. Why waste money on something so stupid? Cakes. It's like that . . . that Queen in France who told the poor to eat cake. They killed her for that. Those people knew what they needed. Real food. Cakes don't fill their stomachs or help them with the things that really count. Why would El support something like that? Stupid.

24

THE VISIT

ABAN is in her kitchen, washing dishes, when she hears a rapping on the front door. The raps reverberate through the house. They sound threatening, not-to-be-thwarted. She stays where she is.

Thump, thump, thump. It sounds like the side of a closed fist on hard wood.

She doesn't move. In a moment, she hears the door open, then murmurs. The door closes on a squawk, and El is beside her.

"Your mother is here. I've left her on the porch. But you must go talk to her." His voice tells her he knows how hard this confrontation will be for her.

Aban freezes. Her hands drop into the warm, soapy water, making her sweat more than the air temperature has already. She sucks in air, thrusting out her ribs, and turns to tell El to say that she won't.

He's gone.

Slowly she removes her hands from the water. Shaking the suds off her hands, she rubs them on the front of her grey

T-shirt that announces "body-centered listening resolves conflicts," and walks carefully down the stairs.

Opening the front door, she faces Mom. Mom doesn't look happy. Her face is a mess of harsh lines, hard eyes, firm lips; her hair is pulled back, but a few strands have escaped and stick to her forehead. Aban swallows.

"Are you going to let me in?"

"Uh, yeah, okay," Aban steps back and lets Mom in.

Mom looks around the hall, wrinkling her nose. "Well, I must say, this is dingy. This is what you chose over your own home?"

Aban ignores her and turns to climb the stairs back up.

"Where are you going?"

Aban keeps climbing, one stair at a time, gripping the handrail, suddenly needing to put both feet on each stair before she can ascend to the next one, one foot at a time.

"Come back here. I have no shame in what I want to say to you."

Aban is at the top and turns to go down the hallway to her living room. Mom is forced to follow. Her footsteps are angry bangs on each step. Aban moves into the living room. Since there is only one chair, she goes to stand by her favourite window directly across from the front door. She stares out unseeingly. She can hear Mom looking in all the doors on her way to stand beside her. Aban senses Mom's displeasure. She knows it well. And suddenly, she realizes how freeing it has been to live without it. She thrusts the realization away, along with her emotions.

"This is a shabby house, Aban. But it doesn't surprise me. Your grandmother didn't take care of things. She was more interested in upsetting people. Look at how she raised your father."

"How did she raise Dad?" Aban asks, crossing her arms. Aban can see Mom in her peripheral vision, though she tries to shut the vision out.

Mom turns to face her directly and slides closer until her body's heat blasts Aban. Mom is taller than Aban, and she stretches her back vertical to emphasize it. "You know how she raised him. In a rundown house like this on a rundown street in a dangerous city, with no thought to his safety or comfort. He had to fight for everything he wanted. She didn't do anything for him."

"Was that so bad?"

Mom raises her chest and glares down her nose, "Of course it was. We cared about you. We gave you everything you needed. We made sure you were safe. Not like her. She would not respect me or our way of raising you. She didn't like it being pointed out how wrong she was with your Dad and with you." Mom jabs her opal-encrusted finger in Aban's face. Her eyes darken, their pupils shrinking into points. Aban doesn't flinch. Mom is nonplussed, and her hand slowly lowers. She regathers herself and says, "You know perfectly well we made the right decision for you. It cost your Dad, but he knew what was best."

"Yeah, it cost Dad. And me. But he had a choice. I didn't. Why'd he let you take us away from Grandma? He's so weak."

"Your father knew what was best. He knows what is best. He made the right decision. You are not."

"Yeah, the right decision. What's that? Obeying you? Doing what you want?"

"I know what's best for you. How can you know? You think coming to Toronto makes you a big shot now? Your grandmother used to flaunt her Toronto airs in our faces. I showed her."

"Yeah, you did," Aban turns her eyes right into Mom's. She looks into them blandly.

Mom blinks and rears back. But not for long. "Yes, I did show her. I did it for you. I did it to protect you, you ungrateful wretch. I did it to keep you safe and to let you enjoy your childhood years. She was talking to you about things no child should have to worry about. She was making you upset and then making you fight with me. Every time she came over, it was unpleasant. I wasn't having any more of it. And your father didn't like it either. He told you that. But you wouldn't listen even though you know it.

"I am your mother, I raised you, I know better than you. You've spent, what, how many days here? And you think you're an expert on Toronto. Well, let me tell you, I grew up in Toronto. I know what it's really like. You think you're safe here, you'll find a job here, you'll be able to raise a family here in peace and get a good education. You're wrong. You're not safe here. And who will hire you anyway? You have no useful skills. You're lucky you have parents who own a shop that can hire you." Mom breathes harder with each word. And Aban feels stronger with each word.

"Are you listening to me, Aban? Your father and I want the best for you. We were teaching you how to run the store. You have a lot to learn. You're always screwing up the computer and getting the prices wrong. But we're your parents. We're not going to fire you. But you think any employer is going to tolerate that? You're lucky you have us, to guide you and provide you with a roof, money, and a job. You'll get nowhere without us.

"Why are you doing this to me? To us?" Mom compresses her lips and leans in until her breath is Aban's breath. "You're doing this on purpose, aren't you? You're becoming like your grandmother, letting her turn you against me. I warned you about this, but you didn't listen to me, your own mother. I know what's best for you, and you're acting like I know nothing. How dare you? I'm telling you that she—that she—that she is trying to get back at me through you, and you're letting her. You're such a puppet. You'll believe anything you're told."

Mom pauses, struggling to breathe quieter and failing. She raises her voice, "You think you're in control here? Well, you're not. She's controlling you, just like she tried to with you and your father years ago. She's in control here. She's telling you you have to live with a tenant. Did you choose the tenant? No. She did. And she chose a man. She was trying to set you up, I bet. She knew what men are like." Mom rakes Aban up and down with her sharp eyes.

"Yeah, okay," Aban says exasperatedly, uncrossing her arms.

"Don't you mock me, Aban. I have kept an eye on your boyfriends."

"What boyfriends? Anytime I got near anyone, you scared me away. I never got near no boys."

"I knew what was best for you. I saw what they wanted. You were so naïve, you bought their let's-be-friends line, especially that girl. Well, I did not, not for a second. I could see what was in their tiny minds."

Aban has had enough. All the stuffed emotions, all the rage from years of not being heard, of not being allowed to be herself and to know her grandmother, burst forth: "You don't think I can handle my own life, do you? You never gave me a chance to handle it! You never let me have friends! How could you do that to me? I'm your daughter!"

Mom's eyes gleam, and suddenly Aban remembers herself as a child, yelling at Mom in exactly this way. And she remembers how those arguments always led to Mom having the last word and her feeling stupid until she learnt never to argue. It'd been so long she'd forgotten that she'd ever had defied Mom. Aban recrosses her arms and almost growls; she frowns hard, angry at herself—more than at Mom—for being drawn in.

Mom softens her voice, triumphant. "I gave you a chance, Aban. And you failed. Remember that time when you were sixteen, how your father caught you in time? Luckily I saw you in that car and sent your father over to rescue you. If I hadn't, I'm afraid to think what would have happened to you. You're so naïve."

Mom pauses to give Aban a chance to retort. And she wants to; she wants so badly to yell and scream and stamp her foot, to prove that she's not stupid, that nothing was happening. No, nothing was happening, not even a kiss. They were only talking. In his car. The boy had given her a lift home the one dark winter day Mom and Dad had had late deliveries to the store and told her she could walk home on her own. She'd been thrilled and scared to accept. But he'd been so easy to talk to, they'd soon been talking about her favourite biology teacher. But in Mom's eyes, cars are bad places for a boy and a girl to be alone, and after Dad embarrassed her, no boy drove her home again.

Deep grooves burrow into her forehead and along the sides of her mouth, but Aban keeps her lips together. Mom narrows her eyes but cannot wait any longer. "So, do you even know who this man is? I sure don't. He didn't look safe to me. He shut the door on my face. That was unconscionably rude. Rudeness will not get you anywhere and associating with a man like that will make you an outcast. What do you know of him anyway? He could be a rapist or a robber. Your grandmother always had a poor choice in friends. I saw who she invited to her house for drinks. She called them dinner parties, but she made hardly any food." Mom snorts in disgust, "And they'd all arrive thinking she was putting on some big gathering, something nice for them. But she was so lazy, so full of herself, she did the minimum for them. And her tenants. Who were they? I can tell you that they were worse than those silly friends of hers. I didn't have to meet them to know that, and having met that man now, I know I'm right.

"I told you what you were getting yourself in to, and you didn't listen to me. Look at this," Mom sweeps her am toward the chair. "You have one chair. One chair. You have hardly anything in your other rooms. What kind of life is this? I don't want to see you living like this. Do you like worrying me, upsetting me, making me wonder what is happening to you, and I can't do anything about it? You will listen to me now."

The tone is all so familiar, and all of a sudden, its very familiarity makes Aban feel unafraid. "Yeah, I hear you, Mom. I'm listening. Everyone's always telling me to listen. But, you know, you don't give what you ask. You didn't listen to Grandma. You didn't care what Dad thought. But he didn't stand up for himself either. Well, I am, Mom. I'm standing up for me. I've met the tenant. I've met Grandma's friends. They've told me lots of stories about her, about how she helped them, how she saved them, how they left those dinner parties feeling full and, and . . . and joyful because of her and El and what they had taught them."

"El? Who is El?"

"El is Grandma's tenant. He's the one who opened the door to you."

"He's brainwashing you. I can see that now. Letting you come here was a mistake. You've had your little rebellion. It's time to go." On those words, Mom grabs Aban's left wrist with her right hand. Aban tries to wrench her arm out, but Mom tightens her grip and yanks her around and forward. Aban stumbles and using her free hand tries to pry Mom's fingers off. But Mom is a painter and a gardener. She uses the computer for many hours of the day. Her fingers are strong and will not be pried off. Mom drags Aban across the wood floor, unheeding of Aban's bare feet squealing, her heels picking up splinters from the worn oak boards. When they get to the door, Aban stops trying to pry Mom's fingers off and grabs the door instead. But the door only swings toward her, almost knocking her in the head. Aban lets go, and Mom relentlessly continues down the corridor, Aban in tow. Aban stops resisting until they reach the banister. At once, she lets all the strength out of her legs and hooks her free arm around a post as she sags down. She reaches forward to the next one to hold it with her hand. It's awkward. It hurts. Mom, realizing they are no longer moving forward, stops and glares at her, her fingers digging further into Aban's wrist.

"You. Are. Coming. Home. I will not tolerate this. I will not allow it to continue. You understand, Aban?"

"Yeah, I get it. You hafta hold me, to control me. You didn't like Grandma cause you said she controlled you. But you're controlling me, aren't you, Mom? You're such a hypocrite doing to me what you complain Grandma did to you and Dad."

"It is not the same."

"Yeah, how?"

"She was upsetting you. She was going to bring you to Toronto and take you away from me."

"Yeah, well, she won."

"What?"

"Guess where I am, Mom. I'm in Toronto. Yeah, in Grandma's house. I wouldn't've come if you hadn't tried to make me lose my inheritance. You said, 'You are not part of this family anymore.' I only wanted to see the house, not move here permanently, you know. You're the one who made it permanent. You're the one, Mom."

"It was your choice."

"Oh yeah? What choice is it when you give me ultimatums and try to drag me back to your house? Well, guess what? I'm not going. And you can't make me."

Mom raises her eyebrows, her eyes widen, then she leans right into Aban's face, "Home. It's your home."

"No. This is my home. Where El is, is my home."

"You've, you've, you've . . . ," Mom's rage silences her. She rakes Aban up and down with angry eyes. "I can't believe . . . After I spent all those hours worrying and protecting you . . . How dare you? I knew this would happen when you came against our better judgement."

"No, Mom, it's not what you think. It's worse."

"What? Worse? What do you mean," Mom loosens her grip in confusion, but before Aban can react, Mom tightens it as what-she-thinks-is-realization dawns, "You're pregnant. With one of your grandmother's abhorrent friends. Unbelievable. I can't believe you allowed this to happen." Mom rages on, but after her mouth drops open in amazement, Aban zones out, staying focused only on keeping her free arm tightly wrapped around the post. "You stupid, stupid fool!" Those loud words bring Aban back into the present place in which she's trapped.

She snaps back, "I am not stupid! How can you say that to me? You know, you're the stupid one when you say that to me, your daughter. You don't know what happened. And you don't care. You only care about yourself, about your feelings. Well, Mom, it's over. You can't make me do your will no more. Your words don't mean anything when you get your way cause you're not going to."

Mom suddenly stops pulling on her. She eyes Aban warily.

"I'm not pregnant. I can't believe you'd think that. It's worse. Yeah, Mom," she says to the growing look of horror on Mom's face. "It's worse. I'm finding out about myself, about life, about what is important, about who and what I should listen to, and how listening to the wrong person, taking in the wrong lessons has made me not know myself, has turned me into a not-nice person, a person who cannot even take care of herself. I can't even take care of myself, Mom, because you never taught me!

"When I came here, I didn't know how to make my own breakfast. And I didn't know what I was missing. I'm twenty and don't know how to feed myself. I felt so stupid, but that's what you had taught me. How to feel stupid. You told me lies about Grandma so that you could get things your way. Instead of coming here to apologize, to make amends for separating me from her and her from me, you come screaming your own rationalizations, your own lies, and you want to be right so badly. You're stuck in your own hell. It's all about being right, isn't it, Mom? Yeah, well, look at what you're doing. You're dragging me out the door! It's called assault, Mom. If anyone did that to you, you'd beat them with a bat. But your words are like bats, and you're trying to beat me up with them. Well, I won't let you no more.

"Look who's stupid now? You just got mad and stayed mad, and you said I'm not your family. And you come here and don't take back those words cause you're still mad. You've made it worse than before. Yeah, it's my turn to judge. You want me back, you'll have to find the key to get me back. You gotta earn me back.

"El said that daughter and mother will be separated if one of us listens to his stories and the other don't. I thought that was wrong. But you know what? I get it now. If I choose Toronto and El, I lose you. But if I choose you, I lose El—and me. And I'll go right back to having to spend every moment shoving myself down just to avoid war with you. How's that good for me? It isn't. I want to be me, Mom. I want to mean something in this world. I don't choose you, Mom."

Mom looks at her contemptuously and opens her mouth. But Aban forestalls her by strengthening her voice. "Yeah, okay, I don't know how I'll influence the world or nothing. But hearing all those stories about Grandma . . . it made me realize I could, you know. Being stuck in that stupid store of yours means I'll never get a chance. I want that chance, Mom. You told me I could never learn. But I've only been here a couple of weeks and already I've learned so much. It's been so hard, but I want more now. I'm awake now, Mom, and you can't beat me back to sleep again. We're over."

Mom yanks her arm, but Aban holds fast to the pole. They remain in this position, Aban's shoulder feeling like it's about to leave her socket, her face grimacing from the pain. But she cannot let go. She won't. She fears what will happen to her if she does. If she lets go, she's lost. She can't be lost again. She can't. Desperation lends her strength, and suddenly her arm is hers again and Mom is staggering backward. Mom is falling backward. Mom smacks down on her tailbone. Pain lashes through her face, and she bends forward and keens. The sound rises and falls, tears wash down her face onto her bare chest, onto her cambric top, and flow under the fat beads of her necklace. She keens louder. Aban remains where she is. What physical assault could not budge, tears will not either. Mom stops, lifting her top up to wipe her face, at last understanding the truth. She's lost control. Aban grabs hold of the posts and then the banister to lift herself up. Aban stands up in one move, not knowing where she got that kind of strength from but grateful for it.

Mom turns and walks down the stairs, erect. Aban follows slowly and stops at the top of the stairs to watch. Mom grasps the knob of the front door and halts. She turns to look up at Aban.

"This life you so freely talk about, it's yours. That's all you'll have without us. You're never going to be happy now," she rasps.

"I don't know if I will be or not, but it'll be mine," Aban replies as she walks gradually down the stairs. "I hope you have a good life, Mom. I hope Dad does too, but I don't think so. His weakness has made him invisible, like I was. And you need to control everyone around you to be happy. You can't, you know. Control everyone. The harder you try, the more people will want to leave. Dad won't. But everyone else will. God, I'm glad to be free of you. Glad, Mom. Glad! And you know what, Mom? I've learnt how amazing it is to help someone. El showed me that. He kind of took it too far, helping people after that storm. He didn't know when to stop, especially listening to them. But, you know, until then, it was, it was . . . I'd never felt that before. I kept hearing your voice, about how we pay charities and taxes to take care of stuff like that. But El wasn't waiting for money or official people to do it. He went in himself. It was so weird and so . . . I know you would've hated it if you'd known how I was going into strangers' houses and yards to help clean up. You'd have told me to go raise funds or lobby the government to help, stuff like that. But you know what? Being there with El meant I got to meet my neighbours, I got to see the damage and hear what they really needed. I wasn't protected from reality. I felt . . . I felt . . . free."

Aban pauses at the bottom of the staircase and looks straight into her mother's eyes, her aching arms and hands loose at her side. "I'm glad you weren't here. Goodbye."

Her mother's hand drops from the knob. Aban strides forward, reaches around her mother, turns the knob, opens the door, and waits. Her mother is like a statue who has come to life but doesn't know how to move. Aban continues to wait, feeling no fear, no anger, and no resentment anymore. Her mother looks closer and sees anticipation—the anticipation of someone looking forward to a life without her. That moves her, but not to changing her mind, but to walking out the door.

Aban shuts the door and returns to her dish washing, relishing the power.

25

THE LAW

ABAN awakens, feeling bereft. The enormity of yesterday's fight with Mom hits her. She'll never see Mom and Dad again. She doesn't want to, yet . . . she can't never see them again. They're Mom and Dad. They've been in her life since she can remember. These almost three weeks are the longest she's been away from them, and then she had to fight with Mom. Yet . . . it felt so good standing up to Mom. Why couldn't Mom see? Why did Mom always have to have her own way and not let anyone be? Why can't Dad fight for her, his kid? Aren't Dads supposed to stand up for their little girls? Matthew did it for Anne in *Anne of Green Gables*, and he wasn't even her dad! It's not fair! It's all El's fault, she decides. If he hadn't gotten into her head, she'd still have a family. She'd still be the old, familiar Aban. Yet she likes doing things herself, not having Mom boss her around, disapproving of her all the time. But El bosses her, and he disapproves. Maybe he should go too.

She flings herself out of bed and dresses quickly. She storms down to confront El. Yeah, he has to go too. Her T-shirt reads "Meet people where they live." Well, he didn't do that, did he, meet her where she lives. He's always telling her how stupid she is and how she doesn't get it. She gets it. He took her away from where she lived. Time to go. She stood up to Mom—she can stand up to El too. She can stand on her own two feet. She doesn't need him.

"You have to go," she tells El as she enters his kitchen.

He looks up from where he's seated, eating his cereal of psyllium and chocolate rice puffs with oat and wheat brans, drowned in skim milk. "I see." He contemplates her furious face for a minute then says, "You can't evict me."

"Yeah. I can. I own this house, you know."

"Yes, you do. But you are also bound by the terms of your grandmother's will."

"We'll see about that." She turns on her heel and slams out of the house. She's so angry, she spurns the northbound bus she sees coming up the hill and slogs through the humid air to Greenwood subway station. She enters Greenwood station soaked and digs her hand into her wet pocket for her wallet. The wallet's empty. She doesn't have any tokens neither. How will she get to the lawyer's?

"Where do I get money for the fare," she asks the attendant behind the thick glass. He points to a round, mesh black thing above the open slot. She frowns. What's he mean? He jabs at it again, and finally she understands. She leans toward the round, black thing and yells into it her question. He replies, "Turn right out of the station and go to the Danforth. Turn right and go to Greenwood. There's a Scotiabank there."

"But that's not my bank."

He looks at her as if she's stupid, "Doesn't matter, lady. You can get money from any bank." He turns away from her. She stands there a minute, then slowly trails out into the haze of the day. She follows his directions and enters the cold bank. The temperature is a relief. She stands in front of the machines, not knowing what to do. She remembered that woman showing her how to use these things, but she doesn't remember what she did. She pulls her wallet out of her pocket and the card out of its slot. She stares at it, hoping it'll tell her what to do.

"Do you need some help?" A man in a uniform asks her.

"Um, I need money."

"All right, well you can use the ATMs or maybe you'll find it easier to go to one of the tellers inside," he says as he points through a set of doors.

"Uh, thanks," she replies and goes through the doors. She goes up to a woman behind the counter, who points to a metal tent sign on the counter that says, "Closed." Aban frowns. The bank is open. How can it also be closed? Besides, the man said to come in here. She opens her mouth to protest, when the woman says to her as she points to her left, along the counter, "The teller there will be happy to help you."

Aban follows her pointing finger and sees another woman, smiling at her. She goes over and tells her she needs some money.

"Do you bank here?"

"Uh, no."

"Do you have an Interac card?"

"A what?"

"Do you have a bank card?"

"Oh. Yeah! Here," she pushes the bank card across the counter. The woman takes it and says, "Why don't I help you with the ATM." She comes around the counter and walks past Aban. Aban follows her back through the doors to where the machines are. She watches as the woman slips the card into the ATM. "Now type in your PIN."

"My what?"

"Your PIN. You did get a PIN number with your card?"

Aban continues to look blank.

"It's a four-digit number."

"Oh. Yeah. I remember that. Four numbers is easy. I type it in here?"

"Yes."

Aban keys in the PIN and watches the ATM screen process then pop up a plethora of options.

The woman shows her how to choose withdrawal, which account, and how much.

"How much do you need?"

"I need it for the TTC."

"Are you getting tokens or a Metropass?"

"Oh, um, maybe tokens."

"Okay. Go ahead and key in two hundred dollars to be safe."

Aban gasps, "Two hundred?"

"Yes. It isn't much. That'll buy a roll of tokens plus some extra."

Aban obeys and soon has ten twenty-dollar bills in her hand. She stuffs them into her wallet. The woman reminds her to take the receipt and to put her card away. Aban follows her instructions and thanks her. They go their separate ways. Back at the subway station, Aban buys a roll of tokens, wrestles with the token wrap, almost spilling out several little bicoloured metal discs as the paper suddenly rips. She gathers them up and drops one into the fare box. She stuffs the rest and the roll into her capacious pocket that holds her wallet. By this time, she's starting to doubt if she can stand on her own two feet; maybe she shouldn't try to evict him. But then she did get the money, and she did buy tokens. All on her own. "So there, El!" she mouths.

The station platform is suffocating. She's relieved when the train pulls in, and she almost runs into the cold blowing air inside. She sits down, keeping her sticky back away from the seat until her shirt dries. Her muscles release slowly as the train clatters toward Bay station, where she gets off when she sees the familiar name. She climbs the dirty steps to the street and pauses as the blistering air assaults her. Just next to the station entrance, a man with matted hair and dirt-dusted clothes sits with his hand out in a perpetual attitude of begging. A woman in a thin camisole and faded jean skirt with worn-down sandals, carrying a basket, with a plastic bag swinging from her left wrist, stops in front of him. She lifts a small cake wrapped in a napkin out from the basket and hands it to him. His face lights up. His hand, all creased and grimy, holds the small package gingerly as he carefully unwraps the napkin. He lifts the cake to his lips and takes a delicate bite, evident pleasure writ all over his face. He eats the whole thing without touching it with his hands as the woman chats to him. When he's done, she takes the napkin and puts it into a plastic bag and moves on.

Cake. That's gotta be that cake thing that girl was talking about, Aban remembers. She wrinkles her lips. What that man needed was real food, real money that he could use. But, but . . . he looks happy. How can that be? Well maybe the cake is okay, but that woman should've given him money too. She expels disgusted air and walks past him to the bus stop.

Aban didn't know she had to get a transfer and has to pay another token for the Bay bus. It bounces and rattles down Bay street until they get to the tall, white building. This time she remembers where to go. She's been recalling that day all the way down.

At the high wood desk, the same coiffed woman with the headset sits. She remembers Aban and pages Mr. Myerstein for her while the air-conditioned air cools the moisture on Aban's skin. Soon he is out and ushering her into his office.

"How are you liking your new home, Aban?" he asks her as they sit down.

"Fine," she mumbles as she slides down into her chair. Now that she's here, she's not sure about her decision. She twists her hands. "I want El out," she blurts, looking at his desk.

"Ah. I see. I understood from your grandmother that he was a nice young man."

"He's not nice."

Mr. Myerstein leans forward, with concern. "Has he been unpleasant?"

"He bosses me around, telling me what to do, how I don't get it. I can stand on my own two feet, you know."

"Has he assaulted you?"

"Uh, no."

"Verbally abused you?"

"Well, no," she draws out.

"Taken advantage of you?"

Aban squirms. She's probably taken advantage of him more, all that food he's cooked for her, being available to her whenever she wants to talk. And then she suddenly realizes what Mr. Myerstein means. Blood floods her face. "No!"

"Then I can't see any valid reason to evict him, Aban. Your grandmother's will was firm. You are by rights allowed to contest the will and its contents if you so choose. But I must warn you that the process is long and by the time it comes to court, the year of his tenancy will have passed. Remember, you can ask him to leave at the end of a year, less than a year now."

"Yeah. But isn't there anything you can do? Like, she's dead."

"Yes, she is. But a will is not a document you can toss aside willy nilly, else there would be more chaos than there already is. You're lucky, Aban. There is no one who can legally contest it other than your father. But he doesn't seem interested. And the contents are not that onerous. Now if you'd told me that El was being abusive, that would be another thing, that would be a criminal matter. We could evict him under those circumstances. But since you say he isn't . . . ," Mr. Myerstein pauses.

"No," Aban concedes. "He isn't. Just difficult."

"Ah. Well, I'm afraid there's nothing we can do. Is everything else okay?"

"Yeah," she replies, but she makes no move to go. She wants to share her grief and anger over what happened with Mom.

But this guy is a lawyer and somewhere in the back of her mind, she wonders if this is going to cost her.

"I won't charge you for this visit. Your grandmother told me in no uncertain terms that I was to help you in any way I can without charge, for she has given me much business during her lifetime and to remember that. Her wishes weren't put into writing, but your grandmother was a formidable woman, even in death," Mr. Myerstein smiles at her. "I'm sorry I cannot help you with your tenant."

Aban looks up at him and nods. She straightens up in her seat. "Well, thanks. Yeah, okay, I guess that's all I wanted." She suddenly stands up. "Thank you, Mr. Myerstein."

Back outside on the sidewalk, the heat hits her like a wall, and her cooled skin is soon shining again. She wanders up Bay to Queen and then along Queen to the Eaton Centre, her hands jammed into her pockets but her head up, although she does not attend to what's in front of her. She passes homeless man after homeless woman, some draped in layers of rags, their hair matted, their faces greasy, as she thinks about that woman who gave that man a cake and the pleasure that came over his face. A group of three teens bumps into her, recalling her to her surroundings. They are all carrying large brown bags, and there's another group on the other sidewalk. They stop at each homeless person, handing out cakes and talking with them. Aban comes to a standstill as she watches their reactions. Both teens and homeless seem to be happier for these encounters. They even laugh. This is not like those fundraising drives she's done collecting funds for the poor, who didn't live in her town anyway, for everyone knows there's no homeless people in small town Ontario. When collecting money for them she never got this close before, never talked to them before. Aban can't drag her eyes away from them.

Abruptly, she shifts her vision and strides off. An unfamiliar and uncomfortable feeling has risen in her. It makes her unsure and her chest feel tight. She doesn't like it. Always, her life had been laid before her, but now so many questions, so much doubt, so many new feelings. She escapes into the comfortable air of the Eaton Centre.

Aban pushes the revolving door, moving from sticky to sweet cool air, and halts. Her eyes widen. So many shops, so many people, she's never seen so much, so much—stuff. "Ooph," Aban blows out as a young man slams into her back and keeps going. She moves forward again, gazing into the displays of each shop she walks by them, gawking at more when she gets on escalators going down then back up again. For hours, she wanders, amazed at the choice of clothing, of food, of jewellery, of, of stuff. But she likes the clothes best. The colours and styles fascinate her, so different from what she wears. The lingerie shops make her blush, but she leans forward to see the displays better. They look so pretty. She's never had anything pretty.

Suddenly, Aban wants what this mall is offering. As she stands outside one store, she looks down at her T-shirt and her multi-pocketed khaki pants that slouch onto her greyed sneakers. Then looks at the clean, white sandals in the window near her, and the pretty white shirt draped over grey-and-black checked short pants in the next. Mom would be pissed if she knew what is going through her mind right now. Aban frowns. Mom believed in natural fabrics and functional clothing. She didn't like Aban's choice of pants and T-shirts, preferring that she wear loose, flowing dresses like hers. But at least her choice in clothing was not frivolous, Mom had always said, and so she had been prepared to accept Aban's style of dressing, she'd told Aban. These clothes are frivolous. These are not natural, not sold to support a worthy cause, not even good for function, they look so insubstantial.

Aban wants.

Aban's lips stretch wide. Her eyes gleam with sudden defiance. Mom would hate her. She already does; what's to lose? Her head thrown back, Aban marches through the open doorway into her first fashion clothing store.

26

THE QUESTION

ABAN struggles with the front door and her shopping bags. She had not only bought new blouses and shirts, new pants and jeans, but also shoes, shampoo for curly hair, scented soaps, candles, and an iPhone, although she isn't sure what she's going to do with the latter. But the Apple store had looked so full of happy people, she'd wanted a piece of that.

Finally in, she butt-closes the door and hauls her booty up the stairs, bumping and banging the bags against the wall and stair rail. At the top, she pauses for breath, starts up again but pauses at the guest room door. She's had enough of carrying all these bags. It's been a long trip home with them on the TTC, packed with other shoppers and sleeping workers, kids with skateboards, and couples with ginormous strollers, and men slouching all over the seats with their legs wide open and their status gym bags taking up the seats next to them.

Aban dumps the bags inside the guest room door, rubs her hands down the front of her pants, and goes into the kitchen for a large glass of water, not waiting for the water to run cold first. She gulps down the water, some of it dripping out the sides of the glass down her face, down her chin, onto her

T-shirt. With a satisfied sigh, Aban puts the glass down on the counter and smiles at how excited the store clerks were when they realized she wanted to buy and buy lots. They had her trying on pants after blouse after skirt. That was weird, putting on a skirt. She didn't think she looked good in them; she'd never noticed her legs before. They were so white. And skinny. But the clerks had exclaimed over how good she looked and all she needed to do was to get a wax job. She wasn't sure what a wax job was, but she didn't let on to them. And then they showed her how she could pay with her ATM card. She'd felt so liberated when she'd done that.

She walks back down the hall to the guest room and pokes her head in. The bags are still there. Mom would be so mad. El would not approve. Aban grins as she returns to the kitchen, this time letting the water run cold before refilling her glass.

She drinks her second glass of water slowly. She puts the empty glass into the sink, wipes her chin and T-shirt, and wanders out the kitchen door, down the hall, and into the living room to her favourite window. Watching the cars go in two directions, she revels in how good she feels. All that shopping, all that spending with her card. She had no idea it could do multiple things. It was not at all like spending money. She'd always paid with cash Mom gave her when she shopped for groceries or a T-shirt when Mom let her. But today had been all about her.

Aban wonders how much she spent.

Worry infiltrates the corners of her mind. Did she spend too much? It was so easy. That card made it so easy.

But it sure felt good. She beams. It was the closest she'd come to feeling happy in—. She frowns. She doesn't remember feeling happy. Ever. Well, yeah, helping El after the storm made her feel good—for a while—but not as good as today. Today, she feels . . . high! Helping El felt good deep down, but shopping makes her feel giddy. Even after she'd stopped from exhaustion, even as she walked through the tunnel from the

Eaton Centre to the subway station, she had wanted more. She had wanted to turn around and buy more, nothing specific, just more.

Abruptly, fatigue slumps her shoulders. She notices that her feet ache and her back hurts. She looks for a couch to crash on, like at home, but all she has is a chair. She glowers at it sitting there by itself in this vast space. By itself. Laughter breaks from her. Aban quickly stifles it with her hand as tears prick her eyes. She blinks rapidly. Control used to come so easily to her. But ever since she'd met El, she's been feeling emotions, thinking thoughts, doing things she's never done before, that she remembers anyway.

How much money did she spend?

Aban has no idea. She'd stuffed all the receipts into her left pocket without checking them, too much in a rush to go on to the next store to put them properly into her wallet as Mom had taught her.

Guilt tightens her chest.

Why shouldn't she shop? Grandma'd left her a lot of money. It's hers. She can do what she wants with it. It's hers. Aban stamps her foot, then the other, and keeps stamping them over to the chair where she flops down. She'll be seeing that bank person in a couple of days. That lady will tell her how much she's spent. They—she and the lawyer—both wanted her to take money out to spend. So why is it so wrong? It made her feel good! But what about now, a voice whispers, how do you feel now, only an hour after it's over? She turns down the edges of her mouth and throws her head back. Her neck doesn't like that, and Aban sits up. Too much thinking. Thinking, thinking, thinking. She hates it. She wants to do something else. She wants to feel that high again. But the thought of getting back on the TTC quails her.

A sweet scent floats by her nostrils. She sniffs the air. Cake?

Aban follows the scent down to El's kitchen.

"Hi," she says as she stops in the doorway.

El puts down an indented hot sheet on top of the stove, takes off the oven gloves, turns around, and grins at her. "Hello, Aban. How are you?"

"Fine."

"I have been baking Madeleines for the neighbourhood. Your grandmother enjoyed this tradition of baking Madeleines for her friends. She was an excellent baker and used to bake one sheet after another. Then she would pack up boxes of a dozen, and people would come in to pick up the boxes and go door to door to hand them out, including to people they passed along the way. She used to print up cards, which told of Madeleine's story, of why we carry on her work, and of how we all need a moment to experience the joy and pleasure of her inspiration. This last batch is for you."

Aban says nothing.

"Come on, Aban, we will share them together. They are best eaten fresh. I've brewed a pot of Darjeeling tea," he nods toward the table. Aban sees a smooth, ivory-coloured teapot made of unglazed porcelain with two matching teacups waiting at their places. There is no sugar pot or milk jug. El believes in drinking tea black, enjoying its pure taste, unadulterated by any other flavour. Aban slides into her seat while El removes the Madeleines from their shell-shaped hollows in the baking sheet and piles them onto a plate.

He brings the plate over and sits down across from her. He holds out the plate for her to take a cake, and after hesitating, she reaches for the top one. She bites into it. Its subtle orange flavour explodes into her mouth; its airy texture graces her tongue and disappears under the force of her teeth; its smallness disappears in a quick two bites.

"Some things are meant to be experienced slowly, enjoying the flavour and texture for as long as possible. For too soon, it is over. When eaten in a rush, the memory becomes distant in a heartbeat. But when eaten with care, the memory lingers even unto the next day and next."

Aban stops in the middle of taking another cake and studies him. He continues to talk, but she hears not a word. A revelation has taken hold of her mind. Aban knows in this moment that every word of El's is not an accident, that every word he chooses deliberately, and that his words have many meanings like those old books her English teachers had them read in school.

An aching creeps into her forehead. Aban rubs it, and the movement frees her other hand to take hold of another Madeleine. She decides to follow El literally and bites into the edge of the cake. She chews slowly, letting the cake touch every surface of her mouth. At last she swallows and takes another tiny bite. Many minutes pass by this time before she finishes the cake. He is right. Not only does the flavour linger longer, but so does the memory beyond the last bite. Still, she wants another one.

Aban looks at her cup of tea and wonders if it will taste better if drunk in the same way. She sips a small sip. She doesn't grimace from the bitterness, because there is no bitterness and no scalding. This is not like Mom's tea. She puts the cup down, sits back, and lifts her eyes to El, who is watching her.

"Why'd you bake the cakes for me, El?"

"I have come for your life, Aban."

"Huh?" This is more inscrutable than usual. She changes the subject, "I went shopping."

"I know. I heard you struggling up the stairs with your bags. Did you have fun?"

"Yeah. I did," she retorts.

"And now? Are you still having fun?"

"What do you mean? Eating cakes?"

"No, with your shopping."

"Oh, well, I dumped the bags in the guest room."

El eyes her T-shirt. "That is not new."

"No. I didn't feel like changing," she pulls the sweat-stained shirt from her chest. "Thank you for the cakes," she pauses, "and the tea."

"No problem, Aban. While I am here, we celebrate."

"Yeah, uh, what are you going to do with the rest of them?" Aban asks, eyeballing the cakes hungrily.

"That's up to you. You decide what to do with them."

Suddenly Aban doesn't feel so hungry. "Oh." She has no answer.

"When you have found your life, Aban, you will know what to do. Take, eat, and remember me and your day, all of your day, the things you saw, the things you bought, the things you heard, and most of all the things you felt. Do not be afraid, Aban."

Aban doesn't move. "It is okay, Aban. They are yours. My gift to you to remind you not only of Madeleine but also of what you and I have done these past few weeks."

"Yeah, what've we done?" Aban sits up straight abruptly. "I've lost Mom and Dad cause of what we've done."

"I cannot cover false relationships with a blanket of peace. I am here to reveal the divisions between the way of a life with purpose and the way people live. I am not here to help you get along with your mother and father. Though you must show them respect, when they prevent you from following your life, they cannot remain in your life. Only when you have the courage to leave false relationships, only then can you live, truly live."

"You make my head hurt! All I know is that cause of you, cause of Grandma, I'm a, I'm a, I'm an orphan!"

"You are not an orphan when you have me. And not only do you have me, you will soon also have a new family. Your grandmother discovered that after your parents banned her from their—and your—lives. She found succour in her friends' healing; she found comfort in serving others; she found joy in this way of life. To have a relationship based on fear and control and judgement that denies your light, that buries the flavour of your talents, that says you cannot, is no relationship. That is a falseness you do not deserve. No one deserves that.

"Who are you really angry at, Aban? Who do you want to be?"

Aban slouches in her chair, scowling at her upturned hands, and admits to herself that it isn't El who's angered her, but Mom and Dad, for not letting her be her, for being so afraid, for liking control over her better than herself, and at herself for letting them push her down. El may be confusing, but he's given her freedom and made her feel . . . special. Not just special, says a little voice in her head, loved. Loved. Aban chokes.

She stands up, slamming her chair backward with her legs, and reaches to the centre of the table to pick up the plate. As El begins to clear up the table, she scurries up to her living room to sit in that lonely chair, and to eat the cakes, one after the other after the other.

27

THE CLASH

SHOUTING rouses her out of her cake-induced stupor. She listens as she keeps her eyes shut, her head on the kitchen table inside the circle of her crossed arms, where she'd collapsed after putting the cake plate in the sink. She feels grungy and sticky. The voices are coming from the backyard, and she is aware enough now to realize only one is shouting.

She pushes herself up with her arms and her head sways as she contemplates the open window. She'd long since stopped closing it during the day. It doesn't seem to make a difference; night and day the air is close. She staggers up and leans over the table to look out the window. El and some strange man are yelling at each other. No, El's body is loose, calm; it's the man who's yelling and throwing his arms around violently. He's spitting his words out, the spit masking the vowels and consonants, and Aban can't understand him. She turns and makes her step-by-step descent down to El's back door to watch through the safety of its window. The man swings a fist at El's jaw as she arrives at the window. El ducks easily and the man staggers forward as El catches him with his right arm. Aban cracks open the back door and pokes her head around it, almost touching the closed screen door.

"You sonofabitch," the man yells as he pushes himself off of El to stand back up. "You and your stupid cakes. All those women you lead and their stupid cakes. We don't want your help. You hear me—we don't need it!" And he thrusts both hands toward El's chest. But El steps back, and again the man staggers forward, hands and arms flailing toward the ground.

At that moment, Aban recognizes the man. He's the one she and El had helped into his house during the storm. What's his problem? He wanted to stay out in that storm? He didn't want to be helped? Weird.

Does she like being helped? Does she like admitting she's in trouble, to El or to herself?

Aban shakes the thoughts away.

"Stop moving, you mangiacake. Fight like a man!" The man steadies himself on his feet and glares at El, easing one foot to the left, crossing his right carefully over it and shifting his weight to the left, as he again moves his left foot slowly to the side. Like an angry, separated waltz, the two circle, El relaxed and upright, the man crouched down, his arms ready with his hands clamped in fists. Their profiles come into Aban's view. She can't believe how calm El looks, and how ugly the man is. Why'd they help him anyway? And how come he's in their backyard? The thoughts of did she want help creep in again. She dents the screen with her head and deliberately focuses on the men as they dance silently over the fuzzy-green yard. As they dance down the yard she notices two of the boards in the fence that separates their yard from the one next door, the one where they'd rescued the man in that storm, have come loose. One is askew and attached in only one corner; the other is lying on the ground. When'd that happen? A grunt moves Aban's attention back to the men.

Red patches appear on the man's face; the red spreads across his cheeks and down his five-o'clock-shadow neck; his tanned muscular arms turn fiery from his anger. Nastiness covers his face. He halts his movements, looks over at the fence. El follows his gaze. Cunning enters the man's face, and he walks over to the fence to pick up the board on the ground. He grips it with both hands and advances on El, who has turned to face him. El looks unafraid and—Aban realizes—also sad and full of pity for the man who is so angry.

El has looked at her that way too.

The man's harsh voice interrupts her contemplation, "You think you're so smart, eh? Well, let's see who's smart now," the man growls at El as he swings the board at El's head. El ducks and stands back up.

"You got lucky. You're not going to evade me this time." The man swings again. Again, El ducks.

"I am not evading you. I am here," says El.

The man says nothing but swings violently for El's middle. And keeps on swinging past El, the weight of the board staggering him almost to the ground. Aban doesn't believe her eyes. She must've blinked cause she didn't see El move. One minute he's in the path of the board, the next he's off to the side. The man regains his feet, shakes his head, and searches around for El, looking as bewildered as Aban feels.

He spots El, "How'd . . . ?" Confusion quickly gives way to his rage. His mouth closes tight, his eyes sink into his cheeks, his lips compress into his teeth, and his whole face thrusts forward. "You think you're so smart, eh? You think you know everything? You think the whole world loves you and should bow down to you? Well, no way man. And I'm gonna teach you that. You can't get away from me forever. You and your fancy pancy ways. You're not going to get away with this."

"I have gotten away with nothing. I gave you my help in the storm, and your wife thanked me. I offered you cakes, as I offered them to everyone, and you took them but did not share them with your wife. Yet now you say you don't want my help.

You have free will, you have the right to say 'no". Why then are you so angry?"

"I have a right to be angry. How dare you stand there judging me, you freak? You started it. You stir things up, making people do bad things to each other. My wife is leaving me because of you! You're not going to get away with this!" And he lunges forward and brings down the board right over El's head. But El is not there. He is in a different place, his back to Aban, and the man and the board hit the ground hard. El looks down at the fallen. Neither move. The man lies stunned upon the board.

"How can you blame me for something you've brought onto yourself? You have free will to do what you please, as does your wife. You blame me for her leaving you. But have you looked at yourself? You have looked at everyone else but yourself. First, you blame your wife: you are angry because of her; you lost your job because of her; you drink because of her. You say she nags you all the time. Yet have you listened to yourself, how you talk to her? It is easier for you to say these things than to look at yourself and see the rage within. You blame me for your wife leaving you, but it is you who drove her away. It was me who showed her the light within herself, the light you were snuffing out because you had long since snuffed out your own. You wanted her to stay in the darkness with you. But she, like you, has free will. She wants to be in the light, not in the dark. You blame me. But you chose the dark. And yet I helped you when you needed me. What was it about that gesture that so offended you, made you so afraid? You do not want to need others? You want to live in the illusion of one man is sufficient unto himself? Do so, but do not expect your wife to hold on to that myth.

"By my actions, I showed you a different way, and you scorned it. You say my way brings judgement and separation and violence, but it is you who is judging and bringing violence. It is you who drove your wife to separate from you. It is easier to blame others, to say it's your victim's fault or the fault of the one who shows you a different path, than to change your mind and take responsibility for your thoughts, words, and actions. You are angry because I am showing you the consequences of your own will. It is you who chose violence and separation. You who are afraid because you are comfortable with your rightness. It is you who chose not to see the truth. You are angry because I am showing you how futile rage and fear and violence are. They cannot prevail."

The man pushes himself up to his knees, his hands remaining on the ground, his head dropping between his arms, breathing hard. He pushes himself up to a kneeling position, then up to standing, swaying slightly. He turns his face toward Aban, and Aban gasps. Such hatred. If looks could kill. Suddenly, she understands that phrase and steps back quickly, away from the screen door, hoping he cannot see her. But he doesn't; he is too intent on El. How can El not hate back in return?

Why didn't El give up on you?

Why, she wonders. She has no answer.

El remains loose, yet to Aban, it's as if steel has invaded his back. His back proclaims, "You cannot prevail against me." She shivers. A strange phrase she often heard from her classmates in school comes into her mind, "Resistance is futile." She believes. She believes El's back. She believes that El can bend her will if he wants to, he can turn her life into anything he wants to, he can prevail not only against violence but also her own desires. Yet he doesn't force his will on her like Mom does—did. He isn't using violence against this man. He isn't even picking up a board to protect himself. He's remaining open; he isn't giving hate for hate or anger for anger. He's doing something else. She doesn't understand. How can he be so, so . . . ?

She hadn't seen that steel aimed at her ever. Or had she?

Even if she had, El had kept talking to her, like he's doing with this weirdo. Yeah, he gets mad. But he's never stopped trying, not with her. Everything that has happened to her these last few weeks is cause he never gave up on her, never told her he was going to turn his back on her and wash his hands of her, cause he waited until she finally saw and heard what he'd said, what Mom'd said. And she'd woken up. She herself had changed her own mind. Yeah, El prevailed, but not against her, but for her.

El is for her.

The thought paralyzes her, and she no longer sees the scene in front of her while she turns this thought over and over in her mind. Whereas Mom shut her down, and that speaker at the SkyDome, whoever he was, hypnotized them, El opened up her mind to show her herself to herself and to show her another way of being. She hasn't followed really—does she want to?—but El hasn't given up, he hasn't yelled at her or beat her up cause she won't agree with him. He just keeps on talking.

Resistance is futile.

A shout refocuses her eyes on the scene in the yard. The man is advancing upon El, his upraised arms ending in fists so tight his knuckles strain the skin, his eyes menacing El. El stretches his steel-like spine up and thrusts back his shoulders into a powerful stance.

The man hesitates.

The man tosses his head toward El in an "I'll-be-back-later" gesture.

The man steps to the side of El, drops his hands once past El, and strolls off, his gait showing the effort of not running. El watches him disappear into the alley between the houses, his eyes still full of pity and sadness.

The confrontation over, Aban's attention wanders away from El to the yard itself. It is covered in soft, peach-fuzz green. She frowns. The green is bright, like that of new growth, not of moss or too-damp soil.

Aban flings open the screen door. She doesn't notice El turning to watch her as she walks across the small deck and looks down at the ground. Where the soil is packed and the birds had pecked, there is no green. Where the men had clashed, there is no green. Where the creeping charlie and clover hog the ground, there is no new green, only the dark hard green of the weeds. But everywhere else, soft, bright, fresh green covers the soil, even in the darkest shadows, even under the pine trees.

This cannot be.

Her eyes are deceiving her.

"Your eyes do not deceive, Aban. Though you did not believe, the earth did, I did, and even the dew and humidity did as they served to water the seed."

Aban raises her wide-open eyes to his, "But that's impossible."

El smiles, his brown eyes crinkle, his mouth twitches up, his whole face transforms from pity and sadness to pleasure and joy. "Yet there it is."

28

THE QUESTION II

ONE day Aban goes for a walk. She pauses on the sidewalk outside Atasgah and checks out the scenery. This isn't like her woods, the ones she walked in back home while Mom and Dad did their yoga. In her woods, trees hid human life from her; they filtered the sunlight and brought a hush around her ears. On the ground, pine cones and leaves, acorns and lichen, drew her attention, while birds secreted in their nests peeped at her from above. Occasionally, a flash of stripes heralded a passing chipmunk, and in the winter, tracks told her of the animals that had passed by. But here, there are no trees.

As she surveys her surroundings, Aban is forced to admit that there is one across the street and up a little bit, its fat trunk bifurcating into two, ending in a weedy top of dead leaves. But looking south, only one giant is visible from above the rooftops, many houses down. All around her is greyed sidewalk, greyed road with faded paint lines, hard brick walls, some walls painted green and some a natural yellow, small squares of brown grass with edgings of hard green weeds, and the odd struggling bush. She sighs. Why did she come here?

El's questions echo in her head: Who are you angry with? Who do you want to be?

She fists her hands and pushes them into her pockets. She sets off, her feet trudging along the concrete in their dust-smeared sneakers, her head down, watching her feet going one, two, one, two toward the railway bridge. She passes unseeing the two-story blocks of buildings with their neon signs and billboard hats on her left. She doesn't notice the Canadian flag drooping from a long pole attached to a house opposite, its red and white still jaunty through the layer of pollution that's settled on it. She doesn't observe the trees opposite that separate the industrial side of Greenwood from a new residential area. Aban wants to watch her feet; she doesn't want to be here; she doesn't want to think about those questions.

The road dips down to pass underneath the bridge. Then on the other side of the tracks, it rises again. Aban stops. This road is too familiar. She turns around and looks back south. She turns around and looks east. She doesn't remember how El got them to that ravine, where all those trees and shrubs were. But somehow she knows it was east. She turns around again and looks north. They went thataway first. But she doesn't want to go thataway. She doesn't want to go where El took her.

Aban resolutely turns south and heads down Greenwood as far as it will take her, to Queen Street. Tracks splits this street in half along its length. A streetcar rumbles and clacks past as she crosses the intersection to head east and then crosses to its south side to get out of the haze-filtered sun burning her dark curls. Though her hands are sticky from sweat, she keeps them shoved down deep into her deep pockets.

She trudges on, eyes watching feet, one, two, one two, hypnotizing her mind into silence.

At Woodbine the landscape changes and catches her attention. She looks south and sees a wide road filled with cars and houses on either side, some painted brightly, some looking older, edging the sidewalk all the way down. She looks east and sees an energetic street, filled with people hustling and cars creeping slowly. Stores bump up against each other while an old-fashioned fire house with its squat square clock tower remains distant from the smaller structures. The wide nose of a streetcar faces her. The traffic light changes, and the cars cross the tracks on their southbound journey, their tires, one after the other, sounding a snappy rhythm. She turns right and follows their direction, her head up, her eyes scanning this time.

She likes the houses on her right. They look fresh and happy. The road curves right, and she's trekking west, but across from her are trees and, and—a beach? Aban had never heard that Toronto had a beach.

But how to get to it? The road is wide, and the cars fast.

She looks around and finally spots a set of traffic lights ahead. Aban quickens her pace and gets to the lights in no time. She waits, the air's hotness making it easy to stand still. Other people wait with her, some on her side of the road, others across the way. The light changes, and they all cross, walking languidly through the stifling heat. It's the cars' turn to wait. As Aban reaches the sidewalk, a waft of air sifts through her hair, imperceptibly cooling her scalp. She glimpses the water.

Aban hurries into the trees, out of the trees, across the echoing slats of a boardwalk, and onto the sand. She lifts her right hand to shade her eyes. The sun glints off the sand pockmarked with many footsteps, creating an oven of sand and air. She takes off her sneakers, not thinking about the heat radiating off the sand in the sun. Here near the boardwalk where she is standing, the sand is partly in the shade. She digs her toes in and feels the grains oozing between them.

Aban takes a step forward and the sand unbalances her. She hasn't seen many beaches—only the one at the local lake—and this one is big. Off in the distance to her right, rises a strip of land covered in trees. Volleyball nets decorate a stretch of beach between the trees of the rise and the trees near the road. Every net has men and women in the skimpiest of bikinis and trunks, fabrics of all colours, their eyes adorned with shades, batting a volley ball from person to person. The thumps of their hands on the balls fill the air.

A scream makes her jump. Children race across the sand in front of her; one screams again as he tries to follow the kites treading the air high overhead, being pulled by even-faster teens. The kites look like they're about to dive down to the ground. A jogger pounds past behind her on the boardwalk, and she half-turns to see who would be so stupid to run in this heat. The echoes of the woman's running shoes hitting wooden boards have barely receded when a stroller trundles past. A golden fluffy dog pads along, his tail swishing slowly, leading his owners forward. Two skateboarders whiz past. On the paved track, cyclists zip, their wheels whining as they spin the air.

Aban returns her attention to the beach and takes a step forward and another, her feet sinking into the sand. She learns quickly how to push her feet back to thrust herself forward. She steps into the sun, and the sand strikes her feet like a molten metal plate.

"Ow!" Aban yelps. She retreats back into the shade.

But the grey-green-blue water on the other side of the sand expanse entices with its sparkling waves. People are splashing and swimming and screaming joyously in it. Its promised coolness draws her back into the sun. She grits her teeth as she hop-dances across the sand to where it is wet near the edge of Lake Ontario. She pokes one foot into the wavelets along the beach's edge. She sighs with deep pleasure and places her other foot into the water.

The lake's waves roll over her ankles rhythmically. Near her, seagulls and ducks bob along pecking at floating lumps of bread. Children run through the small surf, screeching happily while adults stroll, pant legs rolled up. Some older children are swimming, their heads barely above the water. Some look like they're paddling, not sure how to swim but wanting to be right in the cold of Lake Ontario. Aban looks around for their parents and sees adults watching from under umbrellas up on the beach. Aban looks in the other direction for the trees and for the first time espies the pile of boulders in the water below the land rise. But no one is swimming near them but the ducks.

Aban wades in further. And then tossing her sneakers onto the sand behind her, drops down into the waves.

The difference in temperature shocks her. Gasping, she almost stands back up. But the coolness is so soothing. She paddles forward and lets the waves flip her over onto her back. Closing her eyes against the sharp sun, she floats. The water laps in her ears. It is like her woods, except water hushes the sounds of human life from her.

The questions crowd back.

Aban splashes up. The screams and barks and thumps of hands on volley balls return to her consciousness, and for a moment, the uncomfortable questions recede.

Her clothes clinging to her, water streaming from her hair, Aban returns to the beach, picks up her sneakers and resumes walking east, watching her feet kicking at the water, one, two, one two.

But the biggest question of all won't be deterred: who does she want to be?

Aban stops. And sighs. She doesn't know.

Maybe the question is: who doesn't she want to be?

She doesn't want to be that girl who never smiled, never contradicted Mom, never disobeyed the rules, did what was expected, didn't know how to look after herself, and had shut out her own feelings and thoughts. She doesn't want to be that girl who never asks questions, who was so incurious as to stand outside of life. She doesn't want to be that helpless stereotype. Aban had felt so stupid at first, not knowing all this stuff, El making her breakfast, having to take her mail to the bank lady to explain them to her. But the lady had been so nice, explaining over and over how to pay her bills and to keep track of her money. She'd said that she had a friend who could teach her about computers and things. She'd left feeling—.

And then El had shown her how to bake bread. He'd taken the time to show her—to show her, stupid Aban—.

He had faith that she could learn, that she could do something for herself, not like Mom who'd said—.

Aban veers out of the water, onto the hot sand. She likes the crushed rocks burning her soles; she likes feeling the sun wicking all the wet out of her clothes. The burning obscures her feelings. But they won't be overcome. She's really angry at herself for not telling Mom and Dad she hated working in a store. She regrets not studying hard at high school even though she'd liked it, well most classes, because Mom had said she wasn't a natural student. She had believed her. How could she believe her?

Because she never stopped telling you and making sure you believed.

Aban's chest aches at the thought; she swallows hard. How could she do that to her, her own daughter? She had believed Mom too when she'd told her the girl who'd kept trying to invite her home to study with her was just trying to draw her into drugs and fooling around, and you know where that leads, Mom had said. She had to be careful with teens. They weren't raised right, Mom had said. Their parents didn't love her like she did, Aban. But what is love? Mom's kind of love, never letting her do anything on her own, telling her how, when, where, making her feel stupid? Or El's? Aban shakes her head hard and hiccups down a sob.

Mom had told her that about parents not loving their kids like she loved Aban when she'd first driven Aban to the local high school to start grade nine. She'd been scared yet excited. It was the first time she wouldn't spend every hour with Mom. Mom warned her about everything on the way there, especially the other kids. And just to make sure she stayed safe, Mom had picked her up for lunch and then again after school. The noise and all those people around her and the strange things they talked about scared her. And after a few months when Mom saw Aban kept her head down and didn't "fraternize"—Mom's word—she let her come home on the school bus. The others left her alone on the bus too. But then this girl sat beside her in grade ten homeroom. The girl had been so nice that her fear had melted, and then her new friend had introduced her to some kids at the cafeteria. At first, she'd been happy to be part of the group even though she was too afraid to speak, just sat and listened. Then they'd invited her to that party, a going-back-to-school party they'd called it. She'd snuck out to it but had hated it, and she'd been afraid for weeks that Mom would find out. And then though the school had a no-cell-phone policy some began sneaking them out of their pockets more and more. All the kids had one, but Mom had said she didn't need one and wouldn't let her even look at hers. She soon agreed with Mom; the strange little black things sucked the others into their little screens, got them giggling, and the clicks and chirps coming from underneath the table made her afraid. What would happen if they got caught? What would happen to her? Why'd they need them anyway? As Mom always said, pencil and paper is all you need to do school. She'd handwrite her essays, and Mom would type them up on her computer and correct them after she went to bed. She'd give her the printouts in the morning. And if she got detention for not keeping her head down during tests, Mom would get mad at her.

Her classmates laughed at her. Aban sat alone, and she told herself she didn't want to sit with them. And then when she'd finally told Mom how her new friend had invited Aban over to her house after school, Mom had changed the rules. Dad would bring her to the shop for lunch, and Mom would pick her up from school at the end of the day, or have Dad do it. She hadn't objected. That girl had wanted to be her friend; Aban had liked her. Yeah, she'd liked her. She'd wanted a friend, a real friend, but she hadn't objected when Mom had interfered.

She hits her wet leg hard.

All these years she's been disengaged from life so that she didn't have to think or argue with Mom so as to be who she really was. It had seemed so much easier to go with what everyone else wanted. They didn't seem to want her to be her, so she wasn't. They were happy, and Aban was okay.

But she wasn't okay.

It really wasn't easier.

It was scary.

El had seen that.

A kite thuds into the sand at her feet.

"Sorry," a teen pants at her as he races up to grab it and takes off again, children following, laughing. They look so happy, so free. She doesn't remember ever feeling like that. But she'd been so sure that doing what Mom wanted was best, that she'd never thought of anything else. She'd never admitted to herself that it was fear. She was afraid. Afraid of Mom, afraid of being alone, afraid of what would happen if she tried to be herself. So she hadn't thought, had she? Yeah, she'd rebelled a bit by raising money for causes her mom wasn't into, but what kind of rebellion was that? She'd never gotten involved in a real way. Only handed out pamphlets at the store or to her classmates and asked for donations, which she'd dutifully mailed off every month. If Mom really hadn't approved, she'd never have continued.

The thought constricts her throat.

Aban had never felt happy.

Or laughed.

It had all been so empty.

And lonely.

But today, she is awake. Today, she doesn't fear living apart from Mom. No, she isn't afraid. El is always asking her what she's afraid of, but she's not afraid. Not anymore. Not that way anyway. Aban chews over that thought and after several minutes, nods. No, she is not afraid of Mom anymore. But does that answer El's question?

Living apart from Dad makes her sad though, but she doesn't miss him cause though there in person, he was hardly present. It was like he'd checked out from his own life years ago. She'd been like Dad, all shadow and Mom's slave, she realizes with a start. She'd been like Dad, too afraid to find out who she was in case it meant a big fight with Mom, in case it meant loneliness and not being part of the family anymore. Stupid. She'd been lonely when living with them. And, well, now she isn't part of her family no more. Mom had told her that. And who is she to call her a liar? Yeah, she's done it. She's stood up to Mom, said no to her, said "I want to be me," and is no longer part of the family. And Aban is still alive and not feeling any worse. What was she afraid of? Why's she afraid now? They're just questions, what El asked. How can they hurt her more than Mom?

Aban walks into the surf and stares out toward the deep blue horizon of the formidable lake. Mom and her friends had always said that Lake Ontario was polluted. But there's no garbage here. The sand and colourful pebbles of the lake floor are visible through the shallow surf. She bends to pick a red pebble up. The rock's coolness is a relief against her sticky fingers. But the fevered air evaporates the water and colour quickly. She lets fall the pebble, and it plops into the water where it rejoins its mates and regains it brilliant colour.

No, no garbage here. She sniffs. No, not even a trace of rotting fish smell. Mom was wrong. Mom's friends were wrong. So who is right?

Suddenly El's questions don't threaten her. She doesn't know the answers, but she feels like she can look, she can learn.

Aban pushes her legs against the surf, further into the coldness of the lake, lifts her arms high, a sneaker dangling from each hand, and screams. The air is suddenly silent around her. She closes her mouth and grins. That felt good. Mom didn't tolerate screaming. She picks up her feet and runs through the water, parallel to the beach edge. She leans down and splashes her sneakers back and forth. She leaps up and dances through the water, laughing at it splashing up onto her beige T-shirt that proclaims in black letters, "Weight loss is a spiritual affair."

29

THE FEAST

A BAN runs lightly up the porch steps and slams the front door of Atasgah open.

"I'm home," she yells and laughs. Aban slams the door shut, but it clicks back open. Unfazed, she turns to push it closed and notices its peeling cover of yellowy beige. Her front door needs paint. Aban contemplates her door. A Canadian blue sky colour, she decides, with the depth of the lake blues and the brightness of the hot sun. Liking her decision, she skips upstairs and into a cold shower.

Feeling refreshed, with a towel round her, she rummages through the shopping bags in the guest room next door. She hadn't touched the bags or the clothes in them since she had dropped them on the floor that day, that day that seems so far ago. Thirty minutes later, she's wearing a cambric short-sleeved shirt and loose linen capris with white sandals on her feet. Her feet feel naked. The sandals feel flimsy, strange. She takes a few tentative steps in them.

The smell of burning charcoal and grilling oil, vegetables, and garlic seep in through her open kitchen window and down the hall, to tickle her nose. Sniffing the air, she forgets all about

her strange new sandals. Alive to the smells in the air of a
barbecue in full use, she canters down the stairs to El's half of
the house and out the back door,

"I am making a feast in your honour, Aban," El says as he
flips over the last grilling eggplant slice on the tray of a round
barbecue in which sits crumbling grey charcoals glowing red.
He hooks the spatula onto the side of the barbecue.

"My honour?"

"Yes. You have grown much. You have learnt much. It is time
to celebrate before the work begins," El replies.

"Work?"

El disappears into the kitchen and reappears shortly, carrying
a tray of halved red peppers, wedges of red onions and vidalia
ones, thick slices of fat juicy tomatoes, green asparagus
glistening with oil, and globes of prepared artichokes still
steaming from their boiling water bath.

El removes a bulb-shaped foil package with his
cooking-hardened fingers onto the tray, unhooks a pair of
tongs, shifts the eggplant slices over with them, and hooks them
back up on the side of the barbecue. He places the onions on
the tray first, followed by the peppers and asparagus, then the
tomatoes. He disappears into the kitchen with the empty tray
and comes out again with a bowl of grape tomatoes, a bottle of
olive oil, and a cut lemon on the tray. He splashes some oil in
the bowl along with squeezes of lemon juice. And then he rests.

El and Aban gaze upon the roasting vegetables with pleasure
as they talk about the weather.

Aban looks up at the mustard-coloured haze that lies over
the city, bakes their lungs, prickles their skin, and sticks their
clothes to their bodies. Standing here with El, watching him
cook, feeling secure that she's with him, that haze doesn't seem
so oppressive anymore. And she is surprised to learn, her new
shirt and linen capris are much cooler than her regular garb.

"How did you find asparagus? It's kind of late for them.
Mom—" Aban stops herself and smiles at El. He smiles back.

El says, "For you, I went to the specialty shops that sell the hard-to-find and out-of-season vegetables."

"That seems like a waste."

"When it is time to feast, no expense, no effort will be spared. It is a time for celebrating, not for judging. I have also bought fresh Ontario buffalo mozzarella, parmesan from Italy, creamy Devon cheddar, fresh figs, seedless green grapes, and manuka honey gelato for dessert to serve with delicate almond cookies and airy chocolate mousse. I have also splurged on an ice wine to finish off the meal and coffee made from special beans found in Eritrea. Maple sugar will also be on the table." El grins wickedly at her. "You may find my feast for you more than you expect."

"Um, yeah," Aban replies, not knowing how to feel about someone treating her so extravagantly or what he means.

"You are worth the effort, Aban. For you have understood. You have made hard choices. Though you wondered if it was right and became angry with me, still you decided to leave your old home in order to discover life here. And you stuck to it.

"But this is only the beginning for you, Aban."

"What d'you mean?"

"You have only just begun. But without the first days, there is no life. And so we feast in your honour for waking up and for not remaining on autopilot. The time for work is later."

He goes back into the kitchen with the olive oil and squeezed-out lemon halves and the bowl of grape tomatoes and returns with a large platter. He deftly turns the vegetables with the tongs so that they become charred on every side. He removes them, either with the tongs or spatula, when their colour has brightened but before they turn grey. Once all the vegetables are grilled, he carries them inside. Aban follows. He places the platter down on the counter with the tongs on top of the vegetables. And vegetable by vegetable, he chops them up into bite-sized pieces. The artichokes though he leaves whole and stacks them onto a white porcelain plate.

The kitchen is hot. Very hot. Hotter than outside or the rest of the house.

El opens the oven and takes out a large, yellow Emile casserole dish. He places it on top of the stove, closes the oven door, turns it off, and lifts the lid. Fragrant steam rises into the air.

"What is it?"

"Come. See. I have cooked basmati rice with saffron, cardamons, mace, peppercorns, a cinnamon stick, a few cloves, and a bay leaf. I have mixed in with it quinoa so you have the goodness of the latter with the heady flavours of the former. I will add sultanas and raw cashews that I have dry fried at the end," he says as he gestures toward a frying pan on top of the stove.

El draws an enormous porcelain bowl closer to the stove. Yellow and blue flowers dance along its sides in an abstract fashion. Suddenly, Aban notices what El is wearing, a light yellow and blue checked shirt and white linen pants. His feet are bare. She wants to hug him. She looks back at the bowl hurriedly and cranes her neck forward to see better. Inside the bowl glistens dressing.

"What is it?"

"Olive oil, lemon juice, some turmeric, oregano, parsley, and thyme. I debated adding lavender," he replies as he peels the foil wrapped package open to reveal a roasted beheaded garlic bulb. He squeezes the softened cloves out of their skins into the bowl and mixes the mush into the dressing. He slides the vegetables from their cutting board into the bowl, fluffs the rice and quinoa, and spoons them in. He folds the whole lot together. Letting it sit, he cleans off the cutting board and takes the cheeses out of the fridge. He cubes one of the cheeses, its edges crumbling onto the board, and puts the cubes on top of the salad. He dumps the contents of the frying pan over the rice and vegetables. Again he folds the mixture. He picks up the brimming bowl, redolent with its bounty of colours and scents, and carries it into the dining room. Aban follows him like a hopeful dog trotting on its mistress's heels.

In the cooler dining room, Aban stops, surprised. A glass vase shaped like an opening flower holds enormous blossoms of tulips and roses, gladioli and daisies, sprigs of fern and large lemon leaves. The table is draped in white and holds at one end a stack of plates, glasses, a large pitcher of sparkling pink-coloured punch, and forks wrapped in white napkins. El places the bowl at the other end. In between the plates and bowl, sits a wooden board. He picks this up and goes into the kitchen. Aban cannot move, she is so overwhelmed. El returns with the cheeses on the board nestled next to figs and grapes and a stack of small flat breads. After placing the wooden board back where it had been, he returns to the kitchen and comes out again with the plate of artichokes, surrounded by the dressed grape tomatoes, and a bowl of shiny yellow sauce. Aban draws in its fragrance as he walks past. It smells lemony.

"Hollandaise," El explains. "You peel off the artichoke leaves one by one, and dip them into the sauce. You'll like it." El beams at her tenderly.

At that moment, Aban hears the front door open, a person calls out "we're here," and soon the room is filled with chatting and laughter. The table's bounty increases as people place their own offerings on it, one of whole nuts and olives from their relatives' Greek groves, another of a bowl of coconut curry that speaks of a different kind of heat, another with plates and bowls filled with unfamiliar kinds of breads, others of chocolate truffles and sweet sugar cookies that they take into the kitchen ready to bring out when the main part of the meal is done. They tell Aban the stories of the food they have brought and urge her to try it all. Someone thrusts a plate laden with the rice salad, a wedge of cheddar cheese in its lime-green rind, a fig splayed open with a dollop of creamy thick something and a thread of honey on top, and a small sprig of grapes. She hears the walnuts and almonds being cracked open, and as she's talking to one of the people she'd met at El's dinner party, someone else places a few nuts on her plate and at the same time notices that she didn't get a poori or any of the curry. She has no idea what that is; oh you must try one and just a little curry, the heat won't hurt, the person insists and drags her back to the table. The mentioned poori and a spoonful of curry goes on her heaping plate. She hasn't touched any of her food yet. Her stomach is both hollow and overflowing.

Aban carries her plate outside to the back, where it's quieter, where she can catch her breath. She's alone but not lonely. She delicately plucks a grape from its stem and bites into it. Its sweet juice sprays over her tongue. Giggling, she finishes it off. After that, she eats with relish, licking the cream off the fig and liking the sweet, salty taste, before picking up the fig and what's left of the creamy cheese to pop it whole into her mouth. She picks up the poori and takes an enormous bite. Her eyebrows rise at how good it tastes, at how the soft-crisp texture dances with her tongue. She forks up some of the salad, and it's like all of El's qualities come through in the explosion of hot and cold, of sharp and sweet flavours, of giving and resisting textures. When she's had her fill, she hears the screen door behind her squeak open and bang shut.

"Hey, you cleaned your plate. Me too. I'm so stuffed. But I always have room for chocolate. How about you? I hope you left room for some and dessert too. Mona brought a lemon meringue pie from Wanda's. It's the best!" At that moment, the door squeaks open again, and more join them.

"Hi, I'm Adam. That's Emily—"

"And I'm Katie, and this is my husband Rustum."

"Oh hey, I didn't introduce myself. I'm Cathy."

"Hi," Aban says shyly.

"Did you see the latest?" Katie asks Cathy.

"Yeah, wasn't it good?" Seeing Aban's confused expression, Cathy explains, "It's El's blog."

"Huh? I mean, what's that?"

"You know, a blog, a website where you post regularly? No?"
Aban slowly shakes her head.

"You read it on your computer—"

"Or iPad," interrupts Rustum.

"It's an addiction with him," Katie whispers to Aban before saying, "The iPad."

"I tell you, it was a computing revolution. Everyone's copying them now. But—"

"What's an iPad?" Aban blurts out.

The chatter stops.

"Is it like a computer?" Aban asks.

"Yes, exactly," Rustum replies loudly.

"This lady . . . my friend," Aban stumbles over the unfamiliar and pleasing word. Stronger, she continues, "My friend said her friend is going to teach me computers."

"Hey, that's great," Cathy exclaims.

"We'll teach you too," Adam tells her.

"If you want," Cathy adds.

"Of course, if you want," Adam corrects himself. "We'll all teach you or answer your questions any time. Any friend of El's is a friend of ours."

"It'll be fun!" Katie chimes in. "You'll love it. You'll be an old pro in no time, you'll see. And then you'll be able to read El's blog. It's like a Wikipedia really, but with a blog. We call it El-a-pedia. Get it? El-a-pedia."

"She doesn't get it," Cathy says. "Geez, give her a chance to get to know you first before you inflict your bad puns on her."

"Okay, okay."

They laugh.

"Look," Adam says. "We meet for breakfast every Friday."

"It's a great place we go to with lots of room and good food," Cathy adds.

"Why don't you join us?"

"I'll show you my latest iPad," Rustum adds. "I just bought a new stylus for it."

"Um, well," Aban hesitates, feeling bowled over.

"Hey, you don't need to decide now. Adam, you have a card from that place, don't you?"

"Yes, here hold my plate." Adam shoves his plate at Cathy and pulls a slim black wallet out of his pocket. He unfolds it and retrieves a business card, which he hands to Aban.

"Thanks," she says, taking and examining it.

"Join us anytime," Katie tells her. Aban raises her head to look at her. Katie continues, "We're always there from seven to nine in the morning, rain or shine."

They laugh. Aban is perplexed.

"Well, okay, shine only these days," Katie burbles out in the laughter. Finally understanding the joke, Aban joins in briefly, feeling a bit unsure but enjoying this free-for-all, their camaraderie, and their easy inclusion of her. Is it real, she wonders.

Adam starts jeering Rustum about the new Blackberry. Rustum hotly disputes him, and the friends' circle around Aban tightens. Aban suddenly bursts out laughing. The others are confused but are infected by her exhilaration with life and join in. None notice El. He regards Aban from the hallway through the screen for a long moment, then nods.

30

THE DREAM III

THE black silk waves swirl underneath her. She looks down into the familiar nothingness, yet this time she sees it not as emptiness or a void but a vain wasteland. Motion flutters on her left, and she swivels her eyes in that direction. The maggots are swimming into view, two by two. Their ribbed little bodies are wiggling in delighted anticipation as they swim first in a straight line toward the centre of the deep and then in a circle round her. She watches in disbelief. Disbelief: not fear, not disengagement, but disbelief. Why are they still coming? These familiar mushy white creatures no longer scare her, yet she had thought after yesterday that they would no longer haunt her.

Aban is angry. She kicks at them. But, like before, the wasteland grips her feet, yet that does not stop her this time. And neither does she disengage to avoid the fear, for fear isn't driving her, but fury at their siren song of ease and disengagement. She will not be held down.

She wiggles and stretches. She undulates her body. She pours out resistance. Suddenly, her foot swings sharply, violently forward as the wasteland lets go. Her freed foot startles the maggots, and they swerve out of the way. Their unbroken line is broken. But not for long. Recovering their cool, they resume their journey.

Aban focusses on her other foot, and quicker this time than with the first, it too is free. She scissors herself up into the welcoming space above. The maggots stop; they raise the front of their soft bodies. They turn to each other, and then they snake up to close in on her on this different plane. But she does not give in, and she changes course. And as she does, she becomes stronger, faster, quicker in anticipating their moves and persisting against both them and the wasteland.

Suddenly, the space around her changes from insubstantial white to hot gold. A beam shines from above her, blinding her. Her right arm leaps up to shade her eyes. Like sunlight the beam uncovers the black silk surface of the black sink, the nothingness, the void, the wasteland, the vanity of it all. Like a searchlight it moves toward the encircling maggots until it reveals them. A scream shoots out. A high-pitched primordial scream vibrates the air above and the void below; the air and void sing back to each other in harmony. She lifts her hands to cover her ears as she bends her head and closes her eyes.

But she opens them again. She has to watch.

The wasteland heaves; its swirling surface suddenly froths here and there. Wisps of smoke emerge from the front maggot couple. They arch their triangular fronts up in a furious spasm. For the first time, she sees they have tiny black mouths, empty of teeth and gums, but rippling with death. They char into white ash. The light moves on to the next couple. She hears a sound and looks over her shoulder to her left. The millipede with its repulsive black and white spike-inflected stripes, the one that normally follows the pairs of maggots, the one that is chief to them all, has entered this space and stopped. It's hard to tell, but it looks horrified and . . . grieved? It folds up into itself as if trying to make itself so small that the beam will not see it. But it knows that it is a futile move, for sharply it turns and scurries its feet faster than ever, away from the carnage of its maggots. The beam doesn't catch it; it doesn't even try.

While the millipede hurries away, the wasteland changes. A white glowing mist settles over it, and through it, Aban can see the white charred remains of all the maggot couples.

The frothing stops. The screaming stops. A hush descends. The golden-lit air around her hums and sings and smells of roses and lavender and lilacs. Her feet feel mass. She stands firmly on top of the mist. She steps over the charred remains and toward the light-filled space.

Aban wakes up. Sunlight is pressing on her eyes. She can feel its warmth; its brightness flushes her eyelids red. She blinks, stretches, and opens her lids, taking in all the colours of her room. Memories of the happy feast the day before fill her stomach. The feast had gone on long into the night, until after the sun had set and the candles had been lit. She had never experienced anything like it before, and she had loved it.

Aban lies there, letting the last of the memories drift from her. She becomes aware that she doesn't feel the heat as she usually does each morning. She has adjusted to it, and her body no longer feels uncomfortable. Another good thing. Hope fills her. For the first time, the future doesn't frighten her: it isn't something to be ignored either. Last night's feast has rendered it exciting. Aban has no idea what her future will contain, no idea about a job or schooling, but she feels a good life is ahead of her, a meaningful life, a fun one. And that life will be here in Toronto, her new home, and with the people she met last night, her new family. The work El mentioned doesn't frighten her. El probably meant a new job or something. But she can face it with El beside her and her new family to get to know.

She jumps out of bed and looks outside. El is not back there. Strange, there's never been a time that he's not been out there, sitting or standing or kneeling. But she doesn't think about it too much. Instead, she showers, races into her new clothes—faded jeans and a red-and-white checked, gabardine shirt she buttons up, before slipping her feet into and lacing up her new light blue cotton-breathable shoes—and jogs downstairs. She wants to tell El about her dream, about how she's finally free. She jumps down the last few steps, her right hand on the newel post, and pivots around it to run into the kitchen.

He's not there. As she stands in the doorway, puzzled, hands hanging by her side, she hears a heavy-duty zip closing. She turns around and walks into his living quarters. El is straightening up from the small olive green duffel bag that he's just zipped closed. He slings over his shoulder a strawberry-red knapsack with sides of grey.

You can't miss that, Aban thinks. Out loud, she says, "Where're you going?"

"It's time for me to go."

"But you can't. I'm just getting to know you!"

"You don't need me here to know me or to live the life you've been given. I've taught you all you need. All you have to do is remember and read and talk."

"Read? Read what, read where?"

"Remember what your friends told you?"

"My friends?"

"Yes, your friends, Aban," El replies emphasizing the word "your." "Your friends," he repeats simply.

"My friends? Yes, my friends." Aban grins as she believes it.

El continues, "Read my blog. Read my stories. Many have written them down. Your grandmother wrote a journal. Here," he says as he offers her a thick bound book. Aban accepts it.

"Many have also shared their experiences with me on their blogs or in books or in their poetry that they rap on a Saturday night. Some tweet their stories about me in bites so small, they'll satisfy in seconds and last for hours. You can put down your stories too, the ones you learned after you came here in search of your grandmother."

248

"I don't understand. I feel like I do, sort of, but . . . ," she trails off.

Excitement blazes into sparks in his brown eyes as El replies with a grin, "You will. Do not forget Aban that my friends, the sisters and brothers who came before you, the ones you met last night and the ones you met at the dinner party, they know me, and they have trodden the walk that you are now taking. They will delight in sharing with you what lessons they have learned. And they will delight in listening to your stories, not only the ones you've learned from me, but, as well, the ones you lived before and after me. In retelling them to others, you will learn more. They will help you unfold the future of your life, a life of learning and sharing and engaging—if only you give them the opportunity, if only you ask the right questions. Or even the wrong ones. Curiosity will drive you forward. Curiosity is not something to be feared. And remember: they won't put you down. And they won't try to control you. You are ultimately in control of your own decisions and your own life. Have no fear."

Aban shakes her head, "I won't. I'm not scared any more. I have so many questions now. Why do you have to leave now that I wanna ask questions?"

El reaches out a hand to touch her face, "Don't worry, Aban. You will receive your answers. And sometimes you won't. That's okay too, to live in a state of patience and in an attitude of active seeking while not knowing."

He drops his hand, picks up the duffel bag, hefts the knapsack further up onto his other shoulder, and walks around her toward the hallway. She follows him into the hall but then stops. He grasps the front doorknob and pauses. El turns back to look at where she is standing frozen in front of the kitchen doorway, watching him leave.

"Walk with me."

She leaps forward, and half-walks, half-runs toward him. As she reaches him, he smiles at her with confidence, she smiles back tentatively, her eyes filming. El opens the door. He leads her through it, and she leaves it open behind her. They cross the porch, walk down the steps, and along the walk to the gate. He opens the white picket gate and holds it open as she crosses its threshold to stand with him on the sidewalk. The gate leans on the sidewalk.

"Where will you go?" Aban asks him.

"Where I always go—to where I'm led."

"Isn't that scary?"

"No. I'm never alone."

"No . . . I guess not. Neither am I?" Aban whispers. She clears her throat and looks up and full into his eyes. "I get it now. But don't you ever want to go your own way?"

"It makes it challenging and joyous being led," El confirms. "And where would my own way lead me other than to the same place I'm led."

He starts walking up the street. Aban remains by his side, her eyebrows drawing together. She looks a question up at him.

He answers, "There is no 'my way' or 'his way' or 'her way.' There is only one way, and that is where I go, no matter that I do not always know where it is or what will happen when I get there. We all have free will, Aban, though not all of us know it and exercise it, and the choices we make not only affect us but those around us in ever-rippling waves that we cannot see. I go where I am led to the people who are in need. They are not always predictable in their response. Some resent me. Some mock me. But sometimes they surprise you with the suddenness of their change, their understanding, their openness. And then it's time for me to leave. And remember, as I am with them, so I am with you to the end, always."

"Oh." She stops to ponder this, looking away from him and off into the distance. She brings her eyes back to where he was, except he's not there. Not ahead, not under the bridge, not crossing the street. She turns her head swiftly one way or the other. But he's gone. She hurries forward to peer down the small industrial street that goes westward. He's not there. She hurries back past the bus stop and the empty corner store to peer down the leafy residential street close by her home. He's not there either. She hugs herself and slowly turns three-hundred-and-sixty degrees, her eyes tracking every movement, every object.

He's vanished.

Yet she feels him, as if he's left his essence behind. She lets go of herself and walks back toward Atasgah, at first slowly, mourning the loss, but then more and more quickly as she sheds the mourning and puts on the excitement that she had felt when the sun had pressed on her face this morning. It's Friday. She'll meet those new friends, just as they'd asked her to. She swings her arms in time with her feet until they're pumping, and her feet are jogging, through the gate, up the path, up the steps two at a time, across the porch in one leap, and through the door with a bang. She grabs her wallet and keys off the hall table and barges back through her front door, closing it behind her.

She inserts the key into the old lock of her front door, and a clap of thunder shakes the house and the old porch she is standing on. All of a sudden, rain pours down in a deafening barrage. Rain pounds the dry grass and forms puddles and lakes as the soil cannot absorb the deluge. Rain spills rivulets along the gutters of the street; it films the sidewalk with cleansing water; and it causes drivers to hurriedly switch on long-unused wipers to smear rain and dust on their windshields. She shivers pleasurably in the sudden coolness as the rain sucks the heat out from her, as the rain flushes the air and the flashes of lightening electrify it.

Aban laughs out loud.

She doesn't have an umbrella. She has to buy one on the way to breakfast downtown where El's friends—her new friends—had mentioned they hang out on a Friday morning. She locks the door and runs into the refreshing rain.

ABOUT THE AUTHOR

SHIREEN JEEJEEBHOY is a Toronto-based author, blogger, and photographer. She is the author of the award-winning biography *Lifeliner: The Judy Taylor Story*, *She*, *Concussion Is Brain Injury*, and *Time and Space*; two short ebooks; articles for print media and online sites; and she is working on her next few novels. She holds a B.Sc. in psychology from the University of Toronto.

You can visit her website at http://jeejeebhoy.ca and subscribe to her blog posts to receive a free poetry ebook. You may also find her on Wattpad.com.

A Plea: Did you enjoy *Aban's Accension*, enough to tell others about it? If so, please leave a review on the online book retailer of your choice—it's the best way to support the work of an indie author like me. Honest reviews by readers are invaluable to authors, and I would love to hear from you. Thank you!

Please enjoy the peeks at my first novel *She* and my first book *Lifeliner* on the following pages, and don't forget to keep an eye out for my next book.

SHE

CHAPTER ONE

THERE WAS ONCE A WOMAN

TIRES HISS AGAINST the road. A gentle bump bump at high speed wakes her up. She stretches against the confines of the seat belt and blinks open her eyes. Pitch night engulfs the car. The glowing numbers on the dashboard clock draw her eyes: 12:54.

"Wow, I can't believe the time." She yawns, "Did I really sleep that long? I can't believe it's that late. Did we run into heavy traffic? That sucks. I thought leaving so late in the evening, we'd miss the Toronto-bound traffic. I guess not, eh?" She smiles at the driver, but he looks stoically ahead. Her eyes drift past the clock again and suddenly widen. "Hey! Do you know what time it is? It's almost summer solstice time. How cool is that, being out in the country at the exact hour?" Still no response.

Sighing, she looks out her window and frowns. Not only are they late, but for that matter, where are they? This country road doesn't look like Highway 10. Pickets of a prim wooden fence fly by, the ground at its feet rising into view and disappearing. The fields beyond vacuum the meagre starlight, and the car's beams cannot penetrate into their depths. She leans toward her window and cranes her neck to look up at the sky. It's a moving charcoal surface with white glitter winking here and there. The moon is nowhere in sight.

She asks him as she continues to stare out the window, "Where are we?"

"I thought we'd take a shortcut."

"Meaning you don't know," she laughs. He smiles faintly as he continues to stare straight ahead, his hands resting in the ten to two position on the leather grey steering wheel of their car. The amber glow of the dashboard lights up the front of his face like some sort of eerie jack-o-lantern. She watches him for a moment.

"Well, I guess we're somewhere in the country. Traffic must've been bad, eh?"

He shrugs one shoulder. She sighs. She's fully awake now and sharing space with a statue.

"I guess it wasn't so bad for you that I dozed off, eh? Silence is golden and all that," she grins. "Well, I can be silent ... sometimes." She chuckles and then stretches again. "That nap did me good. I feel so awake now and refreshed. I'm raring to go, and I can't wait till tomorrow, I mean today. I have all these song ideas bouncing around in my head. This was a great idea of yours, going on this road trip, it's got me going again, and I love visiting those cute Ontario towns." She twists round to the left to check out the back seat, to make sure all the goodies they bought are still there. Pies and jugs of maple syrup sit side by side with pints of fresh Bing cherries, her favourite. She untwists herself and settles back in her seat. She watches the hypnotic yellow line as it snakes ahead.

"I can't wait to dive into those cherries. They were my favourite fruit growing up. Did I ever tell you that? I used to look forward to the end of school because that's when

Grandmother would buy them. And I'd make a big mess, and she'd get so mad." She laughs at the memory. "Now I can make as big a mess as I want." She falls silent for a moment. "I was thinking: they're too good to make pies with. I'd rather eat them fresh like that, but it's almost strawberry season. Maybe we can go up to Andrew's Scenic Acres and pick some berries. I'm in the mood for making strawberry rhubarb pies or maybe mixed berry pies if the blueberries and raspberries are out too. We have enough room in that chest freezer, I'm sure. I gave it a big cleanout the other day. What do you think?" she asks rhetorically. She savours the thought of a strawberry rhubarb pie with crumble topping. Those are always a hit. And they freeze so well. She can almost smell them baking and taste their sweet tartness. She smiles; her eyes focus on the road again.

She looks past the yellow line, past the boundaries of light the car beams create, into the darkness coming toward them, a forest on the right. The hairs on the back of her neck lift up; her stomach flutters.

"Uh, where are we really?" she asks as she sits up straight, tensing her body. He stays silent.

Her nerves feel taut. She urges, "We need to stop and turn around. Now, if you don't mind."

The car doesn't slow down. His eyes don't flick up to the rear-view mirror or down to the speedometer.

Her chest starts to contract. "Look, I know you're all into exploring the side roads, but this doesn't feel safe, and it's really really late. Let's drive home on a faster road. Let's turn around and go to Highway 10."

He says nothing.

"Could you please just stop the car, turn around, and go back to Highway 10."

"We're fine." He stretches the word out. "Stop being so paranoid."

"I'm not being paranoid."

"You are," he replies. The slight put-down in his voice works. She feels silly. They're just trees.

Those trees are beside them; ahead their mates on the left loom. They fill the front windshield more and more. It's 12:56 a.m. She wants to be the one in the driver's seat badly; instead she's being driven inexorably toward the forest, where starlight cannot penetrate. She shifts her gaze back down to the road, to the familiar yellow ribbon and the dusty edges of the asphalt where road meets grass. But then the edges vanish into the shadows cast by the trees standing shoulder to shoulder, leafy branch merging into leafy branch, creating a light-sucking toothy maw. She feels the air hold its breath. Her breathing speeds up. His body remains still.

The trees close in on the other side, only a sliver of rectangular sky between the two forests breaks their starless black.

She leans toward him, her thick, shingled hair falling against her cheek, trying to get away from the trees on her right, jostling his arm.

"What are you doing?" he snaps at her.

"Can't you move closer to the yellow line?"

In response, he steers toward the right.

"Stop it!" She struggles to breathe evenly.

"I'll stop it when you stop being silly."

She leans forward to look up through the windshield, her hair gleaming in the reflected dashboard light, searching for that sliver of glittering sky, looking for the one opening in the lightless claustrophobia without.

"Would you get a hold of yourself. We're fine. Don't worry." He tries to nudge her away with his elbow, but she resists.

She cannot move back to the upright position; she just cannot separate herself from him. She looks ahead, focussing on the end of the forest, even though she cannot see it, where the fields re-emerge beyond the headlights, willing them to arrive there as fast as possible. But their speed drops to 70 kilometres per hour. She begins to see the individual trees, the shrubs sticking up among them, the rocks laying among their bases. The sky is morphing, undulating, changing degrees of grey-black shades. Clouds are rolling in.

"Why are you slowing down?"

He doesn't answer. "Of course not, why need he?" she thinks angrily. He's proving his point. He doesn't usually treat her this contemptuously. Her anger fades into loneliness as memories arise of how he used to always treat her with consideration and respect and love. She remembers the first time they shopped together, how he had insisted on carrying the grocery bags. Or how when she had lost her keys for the umpteenth time and was becoming mighty annoyed about it, he'd used his carefully modulated voice to calm her and focus her memory on those keys. Within minutes she'd found them. But lately, ever since his annual spring camping trip up near the Bruce Trail with his buddies, he's become moody. Grim. Many, many days, he has been his old cheerful self, making her laugh so hard that she snorts water out her nose, or he has run errands by himself instead of interrupting one of her songwriting sessions. But on this weekend's road trip, he'd once again become serious, become watchful of her as darkness inhabited his face. She doesn't understand this change in him and towards her. It's like he's decided that she has to prove her worth over and over again.

She wants to grab that wheel and take back control. But she can't. She's in his hands.

Sinking down into the shadow of her seat, still leaning on him, her eyes reach the level of the clock. It flips to 12:57 a.m.

The landscape flashes sickly neon green. The car heels to the left as a wind screams out of the forest like a ghastly, whirling Northern light, and slams into its right side then dances up on to the hood, on to the roof, down beside them. The car's back fishtails out. She squeezes her eyes and senses the car turn one way then the other. Even through her closed eyelids, she senses the chartreuse-yellow lightning inside the whirlwind. She squeezes her eyes tighter until they hurt. They're speeding up; they're driving to the left; they slow. She opens her eyes to see him manhandling the steering wheel until they're aiming straight down the road again, but the wind, with its ever-changing neon-green-bottom border, with its dancing gold-green veins, streaks alongside and in front of them. They can't outrun it. He presses the accelerator, trying anyway, as she clings to his right arm, as she puts her head between her own arms. Glass cracks in front of her. The cracks glow green. She scoots closer to him and squeezes her eyes so tight, she sees red. Cracks fracture her side window, and she can't help opening her eyes to look toward the sound. Air moves all around her, pushing at her, raising the hair on her arms, throwing up the hair on her head, fluttering her T-shirt, turning her skin sickly green. Suddenly she sees nothing. She closes and opens her eyes and still sees nothing. Panic attacks her. And then they shoot out of the trees and are between open fields. She sees again. Sobs rack her, and she can't stop them.

"There's a patrol up ahead. I have to pull over," he says.

Her sobs quit suddenly. She sits up, wipes her eyes, smoothes her hair off her face, straightens her Black Sabbath T-shirt. The car rumbles off the road to the gravel shoulder and crunches to a stop. He pushes the window button and his window hums down. A policeman with a bright wand in his right hand and a reflective vest walks toward them; the officer leans in, his eyes keen on them. She returns his look emotionless.

"Good evening sir, ma'am. How are you this morning?"

"We're fine officer. I wasn't speeding."

"No, you weren't sir. That's not why I pulled you over. We're the Akaesman patrol."

"The what?"

"Will you step out of the car sir, ma'am. We need to ask you a few questions."

She obeys. Or tries to. All her muscles seem to have seized up; she looks down puzzled, feeling old. Using her hands and her arms as leverage, she turns herself towards the open door, puts her feet on the ground, stands up, and leans on the open car door, apperceiving her balance, before straightening her flared black jeans and walking over to where the policeman has joined a woman standing a metre or so in front of what looks like the back of a white ambulance sitting next to the black and white police car.

"Did you drive through the forest sir?" the policeman asks him.

"Yes."

"Did anything happen?"

"Like what?"

"You tell me sir."

Slowly he shakes his head.

The policeman stares at him for a few seconds, and then turns to her.

"You ma'am. How are you feeling?"

She considers that for a moment. Shocked maybe.

The woman who had been standing there watching them walks over to her, while snapping on blue nitrile gloves. She takes a penlight out of her pocket and flashes it in her eyes. She flinches. The woman is unfazed. She reaches round and lightly squeezes her neck muscles, moving down to feel the top of her shoulders.

"Follow me."

She obeys.

"Please sit here," she gestures to the step at the back of the ambulance. From there, she can see the reflective letters on the side of the police car: "Akaesman Patrol. To Guard and Save." Weird.

She feels a cuff being fastened around her left arm, and then the rhythmic pump, pump as the woman inflates it. Air hisses out before the cuff is ripped off. A stethoscope is pressed against her chest and then her back. She finally looks at the woman as she straightens up and speaks to the policeman: "It's mild, but definitely."

He nods and faces her fiancé again.

"Sir, you did experience something back there, didn't you?"

She watches her fiancé stare back nonchalantly, but he's no match for an officer of the Akaesman Patrol.

"We might've."

"You did sir. I want to know what it was."

He told him all, even how she was whining about turning back.

"You should've listened to her sir. Stay here." He walks over to the patrol car, the gravel crunching under his dusty black boots. He opens the driver's door, gets in, and slams it shut.

They wait.

He gets out with a clipboard and walks over to her.

"OK ma'am, I'm sorry to have to tell you that you probably had a run-in with Akaesman. Now it doesn't look too serious, some sprains, but I must ask you to read this form and sign it. Then go see your GP tomorrow." He looks at his watch. "Today." He writes, his pen scratching the paper on the clipboard. Then he hands the clipboard over to her. The woman aims a flashlight at it, but it's too much to read. She must be tired, and so she pretends to read it. His finger extends into her view, pointing to where she should sign. She signs. He flips the page up and asks her to sign the copy. She signs and hands it back to him. He presses down on the clip handle and releases the top piece of paper. He hands it to her. She takes it, but he doesn't let go until she looks up at him.

"Go see your GP ma'am."

She nods.

He still doesn't let go. "See your GP, your family physician."
She looks up into his face and says, "I will."

He lets go. She carries the paper back to the car, where her
door is still open. She gets in awkwardly and drops the paper
on her lap, wondering why she has to see her family physician.
She reaches back for the seat belt, and pain ratchets up her
neck. She pauses and then turns her entire body right to get at
the seat belt, pulls it toward herself, turns her entire body to the
left, and stiffly aims for the seat belt clip. Click. She sits back,
sighing. And waits, staring at her fiancé, yet not seeing him as
he strides back to the car. She hears his door open, his booted
foot twisting on the gravel, his jeans sliding against leather; she
hears the slam of the door, the feel of the car softly rocking in
response, the slither of the belt as it's pulled, the click of it
going home, the key being turned, and the engine roaring
excessively to life. They accelerate onto the asphalt, the wheels
spitting small stones out, and drive for home.

Keep reading for a peek at the fascinating true-life story
about the woman who could not eat . . .

LIFELINER

CHAPTER 1

BACK IN ONE HOUR

66 I'M SO LUCKY to have a family, adopted or not! I'm so lucky to be alive!" Judy Ellis Taylor tells her three school-age girls out of the blue on this chilly September morning. They roll their eyes, having heard this before many a time.

Judy didn't know her biological parents, a twenty-three-year-old nursing-student mother and a twenty-seven-year-old painter father, nor did she care to. To Judy, her real parents were Marjorie and Percy Russell. Shortly after her birth on March 26, 1936, they had scooped up the little round-cheeked, black-haired baby and taken her home. At first, Marjorie hadn't wanted to adopt this baby. Only six months had passed since their second adopted child had died suddenly; but Percy talked to Marjorie gently and persistently until he convinced his devastated wife that she could adopt again, that she could have her dream of children, children who would live. She acquiesced, and they adopted Judy from a Presbyterian home. To help ensure that both their girls, Joyce and Judy, their first and third adopted children, would have the best chance, they moved from Rosedale to a large house in the valley of York

Mills, where violets flowed up to the door in springtime. It meant a one-hour drive to his engineering job, but Percy made it sweeter by bringing home chocolate éclairs. Meanwhile, Marjorie anchored their family life with big weekly Sunday lunches after church.

It was a good decision, for Judy thrived on life. She attended the prestigious Bishop Strachan School during her junior-high years and joined the young people's group at St. John's Anglican Church. At thirteen years old, this healthy, mischievous girl pledged herself to Christ at Camp Gay Venture in Haliburton—she didn't explain why to anyone, just did it—and became a camp counsellor at the same time. Like a mother bird, Judy took charge of the little girls at the camp, including Sandra, a small seven-year-old. Judy especially loved teaching the little ones to ride. But being Judy's pupil was not an easy thing: she had a tendency to kick her charges out of the nest if she felt that they could handle it, plus she had a penchant for practical jokes.

One sunny day as the group cantered together, Sandra's black horse (known as Blacky) threw her off. Sandra sniffled on the ground, feeling sorry for herself, while the others milled around. They expected Judy to pick her up, dust her off, and plop her back on her horse. Instead, she steered her horse over and, looking down from her great height, demanded, "Well? What are you going to do about it? I'm going back to the barn. You can either walk or get on your horse and follow me." She gestured to the others to follow her and rode off.

Sandra howled. Some of the kids looked back, but not one slowed down. They disappeared toward the barn. Sandra stopped, mouth open. No point howling anymore. She closed her mouth. She stood up, climbed onto Blacky, and trotted back to camp, where Judy was waiting. "Well, if you hadn't done that, you probably wouldn't ever have ridden again," Judy informed the little girl. "Now take Blacky in and groom her."

That fall, Percy decided that Judy would be better off at his (and my) alma mater, Jarvis Collegiate Institute, near the heart of Toronto, and had her transferred there. She did reasonably well. By age seventeen, she knew what she wanted out of life: to find a husband and have a family.

Judy joined her girlfriends at the church picnic near Fenelon Falls that summer, hoping to find a husband. She did. Her friend introduced her to her boyfriend's buddy. Cliff Taylor was a taciturn, slightly older fellow with a sudden smile and a shock of dark hair. He had to grow up quickly after his mother had tried to kill him along with herself, leaving him alone with his alcoholic father while his younger sister was shipped off to boarding school. By age sixteen, he had dropped out of school to work. He developed a philosophy of paying his own way with cash only. He didn't believe in credit cards or debt, except for a mortgage perhaps. Unlike Judy, he didn't live in the genteel areas of town, but he had become successful in sales and was doing well monetarily. Still, the educated, well-off Judy clicked with this man from the wrong side of the tracks. He loved her with a devotion that drove him to cross the threshold of a church, a feat he vowed never to repeat after their marriage on July 27, 1957, in St. John's Anglican, and she loved him with a strength he could count on.

Cliff bought a new house for his bride, and they settled comfortably into Scar-borough life, spending weekends up at the cottage near his father's place in Bobcaygeon, Cliff paying for everything in cash, as usual, and Judy looking after their growing brood: Cyndy, Julie, and Miriam. Judy had grasped her dream. With her family complete, she went on the birth control pill, a fairly new drug back in late 1966. She was wildly happy and having fun.

But God wasn't impressed with Judy's life plan. He gave her the gifts of toughness, generosity, kindness, healing, advocacy, and teaching. Her dream was too mundane for those gifts, and He would call her to travel to unfamiliar places, places so dark, frightening, and unexpected that she would have no choice but to trust in His faithfulness to her.

Stomach pain was the first intimation of the change to come. The stomach pain was so bad that, after three months, it forced her to see her general practitioner (GP) in February 1967. Despite X-rays, blood tests, and referrals to specialists, nothing revealed the source of her pain, although by 1970 her insatiable appetite and loss of weight clued one of her specialists, a gastroenterologist, into the fact that she might have hyperthyroidism. She joked to her girls that she could run up and down the road at ninety miles an hour, making them laugh while she hid from them the wrenching pain deep inside her. By the summer of 1970, her endocrinologist irradiated her thyroid. Perhaps things would settle down now, Judy and Cliff hoped.

But the pain squeezed harder. Her doctor prescribed morphine; Cliff and Judy hid that, too, from their girls, or so they thought. Family conversations took a strange turn. The talkative, joking Judy suddenly would stop mid-sentence; they would all pretend she hadn't and would gamely continue on the conversation without her. Suddenly, she'd pop back up and finish her sentence. Unfortunately, she would soon space out again, and cries of "Mom? Mom!" from her girls would go unheeded. Frightened, the three dared not ask about this phenomenon when she resurfaced from wherever she'd been, and they pretended that everything was normal. Judy had deceived herself into thinking they hadn't noticed, clenching her teeth against the truth, fighting both the pain and the effects of the morphine.

Wednesday, September 23, 1970, dawns cold. The pain had increased during the past weekend. She had spent the time at the cottage, lying balled up on her bed while the children played with their dog, Goldie, under the sunny fall skies. Back at home, she had pushed herself to get through Monday and

Tuesday, but today, Wednesday, she calls her GP. With Cliff by her side, she dials his number. He's on vacation. His partner takes her early morning call. He instructs her to call her endocrinologist, the one who irradiated her thyroid. She calls him, but her symptoms are outside his field of specialty, he informs her. She hangs up frustrated and decides to soldier on. "I'll be fine," she assures Cliff so that he will leave for work and not worry about her. She has toughed it out for over three years; one more day will not be so hard.

But Cliff feels unconvinced. He writes down his work number and commands her to call him.

Later that morning, after her family has left, Judy's neighbour Frances comes over for their usual cup of tea and chat. After one look at Judy, Frances runs to fetch her next-door neighbour Fran. They return to find Judy lying on the chesterfield, wearing shorts and shivering. Fran dashes into the bedroom and grabs a pair of slacks and a blanket. Judy—the one who always does things for herself, who never discusses her health, who never talks of her ailment—now lets her two neighbours bundle her up.

Fran asks her, "Where's the pain?"

Judy points to, but dares not touch, her sore stomach and confesses her whole story.

Fran thinks that maybe it's appendicitis and is livid at the doctor's inane advice. They should call Cliff, she asserts, and she takes the slip of paper with his work number on it and calls while Frances offers Judy some tea.

Judy cannot abide the thought and turns her head away. Fran suggests that she make lunch for Judy's girls at her place. Judy nods.

Frances has to go back home, but Fran stays. Judy feels maybe a visit to the bathroom will help. She rises carefully from the chesterfield and leans gratefully on her neighbour's arm for the short walk down the hallway. But the bathroom visit doesn't help. The pain hangs on, her nerves screech at her every movement. She lies back down on the chesterfield with relief.

It's eleven o'clock. The phone rings. Fran picks it up. It's Cliff, calling her back. "I may be wrong, but that wouldn't cause what she had, right?" she asks him, referring to Judy's hyperthyroidism.

Cliff doesn't know; he says it's all incomprehensible to him, this illness stuff.

Fran gets off the phone as lunch is fast approaching. She has to get it ready and bake cookies for her son and for Judy's three girls. "I'll ask Frances to keep an eye on you till after lunch," she tells Judy. She runs out the door under the scudding clouds and light rain to Frances's place. Although Frances has her own four kids to make lunch for, she pops over several times and takes messages from a worried Cliff. He's coming home early, and she lets Fran know this when she returns after lunch.

At 5:30 PM, Cliff barrels in from work. He watches Fran leave with a worried backward glance at Judy. He unwraps the fish 'n chips he'd picked up on his way home and coaxes his wife to eat at least a little bit. Fish 'n chips. The last meal of her life. If only they had known, he would've gotten something nicer.

Fed and off the couch, Judy takes a deep breath and throws her affliction out of her mind. Life cannot stop just because my innards are screaming, she thinks. Her girls need new running shoes, groceries need to be bought, for it's Wednesday night, grocery night. She tells Cliff to get the car ready, and she steels herself for the drive to Parkway Plaza. There in the middle of the grocery store, she sways.

Cliff grabs her and half carries half walks her to the car with the girls running along beside them. Cliff rushes them home and settles his wife on the chesterfield. He whips across the street to ask Frances if she can look after the children while he takes Judy to the doctor's office.

Frances doesn't hesitate to say yes, and the two race back to his house. They wrap Judy up in blankets.

As Cliff carries her out the door to the car, Judy—ever protective and still trying to hide her illness—calls back to her girls: "We're just going to the doctor's. We'll be back in an hour."

www.ingramcontent.com/pod-product-compliance
Lightning Source LLC
Chambersburg PA
CBHW020608110726
47899CB00002B/424